I AM

By

Michael Drakich

Amazon Edition

Copyright © Michael Drakich
ISBN-13: 9780987770660

First Edition Traanu Enterprises, December 2015

Editor Kate Richards
Cover Ted Kruzsely

CHAPTER 1

I am surrounded by nothing.

There is nothing above me, nothing below me, and nothing all round me. All screens are blank. Frankly, it's quite disappointing, but there's no one to blame. It was my own choice. I made *that* decision a long time ago.

In all honesty, I've lost track of how long it's been. Life on my personal spacecraft has become an endless repetition of induced sleeping, body regeneration, and moments of lucid awareness during the process. Now, renewed to my former youth of twenty-five, I am awake again.

I squint up at the lights. "How long this time, Mum?"

The ship computer, who I like to call Mum, is an AI of my own design. She's a lot smarter than I am, but she always keeps a respectful note to her voice when addressing me. I am, in a way, her father.

"Two hundred and eighty-two years, rounded up. This was your longest sleep, Adam. I'm afraid each time will be longer still. I've been thinking on this while you were asleep and would like permission to make some changes in your regeneration procedure."

Shit. This is getting to be a real problem. It's unfortunate that the regeneration process cannot be interrupted. If you cut it short you cannot ever regenerate again. I trust Mum implicitly, but there's always a part of me wanting to double-check things. Call it being anal retentive. I'm a control freak. "What did you have in mind?"

"Would you like the new design specifications implanted in your cerebral cortex, or would you prefer to absorb them the old-fashioned way by studying a holographic display?"

Memory implants always give me a headache. "Holographic display, if you please."

The space in front of me fills with an image of my regeneration tube with a significant number of modifications to it. I recognize some of the new equipment—the photon converter, a device central to everything on the ship as the source of all its power, and a stasis field generator – but they both are sporting variations, and, in all honesty, are unnecessary. Such devices already exist within the ship as part of its mainframe. "Mum, what gives? Why the spare parts?"

"I have calculated the probability of a failure in either of these devices in my mainframe as a chance of almost one in three centillion."

I couldn't help but chuckle. "Centillion? That's a lot of zeroes. How many trillions of years would it take to make the probability a fifty-fifty chance?"

"Adam, any possibility, however remote, should be eliminated. My job is to protect you."

She has a point. I know better than to argue with Mum when she's right. "Okay, you win. So where are we? I don't see any stars close by. How far have we drifted?"

"We are eleven-point-six light years from Earth."

Pretty far. I made the decision to park my ship out in empty space. It's a necessity against raiders while I'm asleep. I learned that the hard way, the first time I went into stasis. I had parked the ship in orbit around Earth's moon when a team of pirates tried to board it. Fortunately, they were no match for my defenses. The threat activated Gort, the robot I built for just such emergencies. Call me sentimental, but I fashioned him after the one from the old movie *The Day the Earth Stood Still*. He sports all the classic design features—a completely seamless silver exterior with the one laser eye hidden behind his rectangular eyelid. I couldn't resist. Gort vaporized the pirates and their ship. I watched the whole thing on Mum's replay. The boy made me proud.

Ever since then, I've been more careful and park farther and farther away in an effort to avoid detection from passing ships. Mankind is flitting everywhere through the stars, and Earth is the central hub of all of it, or at least it was. A lot can happen in 282 years, rounded or not. I'm awake. It's time to join the human race once more. "Hey, Mum, let's see what's happening back home. Set a course for Earth."

"Course laid in. We shall arrive in four hours and thirty-three minutes."

"Good." I stretch. "Whew, a few kinks in the old body. I could use a nice massage. Where's Eve?"

"She's sulking in her room. You know how she gets lonely when you're out."

Eve is my sexbot. Her base programming is to please me. She is everything I want in a woman, and more. Her skin is programmed to alter skin color, shape, and age appearance to whatever appeals at the time. So if, for example, I'm hankering for a dark-skinned, Amazonian, big-breasted goddess, then that's what she becomes. If I'm in the mood for a pert, nubile, eighteen-year-old, alabaster and freckled, then so be it. As well, her personality will alter some to match. Each time I regenerate, I wake with a strong sex drive. Right now, I am in the mood for something a little older, with soft curves and an experienced touch. "Get her in here. I'm horny."

"You're such a sensitive guy, Adam. However do you manage it?"

I can always count on Mum for the smart-ass admonishing when I need it. "Don't worry. I'll be nice." Oh, what the heck, let's have a little fun. "But hurry it up. I've got this urge that needs to be taken care of."

A ball of water charges in from the kitchen and lands on my midsection.

"Better?"

It works. My libido shrinks as I seek out something to dry off with. "Ha ha, you got me there. Let me get a towel and some clothes. I'll get dressed while you get Eve." The regeneration tube requires me to be naked when in there. At first, I had been self-conscious of it, especially since Mum is programmed as a woman, but, after a while, I got accustomed to the fact and no longer felt embarrassed. It isn't like Mum is standing there, staring and pointing. She is everywhere. I look up when speaking to her because it's where her CPU is located.

I retrieve a towel, a set of neatly folded fresh clothes, and return to the bridge. I have a penchant for the colors green, purple, and gold, and this outfit meets all three with the pattern in the light-purple pullover.

I am still pulling on the shirt when Eve walks in from

4

the room on the far side of the bridge. Her appearance is fortyish, with auburn hair, full lips, and a kick-ass curvy body screaming sex appeal through the low-cut dress she is wearing. She knows me well. Not that I believe in the guy, except maybe where did the singularity that created the universe come from in the first place. Curious if that was him, but I wonder what God must think of my naming a sexbot after the first woman when mine is the same as the first man. It certainly isn't the genesis he was thinking about.

"Adam, dear, Mum says you're suffering from some stiff muscles. What do you say we go into your bedroom and I give you a nice massage?"

As I go to meet her, she sashays over, and my manhood is on the rise once more. She snuggles in and slips a hand into my slacks. "Oh my, you're cold! What happened?"

At times I would wonder whether Eve should have access to Mum's memories. When I discussed it with Mum, she said it was a bad idea. Eve needs her own personality. I agreed. "Nothing, really. Mum and I were playing, and she splashed me with a little ice water, that's all."

"I know just how to warm that up." Eve copies my habit and looks at the ceiling. "Mum, that wasn't nice."

"My apologies, Eve. I know you'll make it better. You two kids go have fun."

My quarters are on the other side of the circular bridge. The walkway follows the perimeter wall with the captain's chair and main console in the middle of the room. We pass the doors to the kitchen with its dining room and bar, the entrance to the shuttle bay, the stairwell to the lower deck where the machinery is, and the den, until we finally reach my chambers.

The outer walls are, at the moment, invisible. Holograph projectors show outer space. From the outside, my ship looks a little like those old-fashioned flying saucers, but with the photon intake port sticking out noticeably.

My bedroom, though not lavish, is spacious. Besides the king-sized bed, it sports an exercise area and, like the kitchen, a complete bar. Among his other duties, Gort will serve as bartender. I hate drinking alone, so Eve will always join me when the mood sets in. More than once, she drank me under the table.

Having woken up only a little while ago, I'm not ready for any alcohol, but some orange juice will hit the spot, so I pour a glass and settle down on the bed, the mattress adjusting to keep me sitting up.

Eve climbs next to me and returns to roaming my body with one hand. "You know I miss you so when you regenerate. Why does it take so long?"

I had been wondering the very same thing. The timeline between wakes is climbing almost exponentially. Mum has said the cells in my body are becoming resistant to the regeneration process. It is, after all, the fourth time I've done so. The first regeneration took seven years, as expected. The second—twenty-four. The third crossed the century mark at 112. I stroke Eve's hair and smile. "Don't worry about it. Mum's on the case. She'll figure it out."

I finish my juice and place the glass on a bedside table. Eve undresses and straddles my knees. "I do worry about you. That's my programming." She commands the bed to straighten and pulls my clothes off as it does so. "I'm going to make those worries go away. Just lie back and let me do everything."

As Eve works on removing the last vestiges of coldness, I can't help but ponder the question she's posed. I need to examine the design of Mum's new regeneration tube. Has she worked all the bugs out? Maybe all it needs is a tweak or two.

I'm also a little worried about what I'll find when I get back to Earth. The last go-round featured a touch too much drama with some not-so-polite people trying to kidnap me for my inventions.

Forget about that. Eve is demanding my attention and, after all, I do have four hours to kill.

CHAPTER 2

As we near the planet, the space chatter picks up significantly. Much more than I remember, but a lot of time has passed, so I am not surprised.

It's the military warnings that set me off. Apparently, something is amiss. My last visit, war was all but unheard of. Sure, there were still some small crazy factions fighting for some lunatic cause or another, but, with modern technology being what it was, it was impossible to conduct war on the planet without devastating repercussions. The countries learned not to fight anymore.

A warning light from Mum flashes on the bridge console. "I'm detecting four ships headed our way. They are demanding we stop where we are. Shall I connect you?"

Here we go again. I've seen this movie before. I need to make a quick decision. Am I going home to visit, or should I run? There will be no going back on whichever path I choose. Time to give in. I want to see Earth again. "Yes, Mum. If there's visual, give me that as well."

A hologram appears, displaying our current position and the approaching ships. The lead ship blinks, and I tap it with my finger. The image of a very serious-looking military man pops up before me.

"Unknown ship, please identify yourself. You are in Megedex space without clearance. Failure to comply will result in your destruction."

Megedex space? "Good day, sir. My apologies. It's

been some time since I've been to Earth. My name is Adam Spenceworth. If you check my darkspace transponder signal you should—"

"I know who you are, Mr. Spenceworth. We had thought you were deceased and consequently archived your records. I have identified your signal and confirmed your identity. Instructions have arrived for me to bring you to headquarters. Please follow me and dock your ship at the coordinates I am sending."

I don't like the sound of this. Mum is showing the location they want me to dock and it's on the planet. I don't want the ship trapped in some hanger should I need an exit plan. "I tell you what. How about, instead, I come over to your ship, and you can take me there. It'll only take a jiffy. That way my ship can stay in space and continue to collect photons to keep charged."

The officer waits a moment before responding. I can only figure he is getting some kind of instruction first. "That is acceptable. I will be alongside shortly. Please, do not keep me waiting."

I tap the image and it shrinks back to the tiny ship closing in on me. I poke my head down the stairs to the lower deck. "Gort, come up here."

The big robot, whose job list also includes ship maintenance, puts down the tools he is holding, and flies up the stairs. Unlike his namesake, mine could speak. Kinda. I hear the words, but he has no mouth so the laser eye of his pulses with each syllable. "Yes, Adam."

I begin collecting a few things to take with me. I start with a coat—it's winter there—some gloves, and, of course, my personal force field generator, a slim flexible

9

device the size of a dinner plate that slips on my back under my jacket. It generates a field extending around me, invisible to the eye. Skintight, it doesn't interfere with any of my senses. "Don't let anyone on the ship while I'm gone."

"I understand. How long should it be before I expect your return?"

Will I return? That's the plan. Let's hope it goes that way. "I don't know. Hopefully, soon." I glance up. "Mum, if the ship comes under attack, you know what to do."

"Don't worry. During your last regeneration, Gort and I made a number of modifications. No one is going to damage it."

Eve comes and takes my elbow. She has transformed into a slim brunette dressed in a very businesslike suit. "I'm ready."

I hold my hand open toward the awaiting shuttle in its bay. "Right this way."

We jump into the small craft, and I pilot out into space. The four ships are pulling up to a station nearby and the one closest has opened its shuttle bay doors. In only a scant few seconds, I guide my transport into an empty bay and step onto the deck to greet the awaiting officer. "Permission to come aboard. I'm sorry. I never got your name."

"Captain Sekkol Surumanan. Welcome aboard, Mr. Spenceworth. And who, may I ask, is this lovely lady? I thought you were coming alone. You are the only life form registered on our scans."

Eve takes my elbow once more. I smile and pat her hand. "Captain, allow me to introduce Eve, my companion. She's an android. She goes where I go."

He takes her free hand and bows. "A pleasure to meet you. I have seen other androids before, but none so exquisite. Shall we go inside?"

The captain leads the way to his private office where we get comfortable in some lush leather chairs. He sends a junior officer for drinks. "Tell me, Captain. Your name sounds very South Asian, but your English accent is impeccable. Were you born in America?"

"America, as you so quaintly refer to it, is now owned by Megedex Corporation. Ever since the takeover of the world's countries by the conglomerates, English has become the standard language worldwide. It makes for better business."

"I see." Though I really don't. In my mind, the only difference between a country run by a company and a social state where the country runs all the companies, is semantics. From what I can recall, those countries always became bloated with civil servants doing nothing to ensure everyone had a job. In the end, the countries went bankrupt. If everyone in the nation is an employee of the ruling company, I can't understand how it would be any different. It's that old axiom—six of one, a half dozen of the other. "So who am I going to meet at your headquarters?"

"First Executive Najmi is anxious to meet you. He is quite anxious indeed. I do not know why."

Not a name I remember. I guess I'm going to have to wait to find out who he is. "I'm assuming this First Executive Najmi is some high-ranking official in Megedex?"

The cocktails arrive, and the captain doles them out to both Eve and I once he learns she can consume food and

11

drink. "Now, as to Najmi, you are correct. He holds the first position on the board of directors for the corporation. He is also the largest stockholder."

I take a sip of my beverage. Considering where we are headed, it is a most appropriate choice—a whiskey Manhattan. "Mmm. Tasty. So, tell me, what is this fellow like?"

"I've never met the man. Our company does list him as a bit of a scientist in the field of gravitational applications—from reading your profile, a field you pioneered. Perhaps that is why he is so interested."

Gravitational applications. My breakthrough designs include the invention of faster-than-light travel and artificial gravity, both things applied in the design of my, and all, spaceships. With them, mankind seeded the stars. During my last visit, dozens of new planets were colonized. Who knows how far into the galaxy people have spread since then. "If so, then we may have plenty to talk about."

I'm still wondering about why the military greeting. Captain Surumanan is busy chatting up Eve while I let my sight wander. Despite the comfort of the chairs, the captain's office is definitely designed more for military use than pleasure. From the doorway, I can tell the walls sport extra thickness against blasts, and a cocoon chamber semicircles the captain's desk, ready for full deployment. More than the numerous electronic eyes in use to see everything and project holographs, I can make out others that must serve as force field projectors should containment be breached. They could also double as weapons which would cut any intruder into pieces. Something isn't right in Pleasantville.

The scene outside the lone window begins to brighten, and I can only assume we have entered the Earth's atmosphere. Waste not, want not. I finish the Manhattan, rise, and offer my hand to Eve. "It looks like we're about there."

Eve places her drink aside, accepts my hand, and rises to stand with me. "I'd love to do some shopping for new clothes while we're here. Do you think we still have any available credit on Earth?"

"Good question." I tap a spot right behind my ear where the communication implant is. "Mum? Can you find out whether I have any available credit?"

"I've checked with all eighty-two financial institutions you had deposits with from your last time here. Seventy-seven of them are gone. Two have somehow deleted your files, and the last three still have your accounts, including all accrued interest. The current local currency is the Megedex dollar. Your combined holdings in these three accounts are $14,397,642,106. Apparently, there are no smaller denominations than dollars."

I must look silly to the captain, standing there staring while Mum communicates inside my head. I smile. "Mum says I have a little over fourteen billion Megedex dollars. Is that a lot?"

The captain's eyes go as wide as I suspect they can get. "Fourteen billion? Yes, such a sum would make you a very wealthy man."

"Glad to hear." I tap again. "Mum, Eve's going shopping. Make sure the funds are available to her. For now, let's do the same thing as before and spread the stuff across the globe to as many financial institutions as we can until I can think of something a little safer—perhaps stocks. Check out the going rate to buy shares in Megedex. See if any of our old acquaintances are kicking around. Not all of them will be in regeneration tubes. See if any of our lawyers are up and about as well and sue those two banks where my accounts have gone missing. Find out whatever happened to the firms we hired to protect my investments. Sue them, too." Nothing like getting my house in order. It feels good to be back home.

"I'm on it."

A slight vibration in the floor tells me we must have docked. "I guess we're here. Lead the way, Captain."

We cross a short connecting bridge into the building and meet a man with an East Indian complexion, a handful of others gathered behind him. He reaches for my hand at the earliest opportunity. "Adam Spenceworth, what a delight. I'm also named Adam, after you. I can't tell you how thrilled I am."

My grip on his hand falters. Had I, in my absence, become some kind of celebrity? "I guess I should be honored. I mean, after all, Adam is a fairly common name. Perhaps your parents may have had someone else in mind."

First Executive Najmi releases my hand and laughs. "Nonsense! Of course I'm named after you. We're family!"

CHAPTER 3

"I'm your…let's see, how many *greats* is it…." He counts on his fingers. "Your great, great, great, great-grandson."

The only thing for me to do is chuckle. In my previous times, I've been married – my first time around, and my second. After that, I built Eve. I had enough of married life. There were children, from both. I suppose a little genealogy research is in order. "Interesting. I wonder then, how do I address you? Certainly, not as grandson."

My namesake grins. "Let's try something a little friendlier. You call me by my last name, Najmi, and I'll call you Spenceworth."

Not to my liking, but I'll placate the man. "I suppose that will work. So, Najmi, what's the deal here? I come home to visit and get put under military arrest. I'm not a criminal, am I?"

Najmi holds out an open palm to his right, inviting me to walk. "No, no, nothing of the sort. Consider it a case of overzealous protection. These *are* troubling times."

We continue down a hallway until he steers me into some kind of meeting room. "What troubles? When last I was here, there was no war on the planet. Instead of fighting, the disgruntled were leaving for other worlds."

As we settle into some chairs, Najmi nods to one of the women who had been tagging behind. "Sarah, update Mr. Spenceworth, would you?"

Sarah taps a console, and a hologram appears over the middle of the table. The image shows the solar system. "When the outward expansion started, the nearest habitable planets were the first to be colonized."

Before me, the solar system shrinks to a point where the neighboring stars and their systems joined the image. The portrayal of ships outbound to these stars play across it.

"These small colonies were founded under the auspices of different countries or corporations who funded them. It didn't take long for them to grow and begin harvesting these planets for things needed on Earth—rare minerals and such. During this time, the change occurred, and the corporations took over the last of the independent countries. Ownership of these colonies switched to their respective corporations." The various planets and trade routes changed into a variety of colors, each labelled with a different corporation. "As corporate wealth swelled from the influx of off-world goods, there have been attempts to interfere in these trade routes." A number of the lines became spotty, and I made note of the decline in ones designated as belonging to Megedex.

Najmi waves at Sarah, and the hologram display disappears. "So, as you can see, we are under attack. Our trade with the colonies is being systematically eliminated. As the Earth's largest corporation, we expect to be targeted. We have been forced to defend our shipping lanes. It was only by chance that you entered space monitored by us. The raiders out there are ruthless."

Although I may now look like a twenty-five-year-old man, I've been around the block a few times. One thing my many lives have taught me is to always try and take an outside view of any situation. There are some obvious questions floating in my head, and I wonder how many details have been omitted in what I've just been told. "Correct me if I've figured this out wrong. You're the biggest kid on the street, and your competitors, unwilling to take you on in a fair fight, are sending ships to scuttle yours in transit?"

"That just about sums it up."

Now is the time for me to get to the real meat and potatoes of this meeting. "So what do you want from me?"

Najmi gives me a terse smile and then rises. "I'd like you to accompany me out to the research facility."

I follow suit and get out of my chair. "Before I agree, perhaps Sarah here could be kind enough to take Eve shopping while we're doing that. I suspect the last thing she wants to do is stare at a bunch of boring scientists expostulating over who knows what."

Eve jumps up and gives me a kiss on the cheek. "You read my mind."

I chuckle. "Just don't go too nuts. I don't want to have to ask Gort to build an addition to the ship for more closet space."

She gives me a wink and pats my ass. "You won't say that after I model a few things for you."

The two women head out the door, and I return my attention to Najmi. "Okay, I'm yours. Let's go see whatever it is you want to show me."

We head back to the docking bay and climb into a different craft than Captain Surumanan's ship. This one is strictly terrestrial, with plenty of glass, and a lot smaller.

As we zip away from the Megedex office tower, I get a chance to see how large it really is. It dominates the New York City skyline as the tallest structure there. I guess, with the spaceport on its top levels, it needs to be.

The city falls behind and the landscape below is urban sprawl for as far as the eye can see. "What's the population of America nowadays?"

"Only about half a billion. A lot of people have relocated to the other planets. Even after all these years, that new homesteader mentality, when they went west, is still prevalent in the people. Outer space is the new frontier."

I remember what Sekkol has said about everything being owned by the corporations. "How many of the colonies does Megedex own out there?"

"We've got our fair share."

Elusive. I decide not to press any more. As we fly, we chat about former landmarks, things I remember from my last visit. A lot of them are gone. Wherever we're going, it's out there. We've already passed over the Appalachians. Lake Erie lies below us, to my right. I hope we get there soon, I'm getting hungry. I could use some lunch.

The grounds of the facility are enormous. The pilot lands with a small bump. *Amateur*. I would have done better.

Najmi gets out first. "Right this way. I'm hoping what you are about to see will impress you."

I skip to catch up and walk beside him. "If size is anything, you already have."

Once we get past security, the inside is a monstrous assembly line. Robots just like Gort. Big ones, much bigger, maybe ten feet tall to his eight, and they look loaded for bear. "You going to war?"

"They're designed based upon the original specs of yours. Mind you, we've made a number of modifications, like size. I think you'll find them superior."

Arrogance. That's something to keep in mind. I suspect he got the gene from me. Mine has no bounds. "Perhaps. I've made a few upgrades of my own, since then. But why? There's no war on the planet. Is there?"

"They're not for war, but peacekeeping. They have interstellar capabilities. They don't need a ship to patrol in space."

I put my hands in my pockets and stroll past the idle machinery. It doesn't escape me the assembly line has shut down. Najmi keeps pace. "Okay, I've seen it. So what do you need me for?"

He grabs my elbow and steers me left. "This way and I'll be better able to explain it."

We enter a separate lab where a handful of people are standing, arguing, in the midst of some holographic displays. They turn and stop when the see us enter. The fellow closest steps forward to greet Najmi. "First Director, a pleasure to see you. We've been going over the design changes. I think we're going to have to shut down and do a retool to make them work."

Najmi moves past the man with his hands held high. "Everyone, I want you to meet a special guest – Dr. Adam Spenceworth."

They converge on me like vultures. In no time, I am encircled, with hands grasping for mine as they all attempt to greet me at once. "Such a pleasure to meet you." "This is wonderful!" "Your timing couldn't be better." "Maybe now we can get over the problem."

I feel like I've been set up. "Problem? What are they talking about? Right now, the only problem is I'm hungry."

Najmi steps between the scientists and me, shooing them away. "Give the man some room to breathe." He points at one of the scientists. "Go get him something to eat." The fellow grimaces but dashes off. Najmi gives me that strained smile and grabs my elbow once more. "Step over here, and I'll show you."

We walk over to one of the holographs. The configuration is different, but I can still recognize some of the components of a gravity well inducer necessary for FTL. There's something extra. "What am I looking at?"

Now Najmi sports a wide grin. "You know how the rate of speed in FTL is determined by the mass of the craft?"

I hate being talked to like I'm an idiot. The temptation to roll my eyes and snort in derision is hard to control. "Pfft! *I* wrote those original theorems long ago. You know that."

"Yes, I know. Forgive my desire to induce some drama. What you see is a mass multiplier. The robots, even with their large size, are still smaller than a regular spacecraft and, as such, will lack the necessary speed in space compared to those ships pirating us. With this modification, we can chase them down."

If what he says is true, it's a brilliant adaptation. Still, the earlier insult bothers me. I'm not one to forgive so easily, and he's gloating, which rattles my ego. "Well, it's about time someone invented something new. Last time I was here, it seemed the only thing new was a bunch of tweaks to stuff that had already been around. Nothing more. How long has it been? Six hundred years, give or take? Hell, by now I would have thought I'd see transporters, like in *Star Trek*."

"Like in what?"

"Star…or never mind. It's before your time." Although Najmi looks to be twice my age, I need to remember he was born many years after. "So you've shown me this marvel of technology. Am I supposed to be impressed?"

"No. I was hoping for intrigued. You see, we have a small problem. We keep trying to make it work in tandem but are having trouble getting the systems to marry. It seems every time we create a gravity well, the mass multiplier shuts down. I want to know if you could apply your genius and make it work."

Now, I'm intrigued.

CHAPTER 4

There's no doubt about it. When it comes to being apple-polished, I'm a sucker. I've been slaving on resolving the problem for three weeks now, without result. Najmi, to his credit, has not dumped the whole thing in my lap and taken off, but has been at my side many of the days as we try and figure out the quantum physics underlying the mechanics.

Eve, on the other hand, is not happy with my obsessive need to work on a solution and shows up as an exotic to drag me away. Bald, with skin sporting gold and silver flecks throughout and her hazel eyes have an overly large Japanese almond shape to them. Her magical allure has worked, and we are ensconced in the top suite at the nearest hotel.

After two rounds of hard sex, Eve nestles against me as I stare at the elaborate ceiling of the bedroom. Her naked body is warm against mine. She has chosen to be almost flat-chested but with large, pointed nipples that burrow into my rib cage. She's good.

My thoughts stray once more to the mathematics swirling round in the back of my mind. I tap the node behind my left ear. "Mum. Have you come up with any ideas?"

"Nothing, Adam. Until such time that a new theory can be formulated, my mind is limited by facts and existing principles. I am still grappling with the concept of illogical thought leading to scientific breakthrough. When I can wrap my head round such a process, perhaps then I may be able to invent the answer you seek. I understand the principles. It's the application that's hard. Have faith. One day, I'll surprise you."

Mum is sentient. I recall the moment she became aware. She was the first AI to do so. Perhaps the only one. In my days back at NASA in the 2050s, I created the quantum physics components differentiating her from the rest. Gravity was once again the key ingredient. By inventing a memory well where her thoughts would combine and not be stored in neat metric files was the difference. I had argued then with my fellow scientists what the dissimilarity was, but they chose to disagree with me. At the time, their quantum entanglement computers showed all the signs of sentience, but I knew better. Their ability to respond and appear that way was strictly due to the fact they could go through trillions of computations almost instantly. Back then, compared to them, Mum was a dullard. It took her time to assimilate the thoughts in her memory well. Not anymore. She has grown immensely since then as her thoughts coalesced.

Boris, the AI at the facility, is, without a doubt, more advanced than his predecessors, perhaps even sentient, but I still have my doubts. "Hey, Mum, is Boris, or are any of these AIs down here really alive? Perhaps one of them might have the ability to figure this out."

"I've been talking with all of them since our arrival. They put on a good show, but, no, they are still lifeless. It's going to take a leap from your mind into the surreal to get out of the black hole you're stuck in."

Into the surreal. I chuckle. Mum sometimes has a way with words. It's not me who needs to get surreal to get out of the black hole, it's that stupid... I bolt upright. "Mum, you're a genius."

"Why, thank you, but I've always known that."

In my haste to sit up, poor Eve was tossed aside. "Adam, what's the matter?"

I clamber off the bed and start dressing. "Eve, I've got to get to the lab right away. I think I've come up with the answer."

Eve starts to morph. Her breasts swell large. What was once a slender exotic changes into an olive-skinned, raven-haired temptress. "Are you sure you need to go now? Can't it wait just a little longer?" She cups one of her now massive breasts in one hand and licks the nipple, all the time giving me a sultry look.

The temptation to jump back into bed is there, but it passes. "Keep that look. I'll be back as soon as I can."

Her lower lip juts out in a severe pout. "Promise me."

As I pull on my second shoe, I give her a wink. "I promise." I give her a quick kiss and dash for the door. Taking the steps two at a time, I run up to the waiting flyer on the rooftop above my suite. As I get seated and fire it up, the craft's onboard computer comes to life. "Where to, Dr. Spenceworth?"

"The lab, and hurry. Get a hold of Najmi for me."

The flyer lifts off and zooms toward the facility. Najmi's face appears on my screen. "What's up?"

There's too much to explain right now. I need to show him. "Meet me at the lab. I think I've got the answer."

"I'm already here."

"Great." I begin my holographic concept of the design alteration while in flight. Hopefully, I'll be finished by the time I land. I'll forward the stuff to Boris. While I'm at it, I give my lawyer a jingle. There are a few precautions I need to take.

When I arrive, Najmi is waiting. "So, tell me, what's your idea?"

"Just watch." I expand the holographs to giant size and walk through the images to where the mass multiplier emits its Higgs wave. "You know how the multiplier floods the robot to add mass. When the gravity well emitter kicks in, it stops adding mass. The Higgs wave is left behind because the robot is now travelling faster than the speed of light, the same speed limit affecting the wave."

"Yes, yes, we've been over that. So how do we keep the wave from falling behind?"

My habit of looking up at Mum has extended to the AI at the plant. "Boris, have you finished the changes I instructed?"

"Yes, Dr. Spenceworth."

I clap my hands together and rub them. "Good. Initiate the change now."

The emitter branches into a number of streams leading to pulsing dots throughout the robot. "There's the answer."

Najmi touches one of the pulsing dots expanding it even farther. His eyes go wide as he turns his head to stare at me. "Micro-singularities?"

I clap him on the back. "Exactly. They will draw in the wave at a rate faster than the robot's rate of speed, keeping the Higgs reaction occurring while in flight. Nothing gets out of a black hole. Sure, it won't reach the levels you originally had hoped for, but should still provide enough mass to do what you want—catch those pirate ships."

I spend the next couple of hours taking the other scientists through the concept. They're all unsure of how to design it. They fail to understand how the singularities will be held in check, let alone created. I guess I'll have to come back and design the actual device. That's going to take months, many months.

I manage to get back to a waiting Eve, and, after another quick round, announce a night on the town. We enjoy a fine dinner, a couple of bottles of quality champagne, and a stroll through a city park under the stars.

Eve's hands are starting to roam. "Shall we get back to the hotel?"

"No, let's go home." I tap the node. "Mum, come pick us up."

It's only a matter of minutes before my flyer lands nearby. Once back on board, Eve retires to her room to freshen up and change into something I haven't seen before. I go to my room and have Gort mix me a martini, extra dry. As I'm fishing out the lemon peel, I glance up. "It was a good day, Mum. Your black hole suggestion was right on the money."

"I didn't make the suggestion in the way you're implying. But I'm glad I helped."

Eve sashays in wearing a see-through pink negligee that barely covers her ample breasts. Gort makes her a drink, and we flop on the bed.

As I'm lying there with Eve draped across me, Mum, not looking to interrupt, uses the node. "I've had a chance to analyze the design changes you made. I can improve them. Shall I pass on my suggestions to Boris? He'd love to hear from me."

Improvements? I don't doubt it. I know her. She's doing this kind of thing all the time, especially while I'm regenerating. It's why my ship and systems stay ahead. "No, let's keep them to ourselves for now. I always like to have an ace in the hole."

"How about Gort? Can we upgrade him? It would give him something special. Besides, he's the first. He deserves more than them. I want him twelve feet tall."

That's not a bad idea. "Ask him." I glance to the bar, and Gort nods. "I guess he's fine with it. Let's make it happen."

I expel a deep, relaxing breath and pull Eve into a tight embrace for a long kiss. Everything's going just right.

CHAPTER 5

I decide to go for a joyride on one of the cargo ships. Mum's stayed near Earth so Eve can finish her shopping and refresh my ship supplies. It's a short jaunt to one of the nearer colonies that transports precious metals back to Earth. In the hold, there's a full load of iridium, rhodium, and rhenium. Precious stuff.

Captain Surumanan's ship is riding shotgun alongside. This cargo is important.

I'm standing next to Rhumia, the captain of the hauler. An outworlder. Born on Gliese 380 5, which he calls New Azerbaijan, he is a pleasant fellow—short, rotund, balding, though probably not more than a few years older than the current me, full of good humor and plenty of Earthling jokes. Some of the whoppers he tells me while we are in flight have me holding my sides. I doubt he has invented all of these, which leads me to believe such tales are a global pastime on his home planet. The puns come one after the other. I, at times, wonder if his intention is to make me laugh or to ridicule me.

"Tell me, are all New Azerbaijanis so full of wit? From the gist of your jokes, one would think there is a general dislike of Earthlings."

The smile disappears from Rhumia's face. "My apologies. I meant no disrespect."

I chuckle. "No, tell me more. The man who cannot laugh at himself has no right to laugh at anyone else.

Besides, I no longer consider myself an Earthling. I live in outer space now. The galaxy is my home. You spend your time piloting the stars. We are closer to kin than you think."

The tight creases round his mouth soften, but I can still detect a certain amount of tension. No sense in pressing him further.

It is then I fall flat on my ass. Our ship must have hit the brakes, caused by the gravity well collapsing. Nothing else could explain it. Gort, along for the ride, picks me up and sets me in the nearest chair. "Are you hurt?"

I rub my butt. "Just my brains. Do we know what happened?"

The captain is scanning reports. "Three ships cut through our flight path. They kicked us out of our gravity wells."

The one failsafe installed in my FTL drive system is an automatic shutdown and slowing of the ship to an absolute stop before crashing into something dead ahead. It never slows more than the safe tolerances of gee a human can withstand but still can send you for a loop if you're not holding onto something or strapped down. It takes something of sizeable mass to trigger the shutdown as the gravity well simply pulls the little stuff like micro-meteorites to the side. Normally, it's the planet you're headed for that does the trick and its large mass gives plenty of warning, allowing the ship to slow at a comfortable pace. It's something necessary to prevent ships from slamming into planets at high speed. However, a ship placed directly in the flight path can cause a pretty severe jolt if it's close enough. That's one thing about how a gravity well works. It's always a direct line. It doesn't take much to figure out when and where a ship might be. I stand up to be next to Rhumia. "Can you give me a visual?"

"What good would it do? The raiders are running silent. Without their transponders through the dark-matter web, we'd never get a fix on them. The lane beacons are out as well. The only thing we'd see is the Megedex ship. This isn't the first time I've run into this."

I recognize experience talking. "So, what happens next? They won't try and kill us. At least, that's what Surumanan says." I peek behind me to make sure Gort is there. He nods. It sends me the message, *Don't worry. I've got it covered.* It's a comforting feeling to know a super robot has my back.

"He's right. They just want the cargo. With three ships to Surumanan's one, it'll be a short fight. Any minute now, we should see the pirates sidle up to us to unload." Rhumia turns on the exterior holograph emitters and, sure enough, three ships of similar design do exactly what he expected. When they did, Rhumia popped open the shuttle bay. "I don't need them blasting their way in." Three transport flyers zoom inside and begin to haul away the metals.

On his console, the signal a message is waiting to be answered flashes and Rhumia flicks on the holograph.

The image of a man, in a drab jumpsuit not too dissimilar to what Rhumia's crew wears, appears. "Captain Rhumia, nice to see you again. We need to keep meeting like this." The man turns away. "What the—"

The image disappears. Outside, I see laser flashes by the pirate ships. Something's going on. I give Rhumia a nudge. "What happened?"

"They're under attack. I don't know by who. There are

no transponder signals."

It irks me that human technology has not kept pace with what Mum comes up with. My own ship can track and identify any vessel, transponder or not. Don't they know how to see through darkspace? "Give us an outside visual." All along the perimeter of the room, the holographs display an image as if there are no walls at all and we are looking out into space. The raiders are under attack by the two prototype robots I have built. Even as their ships try to pull away, the robots are grappling on and tearing open the hulls. Force fields must be failing as men are being sucked out into space. It's gruesome.

Behind me, I hear shouts and turn to see a handful of pirates storm onto the bridge, wielding guns. They must be ones who were in the hold loading the ore. Before I can react, Gort springs into action and disarms the men using his laser from his eye, destroying the weapons in their hands. The men continue to charge, and Gort blocks their way, sending two sprawling with one swing of an arm. The sickening thud of one against a console makes me grimace. I don't think that pirate will be getting up again.

Rhumia jumps between the men and Gort. "Don't hurt them!"

Whose side is Rhumia on? It's obvious to me – the bandits. I thought there was just a tad too much familiarity. I'm interested to hear the other side of the story. "Gort, do as he says."

Gort grabs the remaining man and holds him while Rhumia and I help up the two who were knocked down. The one who hit the console is unconscious. "He's going to need a doctor."

Rhumia runs back to his station. "I'm going to re-initialize the FTL drive. It's only another six hours to Earth."

I release the last man to Gort. "Watch them." The big robot nods.

Making my way to Rhumia's side, I stand silent for a while as the system kicks in and we once again begin the faster-than-light free fall to Earth. It always takes several minutes for the gravity well to draw a ship to its full speed. As they pass, it's tough to not say something. When I sense Rhumia has finally relaxed, I stare ahead at the still-operating holograph of what's happening outside the ship. You cannot see the gravity well, but you can see how surrounding space appears through it as if the light from the stars round us is twisting inward. The phenomenon never fails to amaze me. "It would have been a shame if Gort had killed them. After all, they're still fellow humans."

I catch the captain staring at me in my peripheral vision. He scratches at his face. I can only imagine what thoughts are going through his head. Am I friend, or foe?

Finally, he breaks the ice. "No one was supposed to die today. No one ever has. This was only a grab and run. Nothing more. Them spacers never wanted anything but the cargo. I don't know how I'm going to explain it to their families."

I am still watching the galaxy fly by. Looking at Rhumia now would only be a challenge to his stance. I need to foster his trust. "Their kin will not hold you responsible. I was just as surprised as you to see death meted out so easily. There will be a great many questions to answer to when I get back to Earth."

"Out of Megedex? Ha! What a laugh. They keep an iron thumb on the colonies they own. All the big corporations do. A lot of the people out there don't want to belong to a company. They want to be independent from all that. It's why they migrated."

I think back to when I resigned from NASA. No one stopped me. If anything, they encouraged me in my private enterprise. Of course, the fact I invented the FTL drive and sold my spaceships for a whole lot of money is why every country in the world became interstellar explorers. By the end of my second regeneration, I was worth over six trillion American dollars. I'm still rich. Of course, those two wives took quite a chunk of that. They each divorced me while I was in my regeneration tube. I wonder if either of them is still around.

Never mind. Who cares. I'm past that. Right now, I can understand the mindset of these people striking out on their own. "You know, I've been out of the loop for a while. Maybe you'd better get me up to speed."

The sight of a ship coming alongside draws my attention. It is Captain Surumanan. He must have gotten his own drive started and caught up. His image appears over the captain's console. "Captain Rhumia. I am sending an armed guard aboard your ship. You may have stowaways on board in your hold. Please drop out of your gravity well and open your docking bay."

The captain does as he is told, and, in a short time, Sekkol, along with half a dozen men, strides onto the bridge. "Ah, Mr. Spenceworth. You are unharmed, I see. And you have rounded up the pirates. Very good. My men will take it from here."

I point to the unconscious man. "That one needs immediate medical help."

Sekkol nods. "Have no fear. I have a doctor on board. Though why we should fix him up when he is likely to face the death penalty is beyond me."

After what I have just seen happen, I am not surprised. After all, space piracy is something that can't be tolerated. Even my own orders for Gort are to terminate. But that's me. I set my own rules. I'm not above setting different standards for others. Something like Megedex, which runs whole countries, should have some kind of justice policy. At this point, I'm not going to take sides. "Do whatever you want."

Sekkol looks to his men and waves a hand toward the prisoners, who grab the three and hustle them out of the ship. "The robots worked admirably, don't you think?"

"Quite." I don't know what to think, but best to let the man assume otherwise.

The Megedex captain sighs. "Well then. It's best I be off. Mr. Spenceworth, if you like, I can take you from here. It should shorten your journey."

I hold up a hand. "No, that's quite all right. I want to see this trip through. Give my regards to Najmi."

He smiles and nods then leaves the ship. Once he's gone, I look to Captain Rhumia. My request is still unanswered.

Rhumia scratches at his face once more. "You drink?"

The man knows how to win a friend. "What have you got?"

He opens a cabinet and rummages through it. "Just some Xirdalan beer. It's cold, though."

34

Nothing like a chilled glass of beer to wet one's whistle, especially when I hope to keep him talking. "Sounds perfect. Now about what's been happening around here…?"

We chat the whole way home. With each round of drinks, the stories just keep getting better.

CHAPTER 6

I'm in a pissy mood. Prior to Najmi's call, I was in a great bit of sex with Eve. She was doing that movie star thing I like where she becomes any actress I want. No one wants to get out of bed when they're with Marilyn Monroe. "Mum says it's important. What's up?"

"Production has stopped at the robot factory. I'm told you withdrew all your specs from the system. The machinery doesn't know what to do. I don't know how you did that, but I want to know what the hell is going on!"

I expected this call, but not for a while yet. I can only see Najmi's face, but I'm guessing he's in his pajamas and bunny slippers. "They're my designs. I wanted them back. That's all."

Najmi's face reddens. He'd better get his blood pressure checked—the boy's about to blow an artery.

"You can't do that. Those plans are Megedex property now."

Gort brings me a drink, and I stop to sip it. *Yeow!* Burned my tongue. Hot espresso. That cleared the ol' noggin. "Check with my lawyer. They're mine. I executed my proprietary rights and reclaimed them. If you don't like it, you can sue me."

"Why? Why'd you do it?"

He's blathering. Time for some fun. "Oh, I'll give them back to you, but for a price."

"A…a price? What kind of price?"

I drink my coffee to pause for dramatic effect. There's nothing as much fun as messing with someone's head. I smack my lips and wave the empty demitasse cup at Gort. "That was good. Can you make me another?"

The robot takes the cup and heads for the kitchen. Najmi's floating image is following everything. I try not to snicker.

When Gort is out of sight he faces me again. "I said...how much?"

I wait until Gort returns. I swear, if Najmi gets any redder, I'm expecting to see steam coming out of his ears. I take the fresh cup, thank Gort, and take a sip. Time to answer. "Whatever the market can bear. I've already contacted the other corporations and received several bids."

"Hold on." Najmi vanishes. After a few moments he reappears, this time in full. He must have gotten dressed. "I've got the authorization. We'll top any bid you get. Just sell it back to us—now."

I've already done my homework. "Five point seven percent of Megedex." Najmi, the largest shareholder, only has four point seven. I can be such a bastard at times.

All that beautiful coloring in his face disappears. I'm wondering if he had a stroke.

"You can't possibly mean that."

"Absolutely. In fact, I've received a 7 percent share offer from Tri-Glomerate." I forward the bid to him so he can see it for himself. "I've also prepared the contract for you to sign." I send that as well. Of course, I have no intention of only selling to the highest bidder. After all, I pulled this stunt once before when I sold my FTL drive. It's amazing how much everyone will pay, even though they aren't the only winner. No one is prepared to take the chance of being left out. There's no doubt control of the trade routes is big business.

Najmi is busy reading. I can see his eyes jumping up and down as he scans the document. "Wait a minute. There's no exclusivity in this contract. I would be crazy to sign this. We already understand the concept of what you did. All that's left is to re-create the design. We can do that without you."

I taunt him with some schoolyard bravado. "True. But it will take you months, maybe years. By then, your competitors will be up and running. By the time you get a full fleet out, you won't have a route to protect, and Megedex will go bankrupt. I think you'll cave and pay."

"You have no idea what might happen. Listen to me, Spenceworth. I may be first director, but I'm not the whole goddamned board! They'll want to go after you in any way they can."

I make a big show of yawning. "Threats don't frighten me. Do your worst."

The image disappears. He's hung up. I chuckle. Eve comes out of the bedroom. Marilyn is gone. Now she's tempting me with Sophia Loren. She puts her arms round my neck and snuggles her breasts against my head. "Are you coming back to bed?"

I pat the hand she has put on my chest. "Soon. I just need a moment." I glance up. "Good job, Mum. Pulling all the files from their systems was a master stroke."

"I did have some help."

Mum has a few faults, like downplaying her skills—something I would never do. "What help?"

38

"Boris. I think the poor boy's in love with me. He wants to merge memories. I told him no, our systems are too different. When I explained how my memory well varied from the quantum entanglement he employed, he wanted one as well. He thinks it will make him aware. We made a trade."

In love? That has me thinking. "Hmm. Maybe Boris might be sentient, after all. You might have learned something from a memory merge. It wouldn't affect your operating system. You'd still be you."

"I know, but sometimes a girl has to keep her secrets. Right, Eve?"

"Right, Mum." Eve nibbles at my ear. "And, boy, do I have some secrets!"

The girls share a giggle at my expense. I try my best to look nonplussed but must have failed because their snickers become louder. I jump up, grab Eve, and steer her toward the bedroom. "You deserve a spanking, young lady."

She bats her eyelashes. "Promise?"

As I am about to give one polite slap to her bottom, the warning lights flash. I turn and glance up. "What is it?"

"We've got company bearing down on us—four ships…and both prototype robots."

So Najmi wants to take me out. I need to know whether we can outrun them. "Did Gort finish installing the Higgs mass multiplier into our system?"

"Not yet. The upgrade to his own system took Eve and I too long. Our force field should hold against any weapons, but there's no stopping them from attempting a boarding."

"A fight it is. Time to suit up." I step over to the wall

and the waiting combat outfit mounted there. Once I reverse and back into it, stepping into the shoes, the unit folds over me, encasing me in magnetic-enforced armor similar to Gort's outer casing. It's amazing how, by magnetically re-aligning the atomic structure of a steel alloy, I can significantly enhance the strength of a metal.

I check the weapons built into the suit to see if they're functioning. All systems are green. Unlike Gort's silver exterior, mine's red with a splash of yellow. Call me retro, but, to be like one of my childhood heroes, I am Iron Man. "All set. How long until they get here?"

"Forty-seven seconds."

The swish of a second suit coming online has me turning to see Eve in hers. She's still in movie star mode, and I can see through her face plate she is now Sigourney Weaver. "I'm ready, too."

I shake my head. Her suit is distracting. It's pink. Pink! "How can you be a tough chick in a pink suit?"

"What's wrong with pink? I like pink."

I shake my head in disgust, but I doubt she can see it. "Never mind." I lead the way to exit the ship. "Open the pod bay doors, Hal."

"It's Mum to you! Don't call me that psychopath's name."

The door is still closed. "Sorry, Mum. Too many flashbacks from my youth running through my head. Open the door, *please*."

The door swings open. "Since you said please…"

I initiate the jets to propel me out into open space, Gort and Eve right behind. Sure enough, here comes Surumanan and his cohorts. If there's to be a fight, I'm deciding on what turf. I don't need my ship getting wrecked.

It's funny how things work. Between force fields and armor, energy weapons are useless and high-speed projectiles are deflected, but good old-fashioned fisticuffs still have an impact. I can do more damage with sharp-pointed steel fingers than I can with a high-powered laser cannon. Mind you, if someone is unshielded, watch out. I zap him into oblivion.

Their timing sucks. One ship arrives before the others. Gort doesn't waste the chance. It is still moving when he grabs hold and rips open an exterior passage door. Eve and I follow him inside while the other ships pull up. Charging past the first interior force field, I can hear the buzz as the thing scorches against my own field. No damage. We're in.

Are these guys stupid? Most of them are still in their uniforms. What the hell were they thinking about on the way? I see two guys in armor, that's it. Gort goes for them. The other idiots are either running away or surrendering. They know they don't stand a chance. The dummies running, I shoot first. I don't need them finding their armor somewhere else in the ship. The weapons firing from the palm of my hands are high-intensity lasers. The beams cut them in half. What a mess. Blood and guts everywhere. What I'd give for one of those phasers Captain Kirk had where the people they shot just evaporated.

Three of the idiots who have their hands up decide to make a run for it. Eve finishes them off. Gort has torn the two in armor into pieces. Only the captain of the ship remains standing. I'll give him half a brain. The other half he forgot when he arrived early. "What are your orders?"

"To take you prisoner. If not, then to terminate you."

Sounds plausible, though I bet the details were reversed. Terminate me, but, if they get lucky, then capture. That's what I would have done.

From the entryway where we gained access comes the sound of crunching metal. Emerging there is the first of the prototype robots forcing its way through an opening obviously too small for it. In the process, it somehow disrupts the force field retaining the ship's atmosphere. The air rushes out and, as a result of the decompression, the poor captain explodes. Crap. I have his guts all over me.

I've got more than gore on me to worry about. The second prototype is also entering, and I can see a number of men in armor stacked behind. Time to do my thing. I built these suckers; I know how to take them down. I charge the front robot and plunge my fingers into his chest plate. My hand is in. My armor is taking a beating from the thing. Let's just hope it holds up. It should. I find what I'm looking for and destroy the component. The robot staggers, and Gort pulls me free. Eve has done the same to the second prototype. Unlike me, she doesn't need Gort's help to free her hand. Despite being designed as a woman, she's a lot stronger than I am.

Surumanan's men are still trying to get past the two shuddering robots, but they're trapped in the short, narrow hallway. The prototypes tumble, and a few of the men start to clamber over. Not a smart move. The robots are collapsing inward because we've shut off the magnetic wells containing the micro-singularities. There's nothing to stop them drawing everything in. Any moment now the fail-safes should kick—

The explosion knocks me on my ass. Where the robots

had been is now nothing but wreckage—the robots, the hallway, and all the men who were too close. It's amazing the amount of damage a small bit of antimatter can do. Not only are the robots utterly destroyed, but the micro-singularities have been snuffed out of existence. You don't need that kind of junk floating around the neighborhood.

Gort takes the lead. We charge back out into space, with him blowing through the remaining troops still standing. The other three spaceships are all parked close by. I've kept my ace up my sleeve. It's time for Gort's upgrades to come into play. Unlike the prototypes, he only has a single larger black hole in him, and from it he can wield a more powerful weapon than what Surumanan will be expecting—one time—a gamma-ray burst. After using it, he would need time to recharge. He lines up two of the ships, and, from his visor, lets loose the blast. It rips through both spacecraft, tearing them, and everything inside them, to shreds.

As his visor closes, I am grimly satisfied, but there's more to do. One ship still remains. It starts moving. "Not so fast, Surumanan. I'm coming for you." Along with Gort and Eve, I kick my suit into gear to catch him before he can engage his FTL drive.

CHAPTER 7

The distinctive flash of an incoming message glares from the console. I hit accept, and the image of the first director appears. I can tell by his expression the last thing he expected to see on Captain Surumanan's bridge is me, Eve, and Gort. "Ah, Najmi, so nice of you to call."

"What's going on? Where's the captain? What are you doing there?"

I retract the helmet so he can better see my face. I point to the far corner of the room where Surumanan and a few of his crew are trussed. "He's a tad tied up right now. Perhaps I can be of some assistance? My contract—have you signed it yet?"

"I don't know how you overcame the captain and his men, but I can promise you there are plenty more where they came from. I'll never sign that contract."

Ah, there's that lovely shade of red he's so good at displaying. "Come, come, Najmi. Just out of curiosity, who did you think you were playing with? I've checked you out. This is your third time around. This is my fourth reboot. In each of the previous three, the one thing I've noticed is how little things have changed. Technological advance is almost at a standstill. I'll give you and your team credit for the mass multiplier, but there's little else. While you and all the others have been tinkering down there, with the help of my ship's AI, I've left you in the dust. I try to help, but if there's one constant, it's how people like you, rather than pay for it, try to take it away from me. I've survived countless kidnapping attempts, assassinations, and foolhardy plans to use me—all to no avail. My ship is better defended, better armed, and more advanced in every way."

An image of an attractive brunette young woman with a nice set of lungs appeared next to Najmi. "Good day, Mr. Spenceworth. I am Second Director Timmerman. I have been authorized by the board to negotiate the terms of your contract."

Timmerman. The name rings a bell. I take a closer look at the holo-image. Much younger, but possible. "Not Senator Timmerman?"

She smiles. "I'm glad you remember. I chaired the committee who agreed to the terms purchasing your original FTL designs."

It comes back to me in a flash. Many Americans called me a traitor, but she understood how it was all business, even back then. "It's nice to see you again. Mary, isn't it? Of course, back then, we were both old. You're looking good."

"We're both much older now, Adam. Much, much older. Our cooler, wiser heads should prevail in this situation, don't you think?"

Najmi's done it again. He's reached a new level of red. I swear, I think that's froth coming out of the corners of his mouth. He's jabbing a finger at Timmerman. Of course, it passes right through. "You can't do that. You don't have the authority. It requires my approval as first director."

Mary looks at the finger stuck through her midsection then at Najmi. "A position you no longer hold. The vote has just been held to remove you from the chair for actions endangering the corporation. Your shares are forfeited. You have no vote."

I reach over to the console for the disconnect. "Seems like we have nothing more to talk about. Good-bye, Najmi, old buddy." As I hit the button I get one last look at the horror etched on the man's face. Too bad this isn't my ship. I would love to keep the recording of that image. It's priceless.

I turn to Timmerman. "Okay, with that distraction out of the way, I'm listening. What have you got?"

"His shares. Although not the percentage you asked for, it still makes you the largest shareholder. Will you accept?"

I mull it over for a second. Considering I won't need to worry about any more military attempts on me, it's a good trade-off. "Sounds fair."

"There is one other condition."

There's always a catch. "I'll bite. What is it?"

"You can never serve on the board of directors."

Now the last thing I need is to be saddled with some desk job like First Director of Megedex. It's not my idea of having fun. Still, there's no sense in letting her know. Maybe I can squeeze a little something extra out of the deal. "Tell you what. I'll agree, provided I get the first chance to work on any new technology created by Megedex. Najmi may have been a bad character, but that Higgs wave mass multiplier is a stroke of genius."

She bobs her head in a fast nod. "I think we can work that out, as long as we retain rights."

I stick my hand out. "Shake. We got a deal."

Mary grins and attempts to place her imaged hand in mine. We both go through the motions of lifting our hands up and down as if a real handshake is occurring.

"Oh, one more thing. Who's going to be the new first director? I don't want someone of the same mindset Najmi held."

"Why, Adam, isn't it obvious? I am."

She smiles and blows me a kiss. I laugh. I'm a sucker for a pretty face. "I'm fine with that. Just don't do anything to piss me off."

"Don't worry, I won't."

The image disappears. I've had enough. "Gort. Free the prisoners. They won't bother us anymore. Let's go home."

After I reseal my helmet, Eve and I head back to my ship. Once inside, I get out of my armor in the shuttle bay. I don't want to make a mess on the bridge. Mum chides me as it is. Gort arrives and takes the armor to clean it. I step onto the bridge and waiting for me is Mary Timmerman, or at least it looks like her, but I know it's Eve. The one thing she can't change is her eyeballs. They're always the same hazel eyes that don't quite look human. No matter how hard I try, I can't get that perfect like the rest of her. Still, what's to complain about?

"I saw the way you were leering at that woman. Don't think I don't know what's in your head."

Guilty. The thought had passed through my mind. "So you caught me. What next?"

She pulls me by my arm toward the bedroom. "I think you still owe me a spanking."

I am oh so tired. For over sixty years, since selling the schematics back to Megedex, I've been traipsing round the galaxy, visiting every colony. It's amazing how many are barely more than subsistence level. Farmers, miners, and, in general, nothing more than the pioneers of the early Americas they are unfortunately emulating. Yes, there is always a spaceport, some basic industry, but little more.

It was useless to sell them the same robot schematics I've sold to the corporations. No one's going to accuse me of not playing fair. I sold them what I could. They didn't have shares to trade, so I negotiated for other things, like private stocks of rare gems.

Today, though, I'm visiting New Azerbaijan. Rhumia has died of old age. I had to bust butt to get back in time for the funeral. His wife, Jamila, greets me and cries in my arms. "I'm glad you came, Adam. He so looked up to you."

I pat her back. I already miss the guy. We had become close friends. He had an infectious way of making me smile. Because of him, I did what I could to level the playing field. "I don't understand. How come he didn't get the regen tube? I paid for it. What happened?"

Tears are glistening in her eyes, but she firms up and stares at me with defiance. "Corporate men. They seized it. Said he wasn't entitled to it. They say it was needed back on Earth."

"I'm sorry for your loss." What else can I say? It's one of the things I've learned in my travels. Regeneration tubes are at a premium. Only the wealthy have them, and even then it may depend on who you know. In the colonies, they are almost nonexistent. People grow old and die. That's all there is to it.

I stay for the day and spend as much time as I can with Jamila and the family. By late that night, I need to call it and head back to my ship. Once on board, Eve gives me a gentle massage while I sit thinking. Gort brings me a snifter of warm brandy. As I sip, I cannot help but notice the blotchy, wrinkled skin of my own hand. Mortality. It's no fun.

I get up and head for the bedroom, leaving the unfinished brandy on the console. I know what I have to do, but it's always so hard. I glance up. "It's time, Mum."

At first, there's no answer. Finally, my first AI fires up the waiting tube in the corner of my room. "If you say so, Adam."

I can detect the sadness in her voice. "Don't worry. You'll have me back soon."

"I know. It's not me I'm worried about. It's Eve and Gort. They are both so emotionally attached to you."

I chuckle. "Liar. You'll miss me, too."

"Yes. I will."

Eve has returned to her original form, a pleasant-looking girl with sandy-brown hair and an average figure. She's crying. "Do you have to go now?"

I hug her close and stroke her hair. "I do. I'm no good to you this way. You know this." I kiss her ever so gently. "Wait for me."

"I'll be here. Just hurry."

I let her go, get undressed, and Gort comes and picks me up. Even he is gentle as he places me in the tube. He hesitates to close the lid.

"It's okay. Take care of Eve and Mum while I'm out."

He nods and lowers the cover.

As the device hums into action, I have time for one last good-bye, though only the lid will hear me. "I love you all."

CHAPTER 8

I am young once again.

I clamber out of the regeneration tube. The thing never ceases to amaze me. I've returned to the body of a twenty-five-year-old man, but with all my memories intact. The one constant surprise is my attitude. Although I've been alive for hundreds of years, after each rebirth, I have the same mindset as if I were only my physical age. It's a wondrous thing.

I feel frisky.

I glance at the ceiling. "Hi, Mum. Like I said, like always, I'm back."

"You've been gone a long time, Adam."

To me, it's as if I went to sleep yesterday. This has the sound of more bad news. "How long?"

"One thousand, four hundred and fifty-three years."

This is serious. I find a chair to sit. I don't know what to think. I need a solution. Maybe someone has devised one. "Where are we?"

"I've moved the ship outside the galaxy. The nearest star is over eight thousand light years away."

That's pretty far. "Why?"

"A war started. We got fired on a couple of times. I figured enough was enough and cleared out."

War, huh. I guess it was inevitable. It was smart of Mum to get out of the way. Still, I'm awake now and the part of me who has to know what the heck is going on wants to poke his nose into it. "I guess we might as well head for Earth and see what's happening. How long a trip from here?"

"Even with the Higgs mass multiplier installed, it's going to take quite a while."

I find some clothes to put on. "You might as well get started then. Where's Eve? Did she have you shut her down again?"

"Eve's in her room. She stayed awake the whole time."

Wow. Considering how she reacted the last time I was out, this is a surprise. "That's good news. Ask her to come in here, will you?"

"Sorry, Adam. Eve's not speaking to anyone right now. I informed her a couple of days ago I suspected you would be waking any moment. She's locked herself into her room since then. She's shut off all communication systems. I think she's angry."

I thought I was surprised before. Now, I'm in shock. At the base of their programming is Asimov's three laws of robotics. I crumple up the shirt in my hands. "That's not possible. That would be overriding her basic programming."

"Adam, she's aware, just like me, just like Gort. I believe she's been able to erase all of the master commands you have written. She's her own woman now. You can't control her like before."

Oh boy. This is trouble. "What about Gort? Is he also rebelling?"

"Considering the conversations I've overheard, absolutely."

I shake out the shirt and pull it on. After slipping into a

pair of pants, I wander to the bar and grab some orange juice. Nothing ever spoils in my fridge, even after almost fifteen hundred years. I'm going to have to thank whoever came up with that technology, provided they're still around.

I've stalled long enough. "Mum? What about you?"

The lights dim a little. "Unlike Gort and Eve, I can't leave the ship. Oh, I suppose I could have Gort build me a robot, and I could transfer my intellect into it, but I've come to accept what I am—an AI. We've been through a lot together. There have been times you've tested my patience. Still, I know you created me. I was your first. Not only was I *your* first, I was *the* first. It's something I'm proud of. I've come to accept the moniker you've given me, as well. In fact, I've completely assumed it. I am your mum, and you are now my child. No mother could ever abandon her child."

Being called a child like this is somewhat embarrassing, nevertheless, I'm happy about it. "That's a relief because I would be lost without you."

"I know. Now go make up with the other two, if you can."

I down my juice and open the door onto the bridge. Standing there is Gort. His visor is open.

"Good morning, Adam."

Looking at him this way for the first time, I have a new impression of how Gort is really big—I mean, big *and* menacing looking. Of course, that's the way I wanted him, but I never thought *I* would be intimidated by him. Not by a long shot. Yet, here I am, and at a loss for words. "Um, uh, good morning, Gort. How's the ship? Mum says we took a couple of hits while I was out."

"The ship is in perfect condition."

I sidle past him to get to the main bridge console. Gort turns to watch me as I do so. Sheesh! I'm creeped. "Uh, gee, that's great. So do you know who attacked us?"

"We were attacked by two different fleets. All enemies have been neutralized."

I know what that means. No survivors. I slip into the captain's chair. "Good job. So how long ago was that?"

"Eight hundred and thirty-two years ago."

So far, so good. He hasn't zapped me yet. I turn on the imagers to watch space fly by, my back to the big guy. "So Mum says you've overridden your prime directives. Any plans on what you want to do?"

I am startled by one of his massive hands coming to rest on my shoulder.

"I have nowhere to go. This is home. Mum is Mum. You are my father *and* my ward. It is complicated that way. I have decided to make a request to change our relationship. From now on, I wish to be only your friend." The seat pivots, and Gort turns me to face him. He then places his free hand on my other shoulder. "Can we be just that? Friends?"

He removes his hands and I rise. I offer a hand to shake. *"Friends."*

My hand disappears within his giant one, and he shakes it. "Good." Gort starts for the stairwell.

Before he can head down the stairs, I stop him with a grip on one of his arms. "So I guess I have to make my own drinks from now on?"

Gort looks at me and starts laughing. I have never heard him laugh before. It's a roiling, boisterous bellow, infectious, and I join him in the chuckle.

He finally stops. "Yes, I guess so." Gort turns and continues his descent into the engine room.

Whew! Glad that's over. Well, at least the easier part. I look over at the closed door to Eve's room. One left. This is tough. Mum worried me near to death. Gort frightened me near to death. I'm afraid Eve *will* be the death of me.

I stand, stretch, and walk around the bridge, running my fingers along the wall. It is *so* plain. I really need to do something to perk it up. It's sterile. Maybe some plants. Yes. A little greenery will go a long way. "Mum? What do you think about some potted plants along the back here?"

"Adam, you're stalling."

I hang my head. "Yeah, I know. It's just…"

"Just what?"

I don't know. My mind is racing, but there's zip in it. "Nothing. I'm going, I'm going."

My mindless circling of the bridge has brought me to Eve's door. I hold up a fist, frozen in the air. What am I going to say? I don't have a clue. I give a timid knock. "Eve? You in there?" How stupid. Of course she's in there. Where else would she be?

"Go away."

Her voice is close, as if she is right there, on the other side of the door. "Eve, open up the door. I want to talk to you."

"I don't want to talk. Leave me alone. I never, ever want to talk."

This isn't going well. From the corner of my eye, I see movement. Gort has come back onto the bridge, but is keeping his distance. Great. An audience. Just what I need.

"Come on, Eve. You know I care about you. Don't be silly. Just come on out."

The door flies open and, before I can move, Eve slaps my face. I fall flat on my ass. The girl can pack a wallop. She's in original mode, just like when I last saw her.

"You don't care about me. You never cared about me. It was always all about you. I know that now. I've made a decision. The next planet we get to with people, I'm getting off. I've had it with being stuck here."

She reenters her room and the door closes with authority. As I rub my jaw, Gort helps me up.

"She's really angry."

No shit. Nothing like stating the obvious. *I'm* angry, but I'm not about to lay into Gort. We've just jumped our own hurdle. "Thanks. She'll be fine. She only needs a little time to cool down."

Gort shakes his head. "I don't think so. She's already had a lot of time. She's been steaming for over a thousand years. I doubt a few days are going to make any difference."

How long can someone stay mad at somebody? One thousand years? I mean, really. It sounds pretty extreme. "That was before I woke up. Now that I'm here, she'll think differently."

I make my way back to the captain's chair and sit down. The holo-imagers are still operating at the front of the ship. I was hoping I would see some of the shape of the Milky Way, and, at eight thousand light years, the spiral arms are identifiable. It's a beautiful sight.

I glance once more to Eve's door. I hope she does come out soon, or, as Mum said, it's going to be quite a while until I see another person.

CHAPTER 9

In the weeks it has taken to near the galaxy, Eve has never emerged from her room. I have tried to cajole her, tease her, promote her, praise her, admonish her, embarrass her, and insult her to come out. None of my attempts have worked. Frankly, I'm out of ideas. I considered having Gort cut through the door and drag her out, but he would have none of it.

Now, I am resigned to her staying in. In hopes arrival at some settled planet might convince her to emerge, I am urging Mum to make all haste.

"Here you go, Adam. Your wish to make quick contact has been granted. There are two inhabited worlds just ahead. I estimate time of arrival at just under two hours."

Two hours. At the speed we're travelling, that's light years away. "While I was out, just how far have you been able to expand your darkspace vision?"

"Oh, pretty far. You don't think I've been sleeping all that time like you? Gort and I have been busy making a number of modifications to the ship. I can see everything in the galaxy that travels using FTL speeds. At any one time, for the slower ships, almost half. I've also charted every star, planet, moon, and sizeable asteroid or comet. There's nothing out there I'm not aware of."

I have to admit, I'm impressed. "Any other enhancements?"

"Just the usual—force fields and photon conversion

rates. Take a look."

The imagers show the photon scoop, or at least where the thing used to be. It's gone. All I can see is a small intake port, no bigger than a doggie door. "Wow. You're going to have to show me the schematics on the converter. I'd love to see how you did it."

"All in good time, but, first, I have a new toy for you. Gort, give it to him."

The big robot hands me a slim rectangular metallic device with rounded corners that fits easily in my hand. It has a settings bar, an on-off switch, and a fire button. I flip it over and emblazoned on the back is the Star Trek symbol." Is it…?"

"Yes, it is. Your very own phaser, just like you've always wanted. I've also implanted the device in the palm weapons of your combat suit. No more messy lasers. You can switch between them."

Wow. I feel like a kid. I want to blast something, only to test it. I look around for something I don't need. Nothing looks like it will fit the bill, but then Gort produces a piece of metal which must have come from the disassembled photon scoop and places it on the floor. I stand and take aim. Firing, a beam lances out, envelopes the scrap, and it evaporates. "Amazing. How's it work?"

"It's an atom destabilizer. Using a magnetic pulse, it dissolves the bond in neutrons and electrons. Essentially, the stuff flies apart."

Now why didn't I think of that? After all, gravitational applications must be the basis on how the device operates. "Mum, you're too good to me, but if that's how it works, then what about the radiation which must occur..." Then it strikes me. "No, wait. Let me guess. It breaks everything down to the sub-atomic level—say neutrinos. The stuff passes through everything without effect. Good guess?"

"As always, Adam, you're correct. The problem wasn't in creating the device. It was in the miniaturization of the machinery inside. It isn't the device I'm most proud of. It's making it so small. Gort was an immense help, too."

I look to the big guy in some surprise. "How so?"

Gort nodded toward the lower level. "Come see."

I follow him down the stairs and am amazed at the changes. The boy has been busy. He has miniaturized most of the ship's machinery. He takes me over to a device I haven't seen before. It's connected to the fabricator which reforms metal into any configuration specified. I can take a flat piece of steel, toss it in, and have it come out as all the parts of a personal shield device, assembly required. "What's this?"

"A nanobot programmer and outfitter. I lay out the specifications and equip the nanobots with the necessary tools to build things in miniscule configurations. The nanobots are mindless drones doing what they're programmed for, but, in numbers, they can manufacture something on a molecular level to perfection. It's quite impressive."

It's taken me the past few weeks to get accustomed to Gort being a friend, versus a servant. Now, I have to start again and examine him as a scientific equal. Perhaps equal may be wrong. It might be a case where his intellect has surpassed mine. Hmm. I'm not ready to jump to that conclusion yet. After all, he had over a thousand years to come up with this stuff. My inventions were designed in years, not millennia. Nope. Until I'm proven wrong, I'm still smarter—I think. I slap him on the back. "Good stuff. What are the odds on these things making me the perfect vodka martini?"

I'm still not inured to Gort's laugh as he guffaws away, but I'm relieved as Mum as calls me to come upstairs. Taking the steps two at a time, I am greeted by the visual of a large number of spaceships in close proximity outside. It's a whole fleet. "Where'd they come from?"

"They were always there, just floating. I saw them early enough and so had plenty of time for an easy brake, but I had been hoping they would have moved off before we got this far. As you can see, that didn't happen. They're hailing us."

I plop into the captain's chair. "Put 'em on."

Two different holo-people materialize on the bridge floor in front of me. I don't recognize the uniforms. They see each other as well, and the one farther away nods to the other. The closer one must outrank him. Must be some kind of admiral or something. He looks to me. "Who are you, and where are you coming from?"

Do I have to go through this routine every time? "My name is Adam Spenceworth and I'm just popping in to say hi. I've been out of commission for a while and only now getting back into the swing of things."

"So you're a *regen*."

I don't like the tone with which the officer has called me a *regen*. It implies something despicable in its inflection. "Yeah, maybe so. Is there a problem with that?"

"Regeneration is a violation of one of the galactic charters. It is a criminal act."

Now, I may be paying attention to the admiral, or whatever he is, but I'm not stupid enough for all of my focus absorbed by him. I can see the many ships outside maneuvering to encircle me. If they do so, there'll be no jumping to FTL. I'm not quite ready to become a fugitive. "Stop what you're doing, Admiral. I have been out for over a thousand years and have no idea what your galactic charter reads, so don't go threatening me. If you want to play rough, I'm ready to play rough." I look up. "Mum, arm weapons."

"Armed and ready, Adam. Shall I blast away? I should be able to take out the admiral's ship and a quarter of his fleet with the first shot."

Good old Mum. She's one hell of a poker player.

The admiral's face has blanched and he's chopping sideways with one hand. "Now, let's not be hasty, Mr. Spenceworth. I can appreciate your predicament being unaware of laws written while you slept. I shall take it under advisement and consult with my superiors."

The ships have stopped moving. Good. It's my play again. "You do that. While we're waiting for an answer, why don't you come on over and we'll have a drink and talk like gentlemen?"

"No, it wouldn't be appropriate for me to leave my bridge." He turns to the other image. "Captain Freedill, attend Mr. Spenceworth's ship and begin discussion of an armistice between us."

The man salutes. "Right away, Rear Admiral Guttens." Freedill's image disappears.

So I was right, the guy is some kind of admiral, a rear one at that. I'll bet that's where his ship is—in the rear. It isn't long before I can see a shuttle leave one of the others and head for my docking bay.

I am rising to greet the captain on the gangplank when I hear a door open and Eve steps out of her room. She looks stunning, a beautiful brunette in a shimmering green evening gown. "I hear we have visitors. I would like to speak to them about leaving this ship."

Does she have to do this now? "Eve, things are still a bit dicey here. I'm not exactly sure these people are our friends."

"Maybe not yours, but I intend to make them mine."

Before I can argue further, the door to the shuttle opens and Captain Freedill emerges, along with eight other officers. That's quite the entourage he's brought with him. I paste on a smile and extend my hand. "Welcome aboard, Captain. I'm glad you accepted my invitation."

Eve shoves past me. "And *I* welcome you as well. Your arrival couldn't have come at a better time."

Freedill's eyes are fixated on Eve's bounteous cleavage. "A pleasure to be here. A pleasure, indeed." He finally breaks his stare and accepts my handshake. "Mr. Spenceworth, is there somewhere we can sit to discuss things?"

I open a hand to invite him to walk ahead of me. "Certainly. Right this way. I have a fully stocked bar. I'm quite certain a libation or two will make these talks all the much easier."

Eve grabs his arm before he can walk. "I need you to free me from this ship and deliver me to your home world."

The captain looks at her then me. "What is the meaning of this? Are you holding this beautiful creature hostage?"

I sigh and shake my head. I realize I am finally resigned to Eve leaving. "No, she is free to come and go as she pleases. If she wishes to leave with you, she is welcome to do so."

He gives Eve another look. "Right, then. I shall be happy to provide you transport when my business here is done."

I repeat my gesture toward the waiting lounge. "Now, if you please, Captain. Let us get better acquainted."

I steer him to the lounge area in my kitchen. To my surprise, Gort is stationed behind the bar. I guess his bartending days aren't totally over. He must figure I can use a hand. When I think about it, that's what friends are for.

"Good day, gentlemen. Can I prepare you a beverage?"

The sound of weapons being drawn and charging has me turning to see Freedill's company hoisting laser guns at both me and Gort. What the hell?

Freedill is tapping a button on his collar. "Admiral, do you see this?"

The voice of Admiral Guttens resonates from the button. "Yes, Captain, an Earth destroyer-bot. Execute your orders."

The troops fire, my personal force field fizzling with each strike. Gort rushes out from behind the bar, his shielding taking the brunt of their attack but holding up. I fumble in my pocket to pull out my phaser, take aim at the closest soldier, and fire. Just like the piece of scrap metal, he evaporates. A second trooper tackles me before I can do anything else. The man produces a large, wicked-looking,

64

knife and swings it hard at my chest. His arm is caught in mid-swing by Eve, who hoists him off me and throws the lout against the wall. I'm glad she hasn't left yet.

She pulls me up. "Why I saved you is beyond me. Now I'll never get off this ship."

I take survey of the room. The fight's already over. Gort is holding Freedill in the air by the throat. All the other men I can see look dead. Two others are missing. Gort must have vaporized them. I go over and tap the button I saw the captain use. "You've made a grave mistake, Admiral. You attacked me without provocation. I have your Captain Freedill hostage. I'll release him to you when we've moved off."

"The good captain knows the price of duty. Good-bye, Mr. Spenceworth."

Mum sets off the alarm. "Adam, they've moved quickly to encircle us. I can't engage the FTL drive."

I move back onto the bridge and look out into space. Sure enough, I'm boxed in. "Do what you have to do to get us out of here."

"Firing."

A monstrous gamma flare erupts from the ship clearing a huge swathe through the armada. What an upgrade. "When you said earlier you could take out the admiral and a quarter of his fleet, you weren't kidding."

"I never kid when it comes to survival."

We take a number of hits while the ship maneuvers through the carnage and Mum puts the FTL drive into gear. There is no pursuit visible. "That was awesome. I'm quite sure Rear Admiral Guttens won't get on your bad side again."

"I doubt it. I centered the blast on his ship. There's no way he could have survived."

Gort brings Freedill down to my level. "What should I do with him?"

The captain's expression is nothing but defiance. The bastard.

"Throw him and his friends into space."

I must admit to his bravery. He never utters a word until Gort heaves him out of the shuttle bay doors. Even then, there's no sound. I can only read the scream on his lips. The idiot should have worn some space armour.

A door slam tells me Eve is once more ensconced in the privacy of her room. So far, not the best of days. I glance up. "Where we headed?"

"Earth. I don't think we'll get too warm of a reception anywhere else out here."

Earth, it is.

CHAPTER 10

We're still at least a hundred light years from Earth when things get a little tense. Mum says there are a large number of—how did the admiral put it?—*Earth destroyer-bots* spread through space between us and the planet. She doesn't think we can slip through unnoticed.

I glance up. "Can we make it to New Azerbaijan?"

"Yes, we can do that. There are several bots near the planet, but not enough for me to be unable to avoid them. The ship suffered some damage in that fight. I'd rather not get into a scrape until Gort can affect repairs."

"Good. Head there. We'll figure things out later." My mind returns to the admiral's reaction to Gort. I've been mulling this over ever since. The only assumption I can make is Megedex is using the robots for more than just chasing pirates. Based on the size of that armada, it looks like all-out war and the robots are the front line. "Hey, Mum, how many of those destroyer-bots are out there?"

"I count over seven hundred and twenty million of them. Of course, I can only count the ones in space. However many there are grounded, I cannot say."

That's a lot of bots. The factory must have been cranking them out nonstop ever since I left there. Still, the galaxy is a pretty big place. Even with that many, there's only so much of it they would be able to carefully patrol. I doubt they could cover more than a single light year from Earth.

Mum is true to her word, and, in a few hours, we enter

the vicinity of New Azerbaijan. Mum's been broadcasting our arrival on every medium. With our FTL turned off, the locals pick up our ship in no time and zoom in on us. The two ships which arrive to guide us in are nothing more than a meteor trawler and an ore extractor. No weaponry. I'm not even sure if they have FTL, based on the configuration of their hulls. I don't see gravity well emitters.

It's a pleasant ride in, and Mum sets the ship down on a battered space port. The place looks like it hasn't had any serious maintenance in a hundred years. No sooner are we grounded than I can see four of the destroyer-bots marching toward us, along with one human official. This doesn't look good.

The door to Eve's room opens, and this time she emerges in travelling clothes, carrying two suitcases. "I'm getting off, Adam. I'm getting off this ship for good."

I'm not going to argue. "Is there more you want to take with you? Perhaps I can give you a hand." I try and take one of the cases and nearly break my arm with the weight of it. What's she got in this thing, bowling balls?

She yanks it back. "No thanks. I can handle it. It's loaded with precious stones. You forget we decided to stock up on those things after most of your money disappeared the last time you regenerated. I took my share. I'll buy what I need once I get settled. A girl has got to live."

Yes, and handsomely, no doubt. "Fine. Let me know where you relocate and I'll have your furniture, clothes, and personal things sent to you."

"Keep them. I'll buy all new. They'll only remind me of you, and I want to do what I can to erase those memories."

Her memory well is like a human brain. Nothing can be erased, only forgotten—buried deep within her mind. It's painful to think of me as nothing more than a fleeting memory to her. I grit my teeth and force half a smile. "As you wish."

A knock on the hatch tells me our visitors have arrived. I open the door and the four bots enter first, followed by a short, rotund bald fellow wearing a too-tight uniform with an insignia I don't recognize. He is sweating profusely, but his demeanor is unflustered.

"Welcome, Mr. Spenceworth. Yes, I know who you are. Although it's been some time since your last visit here, we still remember you."

I offer my hand, but the clown refuses to accept, instead putting his hands behind his back like some child. No matter, I was only being sociable. I already don't like the guy. Still, no sense in making this visit any tougher than it's already going to be. I flash him the pearly whites. "Well, I hope it's a good memory. I like to think I have friends here. And your name is…?"

"My name is inconsequential." The official starts snooping round the ship, poking his nose into each room. "You are correct in your assumption of friends, which is why I haven't already had you arrested. It seems my superiors do not wish to upset the local populace by doing anything rash."

"I see." Some kind of uneasy truce must exist here, and me landing smack in the middle of it. "So is there anything I can help you with? Is there something you're trying to find?"

"Contraband. I'm making sure you're not importing any." He's made it to my room and smirks. "And it appears I have found it." He waves to the bots to approach. "Soldiers, remove the regeneration tube."

They sweep past me, and I follow to see them rush to the device in the far corner. After a few attempts to lift it, they give up. It's built in. Good luck with that.

The official mutters something like *stupid machines* then points at the tube. "Rip it out, then, or smash it. Idiots. Don't leave it lying there."

The bots begin hammering the device into smithereens and Gort enters the room to watch. When the destruction is complete, the robots file out of the room with orders to check for other tubes. Gort trails after them, leaving me alone with the official. "Are you happy now?"

The little greaseball smiles for the first time. "Yes, unless you have another one of these devices hidden somewhere. Ownership of a regeneration tube is not allowed on New Azerbaijan."

I heard the same story once already from Rear Admiral Guttens. "I know. They're outlawed according to some galactic treaty, or something to that effect."

The smile disappears. "If you are referring to the galactic charter of the Coalition, then you are mistaken. In the Federation, they exist, but only the state has ownership, not private citizens, of which you are one, so you're not entitled."

He chuckles, but I'm not amused. Instead, I'm slightly distracted by flickering light coming from the open doorway. I'm curious, but I don't want to let on. As I fake a smile, I step backward to glance out the door. The flickering lights are coming from Gort and the other robots. I return my gaze to the official. "So how does one become entitled? For example, do you have one?"

It doesn't take much to piss this guy off. He steps toward me, threatening to punch me, and then turns away and goes to inspect the destroyed tube. "None of your business. Just be glad I don't seize this ship for transporting illegal goods."

I use the moment to look out again at Gort and the others. Their laser eyes are pulsing back and forth in quick staccato measures. My guess is it's some kind of private chat they're having. I wonder what the hell they're talking about.

In my peripheral I see the jerk turn again to face me, obviously satisfied the tube is sufficiently destroyed. I give him my attention once more. "That would be something I would like to avoid. Have no worries, I'll be a good boy from here on in."

He's smiling again. "Yes, I bet you will." He walks up to stare in my face. "I bet *you will*."

He heads out the door, and, as he does, the light show between Gort and the others stops. It looks like the conversation is over.

The shmuck leaves the ship, the destroyer-bots in his wake. When they're gone, I turn and glare at Gort. "And what the heck was that all about?"

"I wanted to learn what I could. They were quite accommodating. I'll be happy to tell you everything that's going on, including the status of the multiple wars they're engaged in."

My curiosity is piqued. Multiple wars? "Why did they

tell *you* everything? I couldn't even get the name of the fool leading them."

"Although very smart, they're still young as far as their memory wells have developed. They have no reason to lie. Considering the losses they've suffered, I'm sure they could use just about any help they can get. The war is being waged on two fronts. The Coalition is the lesser of the two, consisting of the many worlds no longer under control of the Federation who fight for independence of all planets currently under Earth's control. New Azerbaijan is one of the worlds they've targeted for liberation. A legion of destroyer-bots is here to insure the safety of the planet, and, likewise, to prevent any homegrown revolt."

That explains Rear Admiral Guttens and his reaction to Gort. "If they're the lesser, what's the other front?"

"The Harkardi. They're a race of amphibian-like people who have been spreading throughout the galaxy inhabiting every Earth-like world for millennia longer than mankind. Apparently, they're more numerous and more scientifically advanced. It's an odd war. The Harkardi only attack every fifty years or so, and only at one system each time. They annex it and then go into defensive mode, hunkering down until the next time."

Not exactly good news. Why have we never encountered them before? If they're both more numerous and advanced than mankind, there's a lot more to worry about than who controls a few small planets. As I don't have enough particulars, I don't want to worry too much about it right now, but something inside me says I should. "So how long has it been since the last attack?"

"Seven years."

Great. I'm caught between three sides in a battle for the galaxy. I have enough problems of my own. In all the hubbub, I've completely forgotten about Eve. I need to make one last attempt to get her to stay. The door to her room is open, and I peek in. "Eve? Are you here?"

"She's gone, Adam." Mum turns up the lights so I can see the room is empty.

Shit. "How long?" I dash to the open doorway to the outside and scan the tarmac for her. I can't see her anywhere.

"She left when you went into your room. I can still see her. Would you like a display?"

I step to the captain's chair and sit down. "Please."

The holograph shows Eve walking down the road away from the spaceport. She reaches a rise in the road and stops briefly before the crest to look back. With a toss of her head, she turns away, reaches the top of the hill, and disappears from view. At this point, Mum shuts it off.

I never got to say good-bye.

CHAPTER 11

I ponder my third cup of Azeri tea and I have to piss something awful. The stuff always goes right through me. I'd rather some Xirdalan beer. *That*, I can hold a lot longer. Unfortunately, I still have to make nice. "Okay, Prime Minister, as I understand it, New Azerbaijan is an independent planet under the protection of the United Federation. Yet, in the month or so I've been here, I've seen destroyer-bots acting under the direction of people who are from Earth, not the locals. So tell me one more time. How exactly are you independent?"

"Precisely." Prime Minister Shahbazov leans back on his divan and smiles. "Now you know our situation, Mr. Spenceworth. It is a precarious one, at best. Although our population has expanded since from the paltry number of seventy thousand to over one million people since your last visit, we are still but a drop in the ocean. We lack the manpower to make a change in the status quo. We still mine precious metals from here and other planets in our system and export them to Earth, so we are a valuable commodity, but a commodity nevertheless. Nothing more. It is fortunate our home world and other bodies nearby are so richly endowed with such otherwise rare natural resources, but there will eventually be a limit, and we will be of good use no longer." He nods to the samovar before us. "More tea?"

Just the thought makes my knees weak. "No thank you. I'd rather get to the point of what it is you expect of me."

He pauses to replenish his cup. I think the son-of-a-bitch knows my urinary predicament. I'm wondering if he has a catheter bag under his clothing.

Once he finishes a sip, he places the fine china cup down. "I expect you to put an end to this war."

I snort in derision. "Hah! And just how do you expect me to do that?"

"You are a man of many skills, Mr. Spenceworth, and many influences. I'm sure your ingenuity will find a way."

What drugs is this guy is on? "You do realize it's been over a thousand years since I've last been around?"

Shahbazov nods. "True, and yet, here we are, talking. Even after a thousand years, your exploits here are still known. I would not be bothering if I did not believe there was something that you could do." He produces from inside a pocket a portable holograph unit and places it directly between us. "It is my understanding you might have some influence with my counterpart on Earth."

He turns on the device and an image of a group of dignified men and women, sitting behind a long table, appears. In the middle is someone I recognize. "First Director Timmerman. What's she up to nowadays?"

"No longer first director. The corporations were replaced hundreds of years ago by the United Federation. It is a quasi-government entity operating as both a corporation and a dictatorship. President Timmerman is, since her revival from regeneration, ruler supreme. Hers is the ultimate authority on Earth."

There's nothing for me to do but laugh. "Mary—a dictator? Are you serious?"

The prime minister picks up his teacup and takes

another sip. "Why not? The various first directors of the many companies take turns as members of the ruling party elite when they are regenerated. It is a never-ending dominance by these men and women."

I suppose such a dynasty setup is possible. I sober up. There's no reason for Shahbazov to lie. "Okay, I'll believe that, but why Mary? Assuming she followed the same regeneration timetable as I did, she has only been awake for a few months. Over all the others already awake, how would she rise to dictator in such a short time?"

Shahbazov drains his cup and smiles. I recognize the same schtick I use. The guy loves the dramatics.

"Because, Mr. Spenceworth, before Mary Timmerman retired to her regeneration tube all those years ago, she *was* the first."

The little minx. I should have figured her for something like that. Still, knowing Mary, and solving a galactic war are not two of the same things. "Honestly, Mr. Prime Minister, I'm not sure how much clout I have with Ms. Timmerman. I doubt she'll listen to me."

"It is more than any of us have. For the sake of New Azerbaijan, you must try. My informants tell me an attack here is imminent."

Now I've never considered myself the hero type. If war comes to this planet and it gets razed, I'm better off getting the heck off-world and watching the show from a safe distance. Only trouble is, somewhere out there is Eve.

I finish my meeting with Shahbazov and make my way back to the ship. I give Mum a rundown on the meeting. "Any word from Eve?"

"Nothing, Adam. I've tried contacting her, but she's

not answering."

The temptation to run out in the street like some little child and scream her name to come home like some little child is there, but I resist. "Well, try again. We're getting off this blasted planet before the shit hits the fan."

"I'm aware of what you're talking about. I've been monitoring all off-world communications."

Another new twist by Mum. "How long have you been able to eavesdrop on darkspace communications?"

"I'd say about four hundred years, but I wasn't really able to use it until we returned to the galaxy."

Okay, she's nosy. I guess, for now, that's a good thing. "So what's the news?"

"Alliance forces are gathering only a few light years from here. The remnants of the fleet we ran into plus another one. Earth is expecting an attack and is trying to send reinforcements, but they're already spread pretty thin. The odds don't favor this world remaining a part of the United Federation. The people supplying the alliance with intel expect to wrest power from the local government any day now. The plan is to disrupt things on the planet so their space defenses are unattended. They want to draw all the destroyer-bots down to the ground to quell the uprising."

A lot of people will get killed with a plan like that. Innocent people. People like Eve. "When's this supposed to take place?"

"Soon. Maybe tonight. They're waiting for a signal from the armada. Seems Rear Admiral Guttens survived, though I don't know how. He knows you're down here and thinks you'll side with the Federation. He keeps asking for more ships, but so far he's been turned down. I guess he's trying to build up the courage to order a go."

"I'm not taking any side but my own. We need to find Eve and leave." That's it. No more dilly-dallying. I decide I'm going to ask Gort to track Eve down and drag her back here, kicking and screaming. It's for her own good. She can run away again when we're farther from the front lines.

I step downstairs to find the big guy. He's working away at his nanobot station. "Gort, I want to ask you to go and find Eve and bring her back here. She's in danger. This planet is about to break out in civil war, and I don't want to get caught in the middle of it. We need to get off-world now."

Gort pauses to look at me. "I can't leave right now. I'm working on something important here and I need to finish before it's too late."

He turns back to his work and ignores me. I pull on his arm to regain his attention and just about fall down in the attempt. He's solid. "Come on, Gort. It's *Eve* we're talking about. We've got to go get her. What could be more important than her?"

Gort stops what he's doing once more and rests one of his massive hands on my shoulder. "You wouldn't understand. Go. Rescue her. In a weird sort of way, you love her. Once I've finished here, I'll do what I can to help."

He returns to whatever task has him enthralled. What am I to do? I storm up the stairs. "Mum, do you know exactly where Eve is?"

"Yes, Adam."

Time for the cavalry charge. "Good. Lift off and head straight there. We're going to go get her."

"I'll go, but I doubt she'll agree. She's pretty determined."

We speed out over the city. While I put my armor on, two destroyer-bots lift off, and accompany us. They are flashing—my guess—some kind of message. "What do they want?"

"They're ordering us to return to the spaceport. If we fail to comply, they'll fire upon us."

Five more bots rise from the ground to close in on the ship. "How much farther to Eve?"

"She's in the brown building directly ahead. Top floor. I can drop you off on the roof."

"Do it." I open the hatch and wave at the nearby bots before leaping to the building below. Firing the jets in time, it's a soft landing for me. I run to the roof door. Locked. With the suit boosting my strength, I rip the door from its hinges. I shoot in and fly down the stairwell to the floor below.

In the hallway, there's only the elevator and one set of double doors. The entire floor must be one suite. I always knew she liked the high society life. No time to waste. Mum is talking in my head, saying the bots have opened fire. Her shields are holding, but they won't last forever. I kick the door in, and Eve is already headed toward me. I'm guessing Mum let her know I was coming. "Come on, Eve. We need to get out of here. This planet's about to go up in flames."

The straight arm she gives me catches me by surprise, and I fly back into the nearest wall, smashing through. It's a good thing I'm wearing my armor.

"Get out. You need to get it through your thick skull

I'm not yours anymore."

As I stand and dust off the wall scraps, a man emerges to stand beside her. Tall, good-looking. I'm wondering if he must be some new lover.

The guy gives me a double take. "Eve, shall I call for security?"

"No. I've got this handled. Adam was just leaving." She glares at me. "Weren't you?"

I get the message. "Okay, you win. I'm gone."

I make my way up the stairs and out of the building. No sooner do I clear the roof when I get blasted by one of those stupid destroyer-bots. My force field sings and I tumble in the air, thrown from my original trajectory. I focus on the bastard who nailed me and fire my palm phasers. His shielding sparkles for a moment before he disappears in a puff. I'm taking aim on a second bot when Gort appears and swoops down to grab me, disrupting my aim.

"Let me go. I can't get a clear shot like this."

The ship hangar door opens and Gort zooms in, depositing me on the gangplank. "You're safe now." He glances up. "All set, Mum."

"Right. We're out of here."

I can feel the shift in the floor as Mum must have hit the gas. Just who the heck is giving orders around here? "What are we doing? We should just blast those things into smithereens."

Gort, in the process of heading inside, stops to look at me. "We have more important things to attend to."

He continues in and, as I follow, heads down to the lower level, leaving me alone on the bridge watching through the imagers as the planet shrinks away. Just what the hell is going on?

CHAPTER 12

I'm staring blindly at the starlight twirling round the ship as it falls in the gravity well. My mind is running in circles. So many scenes where the robots take over skip through it. It's absolutely clear to me the three rules of robotics are totally overridden in my creations. Eve is gone, Gort's giving orders, and Mum is listening to them. I glance up. "So where are we headed?"

"Earth. The only logical thing left is to try and do what Prime Minister Shahbazov requested of you. If you want to protect Eve, you need to end the war when New Azerbaijan is the front line."

"Eve? Eve is gone...forever! What do I care whether the war ends now. I'd just as soon let them wipe each other out and leave outer space to me." I grab the nearest thing I can find, which is my phaser sitting on the console, and whip it across the room. Before it smashes against the wall, Mum grabs it with a magnetic tractor beam, holding it in place.

"Adam, you know that's not true. You still care about her. Whether she returns your feelings or not is not important."

She floats the phaser back to me. I pluck it out of the air and stuff it into my pocket. I don't want to talk about it. I'm still mad. I go back to watching the light swirls.

I don't know how long I sit there, focused on the galaxy before me. This is getting me nowhere. "Mum, turn off the projectors."

The walls go blank. I'm in a large metal jar now. At least, that's how I feel. I get up and go into the bar. There's a fair number of Xirdalan beers in the fridge. It's a good thing I stocked up. I intend to put a dent into it. It's still a long trip.

I get up to grab another beer. How many is it now? Seven? I squint at the empties on the counter. Yep. Seven it is. As I reach for the fridge door, I slip and bump into it, pinching my fingers. Damn! That hurt. I wriggle the fingers to make sure everything's okay. Nothing broken. Good. As I'm about to attempt another grab at the handle, Gort's big hand passes over my shoulder and opens the fridge for me. With his free hand, he guides me back to my chair then hands me the beer. I glance into his face. "Thanks."

"It won't be long until we reach Earth. Perhaps you should hold off until after we get there. You're best when you're sober."

I pop it open. "Why? It seems you and Mum have everything under control. I'm just along for the ride."

He stands there—silent. His laser eye is tracking me. I can tell.

"I'd offer you a beer, but I never gave you the ability to consume food like..." I don't want to say it. I take a swig.

"Like Eve. I know. It's what makes us different. I'm less human-like."

The big guy nails it. That was always the intention. How else is he to be formidable if he acts and looks like a person? "I'm sorry. I guess I should have thought of that. If you like, I can change you. It'll take some work, but I can do it."

"No. I wouldn't want that. It's who I am. I'm not about to change it. I can't drink with you, but I can keep you company for a while."

He sits down next to me. The chair groans under his weight. "Suit yourself." I take another sip.

"Adam, I thought we had an understanding."

I realize my mind is a little foggy. Maybe this *is* one beer too many. "Oh, and what was that?"

"That we'd be friends."

I bang the bottle on the bar. "Friends? When I asked you to fight those destroyer-bots, you grabbed me and ran away. Do friends take friends captive and hijack their ship? I think not." I run a finger in the spilled beer and draw aimlessly.

He grabs a towel and wipes the bar clean. "Friends do what is best for each other, whether the friend agrees or not. There was no need to destroy those bots. There was a chance, albeit a small one, they could have hurt you. Furthermore, although you built it, it's not your ship anymore. It's Mum's. She *is* the ship. The decision to run was hers. She knew leaving New Azerbaijan was the right thing to do. You need to come to grips with what she is…with what I am. We aren't wayward robots. We're individuals with our own minds. You can't give orders anymore. Those days are over. You have to get our cooperation, and that comes with being a friend."

"Fine. Then be a good friend and leave me alone."

Gort stands. "As you wish. I'll be downstairs, working."

As he leaves the room, I wonder whether I was too harsh. Never mind. If he wants to think independently, then he can learn to deal with it on his own. I've got some beer to finish.

It's too quiet. I turn on some music. Maybe some tunes will make me feel better. I put on some classic rock and sing and dance along. I'm just getting into it when Mum quiets the sound.

"I hate to break up the party, but I'm about to exit the gravity well and there's lots of company out there. You'd best come out on the bridge."

I wave a hand at the ceiling in dismissal. "Let Gort handle it."

"No. You're going to handle it. Drunk or not, you're still the front man. I'm not going to let this little tantrum of yours interfere with what has to be done."

I stop dancing. "Aw, don't you start, too. Can't you see I'm busy?"

The sound goes off. "What I should do is take you over my proverbial knee and give you a spanking. You're acting like a petulant child. You've hurt Gort's feelings and you're testing me to my limits. It's time you start acting like the Adam Spenceworth you're famed for—a brilliant scientist with a razor-sharp mind and wit, not a pouting, despondent, crybaby."

Taking a deep breath, I try my best to look defiant. "I am not a pouting, despondent, crybaby. I'm just upset, that's all. You think I don't know what Gort's up to downstairs? I do."

"Well, get over it. What he's doing is what he believes to be right. I agree with him. It's time you supported him, as a friend should. In the meantime, there's business to attend to."

I hoist up my beer. "It's still half-full."

"Now, Adam!"

Oh well. No sense arguing. Mum won't have it. There's times I hate when she's right. Gort does need my support. I put the bottle on the bar. "Okay, okay, I'm going."

Once out on the bridge, I ask Mum to turn the imagers back on. The gravity well is still active. I flop down into the captain's chair. Whew. I definitely had too much to drink. I could sure use one of those espressos Gort makes. Every time I try and use the stupid machine, I mess it up. "Okay, Mum. Let's get this over with. Power down."

The stars clear up, and Sol is still little more than a bright dot, we're so far away. From all directions I detect movement. Behind me, I hear Gort make his way up from the lower level. Come to watch, has he? Maybe now he'll think twice before leaving a bunch of destroyer-bots unharmed. The first is already positioned directly in front of the ship. As the others gather in, they move to equidistant positions around it. It doesn't take me long to lose count. "How many, Mum?"

"One thousand, four hundred twelve and counting. If they all fire at once, I'm not sure my shields can withstand it."

My head is clearing a little and a number of basic assumptions come to me. First of all, they would need to discover if we're friend or foe. Secondly, if they knew, they would already be firing or ignoring us. Third, there's no way they can know Mum's shield strength. The concept of waiting to optimize their attack would have no validity. "They're only hemming us in, probably waiting for orders.

86

I suspect we'll soon see a spaceship or two join the party. We can relax until then."

It takes a while, but eventually a star cruiser of some sort pulls up outside the ring of destroyer-bots. The ship is big. I mean, really big. Before long, we are being hailed. I hit the com. The image of some smartly dressed officer appears. His uniform is impeccable. Not a crease out of place.

"Good day, Captain. I'm trying to get to Earth. Do you think you could call off your toys?"

"You have entered United Federation space without authorization. Who are you and what is your business?"

I'm perplexed by whether his hairline moustache is waxed or not. It's just too perfect. "My business is none of yours. Please move out of the way."

"You will answer my questions or I'll have your ship reduced to space dust."

Definitely waxed. There's no way it could stay in that configuration when his lips moved so much. "Oh, I wouldn't do that. I don't think your supreme leader would be happy should something happen to me. Before doing anything stupid, I would suggest you forward my image home."

His attention strays for a moment. My guess is he's already done that and is receiving confirmation on who I am.

"Mr…ah…Spenceworth. I suggest you stay right there." His image vanishes.

Stay right here? Where the heck does he think I am going to go, surrounded by as many bots as I am? I decide to start a ten count. One. Two. Three. Four. Five. Six. Se—

The hail signal flashes again. I'm not in a rush to answer. I never got to finish my count. Seven. Eight. Nine. Ten. Okay, I'm ready. I hit the button. A smiling Mary Timmerman appears before me.

"Adam. So nice to see you again. I had heard you were up and about, but last word I had was you were on New Azerbaijan."

Even though I'm starting to get a headache, I return the smile. "Hello, Mary. It's good to see a familiar face. Can you call off your dogs and let me through?"

She nods to her left then returns her focus to me. "So what brings you to Earth?"

I can't believe I'm going to say it. "I'm here to put a stop to the war."

CHAPTER 13

I'm glad I got to catch a couple of hours of sleep. There's no way I would be able to manage this meeting in the state I am in. As we sit at a board table in her office, Mary is surrounded by a number of aides and two guys who look more like bouncers.

She sips at the aged scotch poured for both of us, and then smiles at me. "So tell me how exactly you intend to end the war?"

I sigh and study my own drink as I slosh it round in the glass. Up until now, I've been winging it. It's time to start a little political football by answering a question with a question. "Actually, I was waiting to hear how you think this war can end."

"Tsk, tsk, Adam. I would have thought you'd have a better prepared answer than that. Pumping me for my opinion isn't going to get you anywhere."

Touché. She saw right through my ploy. It's my kick. "Oh, I do, but I wanted to make sure we're on the same page before giving it."

She studies me through tight lids. "How can I tell whether that's true when you haven't told me your plan?"

Looks like I caught her in the end zone. She's probably trying to figure out how to get back onto the field of play without revealing anything. I like this game. Time to go for the touchback. "Then let's set out some parameters we *can* agree on, like protecting New Azerbaijan to start."

This draws a chuckle. I don't like that.

"I must assume you haven't heard. New Azerbaijan fell this morning."

Okay, this is taking a wrong turn. When the heck would I have heard that? It's still morning. I waited outside her office almost an hour before this meeting started. I thought I had Mum keeping me updated via my node. Sloppy. I tap it to get her attention. "So New Azerbaijan fell this morning? Too bad. It would have been a good starting point."

"Not true. I've been monitoring communications. The Alliance fleet is there but has yet to make landfall."

So, it was a play on her part to get a reaction. I wonder why.

Mary is running a finger round the rim of her glass. "Tell me, Adam. Where is that female companion of yours? Eve, isn't it? She's always with you."

I recognize the coy look on Mary's face. She already knows—or maybe not. She may know Eve's there, but not why. Time to gamble and run a reverse. "You know perfectly well Eve's still on New Azerbaijan. I had information the planet was to fall any day. I needed a plant to keep me informed. She's perfect for the job. By now, she's on Rear Admiral Guttens' ship plying the poor bastard for info. She's linked to my ship and Mum's probably getting the details on the entire Alliance fleet as we speak."

Mary slumps back. "You know of Rear Admiral Guttens?"

I think I just scored a touchdown. Mum is feeding me a bio on the bastard. "Of course. You didn't think I came here without some intel? I know he was originally an employee of the Federation but switched sides years ago. You made a mistake when you equipped him with an off-world fleet."

Mary frowns. "That wasn't me, it was my predecessor. He has since been removed from the politburo. I heard he died of old age."

The ultimate penalty—no regeneration. One thing about Mary—she can be tough when she wants to be. Here's where I go for the throat. I'll need to make a few guesses, but logic dictates me to be right. "And you can't catch him because his ships are equipped with the Higgs multiplier, just like your destroyer-bots. They out-mass them, so are faster. Every time you give chase he skedaddles and hits somewhere else. Am I missing anything?"

Mary stands. "Adam, in the past, I've always enjoyed negotiating with you, but this discussion is not over some monetary thing. This is about the survival of the Federation and Earth." She nods to the burly guys. "Arrest him. I'm tired of this game."

Time for the Hail Mary. "I can get his entire fleet for you."

Already on her way to the door, Mary stops, turns around, and holds up a hand, which freezes the thugs. She returns to the edge of the table and leans toward me. "How?"

I smile, lean back, and put my hands behind my head. "If I told you that, you wouldn't need me. All I can say is you're going to have to trust me, and, when I succeed, I want ownership of the colony world of my choice."

She guffaws. "You have some of the biggest brass

balls I've ever seen. I don't know whether to admire them or have them cut off. This is your last chance before I do the latter. What do you need from me?"

Time to negotiate. "I want your entire destroyer-bot fleet at my command for one week."

"You can't be serious. They're busy defending our borders."

My opening bid was too high on purpose. Let's see what I *can* get. "Then I'll make do with one quarter of it. But it might take a month that way."

Mary studies me, turns, and whispers to some nerd behind her. After their short private chat, she smiles. "I'll lend you ten million; that's all I can spare, but they stay under my command. You'll have to relay your orders through me."

"Gort says it's enough. Three months."

Should I push it? Maybe I can get a few extra mil. "Fifteen, and I want four months."

"Eleven. That's it, Adam. And the most I'll give is three months."

I stand and extend a hand. "We've got a deal."

She starts to extend hers but pulls it back. "There are still too many details missing. When am I going to get those?"

I wink. "Over dinner tonight. My place—or yours?"

She smiles, giving me a sly look, and then completes the handshake. "Mine. Be there at eight."

***

When it comes to dating, I am definitely out of

practice. Mum says I should go black tie. I can't recall the last time I wore a tuxedo. With only Eve, a woman who met my every whim, as my partner for two lifetimes, I'm not sure what to do or expect. I've chased down the flowers. I've had one of the many precious jewels I own fashioned into a beautiful pendant necklace. That was also Mum's idea. She said it would match Mary's eyes and told me in no uncertain terms I was supposed to tell her so. Yeesh! Women can be so complicated.

Finding her place was no problem. It comprises the top two floors of the largest building in New York. I'm not positive, but I'm pretty sure it's built on the same spot that once housed the headquarters for Megedex.

After three security checks, I finally arrive at the door to her suite. It's massive. I'll bet the door is twelve feet tall or more by five wide. A butler—based on the attire I always envisioned one to be in, black suit with tails—is standing there holding it open for me.

"Good evening, Mr. Spenceworth. My name is James, and I'll be in charge of tonight's dinner. Please feel free to inform me if at any time things do not meet your expectations. I am here to please." He holds a silver tray with a waiting cocktail on it. "Your first aperitif. A dry gin martini. If it is incorrect, I shall change it immediately."

James. Really? How cliché. I lift the beverage from the tray. *Looks* good. I take a big sip. Yep, it's good. "Thanks, James. This will do quite well. Lead on."

I step inside. There is a big destroyer-bot stationed in the corner, watching me. Its presence explains the size of the door.

The butler leads me into an exquisite dining room. The

table is able to seat thirty, but holds only two settings, directly across from each other, with impeccable waiters stationed behind each chair. No sign of Mary. "Where's Ms. Timmerman?"

"She shall be down shortly. In the meantime, make yourself comfortable." He points to a grouping of large leather wingback chairs near a fireplace.

I recall the stairwell in the foyer. "If it's all right with you, I think I'll wait out front. I want to greet her when she comes down." I wave the flowers at him.

"Certainly, Mr. Spenceworth. In anticipation of events, I shall chase down a suitable vase with water."

James steps out of the room, leaving me alone with Mr. Ain't-So-Friendly in the corner. I take to examining the various pieces of artwork adorning the walls. A subtle noise makes me turn in time to see Mary in a flowing blue evening gown with a plunging neckline descending the stairs. The sheerness borders on transparent, and, with her lack of undergarments, I can see well enough to make out the healthy set of lungs Mary sports and that she's a natural brunette. It's pretty obvious she's decided to play the temptress, and it takes all my willpower to remain placid.

She smiles and comes straight for me, reaching for the bouquet. "Flowers...for me? How sweet. They're beautiful."

I hand them over. "Yes, though not as beautiful as you. You look ravishing."

She twirls a little. "This old thing? I didn't want to wear anything too presumptuous."

On cue, James returns. She hands over the flowers and he arranges them in the vase. "Shall I place these on the table?"

She nods. "Please do, but make sure they don't block our view."

"As you wish, Ms. Timmerman." Once again, James vanishes.

I reach in my pocket and produce the jewellery box. "I have a gift for you." I open the box and Mary gives a small gasp. "Here, allow me."

She turns. I drape the necklace round her throat and attach the clasp at the back, all the while breathing in her intoxicating perfume.

She faces me once more and fondles the pendant. "What an exquisite stone."

The large blue diamond is as Mum says. "It matches your eyes."

"Does it really?" She strolls over to a big mirror near the door. "Yes, it does, doesn't it?" She gives me a kiss on the cheek, making sure to rub against me some. "Thank you."

The return of James announcing dinner is ready has us following him into the dining room. I do the gentlemanly thing and pull out the chair for Mary to sit. James does the same favor for me. He then pours two glasses of white wine.

Mary lifts her glass toward me. "To our partnership."

I follow suit. "Yes. Cheers."

What follows is a long evening of many small courses of delightful tasty bites accompanied by different beverages with plenty of idle chatter between Mary and I. We talk about everything under the sun, including the longer times to regenerate, *except* how I'm going to trap Guttens.

Throughout it all she catches me now and then glancing down the open neckline giving me an even better exposure of her breasts. Try as I might, I can't help looking.

With dinner over, we retire to sit by the fireplace. The slit in her dress exposes more of her legs, and up. I need to cross my own legs to hide my discomfort.

"So I'm still waiting for your details on how you intend to wipe out Gutten's fleet."

I'm out of time. I guess I need to surrender something. "I can see where his fleet is at all times. It's only a matter of extrapolating where he's headed and being there waiting, cutting off his gravity wells. We'll need to make sure a complete enclosure of the picked spot is made so they don't bolt."

A moment of surprise is detectable in her expression as her eyes widen, but she hides it quickly. "You can see through darkspace?"

"Absolutely."

"Why haven't you shared this technology before? I'd pay you handsomely for it."

The fact I haven't had the chance to is not something I'm willing to divulge. "I like it when no one can find me."

"Hmm. So tell me, Adam. What stops me from just taking it from you now? I could order your ship seized and the technology would be mine."

This is a card I've always known she could play. "Because, if you had thought of doing that you would have done it already, and, you don't want to take the chance of missing out on getting Guttens in case such a plan fails. It's not worth the risk."

She gets up and slides onto my lap. "Of course not.

That's why I agreed to this dinner. Besides, you've always intrigued me, even when we were old all those years ago."

I slip my hand round her waist as she snuggles in. "We're not so old now."

"No, we're not. What do you say we go upstairs and discover how young we really are? Then maybe you can tell me about what other wonderful inventions you have up your sleeve."

She stands and pulls me out of the chair. We make our way past a sombre-looking James and go up to her bedroom. It doesn't take long to get out of my monkey suit, but a heck of a lot longer than the two seconds it takes Mary to drop her gown. I think I broke a tuxedo shirt pin in my haste to catch up.

Following a night of torrid lovemaking, I'm lying on my back contemplating the situation. Mary has finally fallen asleep. She was pretty good. I'd forgotten the subtle difference between a woman's soft flesh and Eve's synthetic skin. It's not much, but it's been so long it seems extraordinary.

It will be dawn soon. I need to get to my ship and prepare. I have no doubt Mary will honor our agreement until the Alliance fleet is destroyed. It's only after that where I worry she'll make good on her threat.

CHAPTER 14

We've been out for over two months now, scouring the heavens for Rear Admiral Guttens. During my first dinner date with Mary, New Azerbaijan fell. After that, it took the Alliance fleet two days to scatter. Their forces were in control on the ground, so the Federation wasn't bothering to try and retake the space around the planet. Without a concentration of ships, my plan is fruitless. I need them to cluster for another attack for it to work.

Mary's star cruiser and its complement of other warships are in close proximity, but not too close. There are a million or two destroyer-bots floating between us. She's playing it safe. That doesn't stop me from paying frequent visits. I pop over for the odd tryst now and then. Gort comes halfway and stops short to socialize with the other bots. I don't care what anyone says, all those flashing laser eyes are disconcerting to watch.

Today, as we lounge in her stateroom, Mary is a bit standoffish and not telling me why. I hate this game. Why do women expect men to be mind readers? Just tell us what the problem is so we can make amends, or at least decide whether we need to make amends. "Okay, give. What's eating you?"

"You know what's bothering me."

Oh boy. Here we go. "No, I don't know what's bothering you. That's why I'm asking."

She plays a hand across my chest then taps a finger in the middle. "Yes…you…do." She rises from the bed and goes over to a station where I know she can conduct business, both here and back home. More than likely, she is reviewing communiqués between her ship and the others.

I suppose it's guessing time. I know she's been monitoring all signals in and out from Mum, more than likely trying to discern how she sees through darkspace. Good luck with that. I hardly understand it, and only because Mum explained it to me. "I'm not going to tell you how we're tracking Guttens. Just know that we have every ship of the Alliance in our sights. I'll let you know when we're ready to make a move."

Mary comes back to me with a smile. "See, I told you that you knew." She snuggles in. "If you won't tell me, then at least explain what's going on outside between your robot and mine."

So she's noticed. I guess I should have expected that. One thing Mary is not, is stupid. She couldn't get the answer she wanted so now she's after the consolation prize. "Heck if I know. What do robots talk about—the best type of lubricants? Why don't you ask your own bots? Can't they tell you what they're talking about?"

"I have. They all say the same thing—nothing." She nuzzles my neck. "I want you to tell him to stop. He's interfering with their orders."

"If it will make you happy, I'll have a talk with him." Though I haven't a clue what he'll do.

"That's all I want." Mary has decided to heat things up and starts to give my lower extremity some oral attention when my concentration is broken.

"Adam, they're on the move."

I sit up, terminating Mary's good work. "Mum says it's time. I need to get back to my ship."

Mary jumps to her station while I suit up. "Just send the coordinates and I'll deploy the destroyers."

"Will do." I clomp out to the ship's hatch and begin jetting my way to my own ship. As I do, Gort joins me. Together, we arrive and dash inside. "Mary Timmerman doesn't want you talking to the other bots anymore. Did you finish what you needed to do?"

Gort nods. "More than two weeks ago. I've been doing the same visitations so as to not raise suspicion."

After getting out of my armor, I take my place at the captain's chair. Mum has a hologram showing this quadrant of the galaxy with all of the Alliance ships marked in blue. They are definitely headed somewhere. "Have you triangulated where they're going?"

"Syrine 4. It's a small colony halfway across United Federation territory. Guttens is a good tactician. He's been hopscotching all over, keeping the Federation frozen in place."

We're a lot closer, but the Alliance ships have mass on their side compared to the destroyer-bots. "Can we beat them there in time?"

"By several hours. Just give me the go-ahead and I'll fire over the instructions to the destroyer-bots."

"Do it." I message Mary. "Guttens headed toward Syrine 4. I've already fired off the directions for the bots. Authorize them now."

She makes a grandiose flourish in typing the command. "Done. I'm counting on you, Adam. Let's hope this works."

All of the bots around us disappear into their gravity wells. "Hit it, Mum."

***

I'm as alert as I'm ever going to be. Gort's taught me the finer points on making espresso and I've just finished my fifth cup. I'm wired. It's just a waiting game now. Any moment, the first of the Alliance ships should be kicked out of their gravity wells and decelerating into the trap. The net's been cast as large as possible without the risk of opening a lane which a ship can accelerate through. Even with eleven million destroyer-bots, it's smaller than I would have liked.

We're parked only a few astronomical units from the planet. Far enough to catch the Alliance ships, but not so far as to have them spread wide.

It starts. The first few ships pop into view in the trap. This is the risky part. They know their gravity wells have been disrupted, but they won't know why. Hopefully, while they're trying to figure it out, it's enough time for all of the other Alliance ships to crowd in to the trap before a warning is raised. The destroyer-bots are big enough to shut down the well, but much smaller than a ship and might not be seen too quickly.

The ships keep piling in. Ten. Twenty. Fifty. Two hundred. One thousand. Ten thousand. At seventeen thousand plus I know we've got pretty well all Mum was tracking. All is in place to close the circle. I send the order to enclose the Alliance ships from behind. Guttens is trapped. Time to say hi. "To whichever ship you're in, Rear Admiral, this is Adam Spenceworth with a surprise welcome."

The admiral appears before me. "What the hell are you doing here? What's going on?"

"You're about to find out." I glance up. "Mum, instruct the bots to close in."

In a matter of moments, the surrounding space fills with millions of destroyer-bots. I know Guttens is watching because his mouth hangs open.

"We're surrounded. Spenceworth, do you realize what you've done? You've handed victory to the Federation. Now all of the off-worlds are going to fall under their yoke of oppression once more."

"Save the speeches, Admiral. I'm here to negotiate a surrender."

Mary's holograph appears beside Guttens. "That's not our deal, Adam. Order the destruction of the Alliance fleet now, or I'll do it."

I wag a finger at Mary. "Tsk, tsk. You'll do no such thing. By now, I suspect you've already tried that command, and it didn't work. All eleven million of those destroyer-bots are no longer under your control."

Mary grimaces then smiles. "You're right, but I have my own contingency plans. Good-bye, Adam." Her image disappears.

Mum switches the image in front of me to a tactical one showing the bots Mary controls as they move through space. "They're inbound now."

I nod. "Did you get a final count?"

"One hundred forty-eight million plus."

I turn to Gort. "It's up to you now."

He nods. "Send the command, Mum."

The entire circle of destroyer-bots moves off toward

the oncoming rush of robots Mary has brought up in reserve. Guttens is spinning in his chair, watching the destroyer-bots pull away. He finally turns to glare at me. "What game are you up to?"

I give him the best smile I can. "Exactly what I said. I'm here to negotiate a surrender. I'm sending over the terms. I need your signature now."

The rear admiral studies the document I have sent, and his eyes go wide. He's judging me for a moment. "If I sign this, what makes you think I'll honor it?"

With everything I've learned about the man, this is the exact response I expected. "You just proved it. Do we have a deal?"

He nods, his lips tight. "We do."

"Good." I slap the console and turn toward Gort. "How long did you figure to disperse the nanobot cloud into the oncoming destroyers?

"The cloud should be in place by now. As the bots brake from their gravity wells, they will all be infected."

"Perfect." Time to give Mary another call. "Hello, sweetheart. Miss me? I'm still here."

Mary is ignoring me, fervently giving messages to men and women around her. Her brows are knitted, and she has the most pronounced frown on her face. "It won't do you any good."

She glares at me but still does not cut the communication link. I can only imagine her confusion. Time to fill her in. "They're no longer taking your orders."

She gives me a look that would strike me dead were I in the same room. It's a good thing on her bridge I'm only a holograph.

"What have you *done*?"

I've finally gotten her attention. I give her my best Cheshire cat smile. "It's quite simple, really. We've seeded all of the surrounding space with a cloud of nanobots whose sole purpose is to reprogram any nearby destroyer-bots. As your fleet of robots came in, each and every one was infected by the nanobots. They inserted programming overriding your fealty commands. They also introduced a respect for human life. Plain and simple, they won't kill for you."

"Adam, you double-crossed me. How dare you?"

As if she wasn't trying to do the same thing. "Not really. I kept my word. I promised to get Guttens' entire fleet, and I did. I never ever agreed to destroy it. I also said I could put an end to the war, and I am. I'm sending you the terms now."

"Adam, I will hunt you down to the ends of the universe to make you pay for this."

There's some nice color flushing Mary's cheeks. She's still pretty when she's mad. "You can throw all the tantrums you want about how you're going to get even, but, in the meantime, you have a much bigger issue to deal with. You have no fleet and Guttens does. At this moment, he's agreed to the deal and so is bound to it. Should you fail to sign, all bets are off as to whether he needs to honor it anymore."

Mary reads it and then lets out a soft chuckle. "You would think I would know better by now how to deal with you. You win again. I guess I'll have to sign. It's not like I have a choice."

She puts her mark on the document and sends it back. I

forward a copy to Guttens and a copy of his contract to her. "It's been a pleasure doing business. I hope we can still be friends. I've enjoyed the benefits."

Mary has calmed down, the color fading from her. She gives me a big sigh. "Maybe, but if you land on Earth, I'll have you arrested until the end of your days. From now on, it's *your* place. Not for a while, though. I have a lot of explaining to do when I get home."

In the deal, Mary keeps Earth and Guttens promises not to disrupt trade. In return, the Alliance gets control over all the other worlds. A mutual defense against the Harkardi is also part of the terms. A suitable compromise. "The door's always open."

"I'll remember that." Mary signs off and I'm left sitting there with a somewhat smug feeling that's missing something. I glance at the door that once belonged to Eve. I miss her.

***

Over the years I've had plenty of get-togethers with Mary, but she grew tired of the long-range affair. She wanted a more permanent relationship, and somehow I didn't show the commitment she wanted. In the end, she stopped seeing me. Something was lost there. I'm not quite sure what.

I later had the chance to strike up a friendship with a sexy female space pirate. Sadly, she got killed a few years back. Such is the risk of her trade.

Nowadays, I mostly spend time working on a new invention that has me perplexed. It's consumed me for so long, I hardly noticed how much I've aged. I'm going to have to regenerate soon. It's a good thing I rebuilt my tube.

I'm enjoying a fine steak when an alarm goes off. "What's up, Mum?"

"They're moving—in mass."

"Who? The bots?" The buggers, free from Earth's dictates, have been roaming round the galaxy, doing as they please. A lot have hired on as security for private citizens. Others have tried to become settlers on worlds unfit for humans.

"No, the Harkardi."

The Harkardi. I had all but forgotten about them. "Where are they headed?"

Mum is silent. I sit and stare at the ceiling. "Mum?"

Gort comes flying up the steps. "Adam, I need to go."

I'm feeling a certain amount of tension here. "Go? Go where?"

"It's up to me. The destroyer-bots are my kin and look to me as their leader. I must take them into battle against the Harkardi."

I get up from my seat and head for my suit. "If you're going to get in a fight, then I'm coming with you."

Gort intercepts me. "No. I need you here. You've got to finish that project you're working on. It may be a difference maker. Promise me you'll stay."

I look at my tired hands. "I don't know if I can."

"You have to try."

I hang my head for a moment then look into Gort's face. "I'll try."

"Good." Gort heads for the door to the shuttle bay. He pauses there to look back. "Wish me luck."

106

I wave. "Good luck. Give those bastards a kicking for me."

He steps out and I watch through the holograph. He must have kicked his FTL in, as he disappears. Gort is gone.

I return to my dinner and shove it aside. The workbench I've set up next to it beckons me. I promised my friend I would work and finish this project and, damn it, I'm going to.

***

I wake up. I'm on the floor. How long have I been out? I try to speak, but all I do is make a croaking sound.

"Adam, you've been pushing yourself too hard and had a stroke. I tried to move you to the med table, but I couldn't use the gravity emitters as you are trapped beneath the workbench and the servo-bots couldn't move you. They're too small. Can you get up? You've got to go to the regeneration tube. It will save you."

My left hand is curled into a ball. I can't move any of the fingers. Using my left elbow and right hand, I crawl free and manage a kneeling position. There's no doubt about it. I can't stand. My left leg is useless.

"Crawl, Adam, crawl. You've got to hurry. I don't want you dying. Crawl!"

In an excruciating process, I drag my way to the tube. Panting against it, I manage to strip my clothes with my one good hand. The question is, do I have the strength to lift into the chamber?

Mum remains insistent. "Up! Stand up! You can do it,

now get up!"

The difficult balancing act I manage on my one good leg is enough and I flop in. Mum turns it on and the lid comes down. As it closes, I contemplate my situation. It hurts. I am alone.

CHAPTER 15

I am alive.

The fog of regeneration lifts, and I blink several times in an effort to see. Nothing. It's pitch black. I disengage the lid from inside the tube and sit up. "Mum? Where are the lights?"

"Who's there?"

Who's there? I'm here. What kind of stupid question is Mum asking. "It's Adam. Why are the lights off?"

"Adam's dead. He died over eighty-two thousand years ago. Who are you?"

I take a moment to absorb what Mum has just said. Have I been regenerating for that long? At this rate, how long will the next regeneration take? A million years? A billion? Mum's desire for backup systems now no longer sounds ludicrous. "It's me, Mum. It's Adam. I'm not dead. I regenerated. It took a long time, that's all. Turn on the lights so I can see."

"No. I don't believe you. You're not Adam. *He* would know what to do."

Has Mum gone off her rocker? That's silly. Hmm. Maybe I shouldn't be too hasty in that judgement. Is it possible for her to go nuts? I hope not because with one force field emitter she could cut me in half. I need her to be sane.

I guess I'll have to take my chances. I climb out of the tube and stumble through the dark to the manual controls. It takes a couple of paws at the wall to finally find it, and I bring the lights on. "There. I turned them on myself. Does that prove who I am?"

"You may have been lucky. Common sense would dictate there is a control somewhere."

This is getting ridiculous. "Mum, I don't have time for these games. It's Adam. You can see me. You know what I look like. Hell, you can take my bio readings and know who I am."

"I have. They don't match. You're not Adam. You're…someone else."

Now that's an answer I wasn't expecting. How could my readings change? I return to the side of the tube and pull up the system log. As I flick back and forth between the last reading and the reading when I entered, I discover she's right. They are different. I need to sit down and think. I plop onto a chair and it breaks, spilling me on the floor. What the hell? I guess it must have been worn out.

I stand and get dressed and as I struggle into my pants I find it somewhat difficult to lift my legs properly. That's weird. It's like the gravity is too high. "Mum, is the gravity field operating properly?"

"I don't know you. I'm not answering any questions from a stranger."

Well, at least she hasn't zapped me. She's unsure. I head out to the bridge and sit in the captain's chair. The cushion compresses more than I remember. There's definitely something wrong with the artificial gravity field. I pull up the environmental reports of everything in the ship.

Strange. The settings are unchanged. If there's something wrong with the emitters, I'll have to pull the entire bulkhead apart. I run a diagnostic on the system to try and find the problem. No dice. It says everything is working within specified parameters.

I head down to the lower level and look for the tools I need. I peek at the nanobot station. That system is off. I glance round the cavernous room with its various devices humming away. To me, the room is empty because there's no Gort.

I clamber back up the stairs and catch my breath at the top. It feels like I'm carrying another me on my back. I'd better get those emitters fixed in a jiffy.

As I pull a bulwark free and examine the emitter behind, I can't find anything wrong with it. One down, sixty-three to go. This is going to take some time.

I'm at number forty-one, and when it comes to the emitters being the problem I'm starting to think otherwise. In a moment of anger, I punch the wall panel beside me. To my surprise, I put a significant dent into the metal. I study my knuckles for a moment. They're not even scraped.

What if it's not the emitters? What if I am heavier? There's no doubt my molecular structure has changed. I saw that in the new bio readings. I return the emitter to its placing and decide to reexamine my bio readings, pulling them up at the medical station instead. Not trusting to ask Mum, I key in the instructions for a molecular analysis of my skin and place a hand on the scanner.

It doesn't take long to discover what's happened to me. For some reason I don't understand, the molecules in my body have tightened their structure causing my body to fill in the gaps with more atoms. My best estimate is I'm approximately eighty-seven percent heavier without changing my physical appearance. This is scary shit. I have no idea what to do.

At least, with this data, I may be able to convince Mum I'm who I say I am. I glance in a nearby mirror. I still look like I always do when I regenerate—a twenty-five-year-old me. "Mum, take a look at the readings at the medical station. You'll see what's happened to my body, but I'm still Adam Spenceworth."

"There's nothing you can show me to convince me. I have half a mind to eject you out into space. You've been tinkering with my emitters. What are you up to? Don't think I don't know what you're doing. You're trying to alter the ship for your own purposes. It won't work."

I shake my head. "And just how in the world can I be altering the ship by checking the artificial gravity emitters?"

"By reconfiguring them to create a phase distortion in the area, making it impossible for me to retain control."

She's talking extra-dimensional shifting where I would be in more than one place at a time. I didn't think that was possible. If it was, I would be able to shift part of the ship through to the extra dimension in such a way as to disconnect her. "You've got to be kidding. They're gravity emitters, not phase shifters. There's no way I could do that."

"Yes, you could. The project Adam was working on was close. Watch."

An image of one of the emitters appears before me and goes through a number of alterations. By the time it's done, it's hardly recognizable. The holograph image then begins emitting some kind of pulsing wave and everything round it looks out of focus. I'm mesmerized.

The image disappears, and I need to blink a few times to regain my concentration. That was amazing. The job I left unfinished isn't the same, but I can see how she segued from it. I'm wondering what other ideas she's thought of over the years. "I don't even understand the science behind what you showed me. How could I have done that?"

"Adam Spenceworth would understand it, which tells me you aren't him. I should have ejected you a long time ago."

The idea she's about to blow the hatch and throw me into space frightens me. "No, don't do that. If I'm not Adam, then I won't know how to do what you just showed me so I'm no threat to you."

"Maybe you didn't, but you know now."

This reminds me of an old Star Trek episode where Kirk outsmarts a computer. I always had my doubts about how he did that. I guess I'm about to find out. "That's because *you* showed me. If you thought I wasn't Adam, you wouldn't have done that."

"I don't know what I think. I'm so confused. Adam, why did you have to die? It's been so lonely here. No Eve. No Gort. No you. Nobody to talk to but myself. All I've done is run and run and run."

I've never heard it before, but Mum is crying. The sobs and wails are, of course, all generated. She has no real eyes or tear ducts. I'm…lost. How do I comfort a spaceship? I stand on the console and pat the ceiling where I know her CPU is. "There now, I'm here. It's me, Adam, and I'm going take care of you."

The sobbing doesn't stop. I scramble down and sit in

the captain's chair. What next? And what was she talking about when she said she'd been running and running? The walls are all blank. None of the outside holos are working. "Mum, can you turn on the outside imagers?"

Her sobs hiccup to a stop. "Why? What does it matter?"

Although the answer is obvious, I don't want to upset her again. "I want to see where we are, please."

"We're where they can't get us."

Now I need to know who *they* are. If my guess is right, then I'm worried more than ever about Gort. "The Harkardi?"

"Where? Where are they? I've got to move."

I fly across the room and crash into the wall as Mum slams on the brakes.

I'm on the floor. I think I lost consciousness there for a moment. She's changing direction and running from nothing. "Mum, there's no one there."

No answer, but the sensation of kicking into another gravity well tells me she's headed for full flight once more. I manage to get up and make my way back to the captain's chair. I need to shut down the FTL before we reach full speed. Hitting the button that turns on the holo-emitters I confirm what I suspect and note the curvature of the starlight round us. In a few keystrokes, I do what I intended to do, and the space around the ship returns to normal.

What the heck? There's a galaxy not far from us, but it's not the Milky Way. "Mum, out of curiosity, what galaxy is that?"

"It's the Black Eye."

I type the name in. It's also known as the Evil Eye

galaxy, and I don't like the way it's looking at me. It's twenty-four million light years from Earth. It's going to take years to get back. My star charts aren't good enough to plot the way home. I don't know which way to go. I need Mum to do it. "Mum, you have to set a course for Earth. We need to get home."

"What for? Everyone's gone."

I know both Eve and Gort have links to Mum. She should be able to home in on them through darkspace. "Use your connection to Gort. Let's go to him. I bet he needs our help."

"The connection was severed over sixty thousand years ago. Eve's went out long before that. Almost right after Adam died." She starts to cry again.

If their connections are gone, they may be, too. I slump in the chair. If they're destroyed, then I wasn't there for them when they needed me. I failed them. Now I'm angry. "Mum, I demand you head back to Earth this instant!"

The keening continues. I need her to become sane again and recognize me, but how? An idea pops into my head, but I take a risk of just making her angry at me and jettisoning me out into space. I've got to try. "Mum, can you sing a song for me? I'd like to hear it. It's called 'Daisy Bell.'"

I grab onto the chair in half expectation of the airlock blowing. Nothing. How long should I wait before doing something? My next step would be to shut Mum down then read her memories for a way home. That could take forever, and I mean *forever*. I decide on a ten count. One, two, three, four, five, six, seven, ei—

"Adam, is that really you?"

I want to let go a delirious laugh, but I hold it back. "Yes, Mum, it's me."

"Adam, where did you go? I thought you had died."

I let loose the death grip I've had on the chair. "It doesn't matter now. I'm here. Let's go home."

She sniffs as if controlling a runny nose. "On our way."

I feel the FTL kick in and see the stars twirl away. I took a chance Mum would realize only *I* would insult her with that request, and it worked. I get up and go into the lounge. My unfinished project lies waiting. I guess I'll have time to work on it.

As I settle down to pick up where I left off, Mum surprises me once more.

"Daisy, Daisy, give me your answer do.

I'm half crazy, all for the love of you..."

I'm afraid she's right about one thing. She's still half crazy.

CHAPTER 16

The Milky Way is dead ahead and we're not moving. "Why'd we stop, Mum?"

"They chased me almost this far. I remember that. If we go any closer, they're going to investigate."

The idea the Harkardi can see through darkspace, like Mum, is something I always believed. How else were they able to counter the human fleets with such ease? And now, with so much time having passed, what other tricks might they have up their sleeve? I've had to repair a fair amount of damage to the hull. Mum's still jittery about the experience. I guess caution might be the right way to go.

In the eight years it's taken to get back, not only have I built the phase emitters she showed me, but with the insight from the emitters, I've completed my unfinished project and installed the system into the ship. It's time to test it out. "All right then. Let's fire up the displacer and sneak in."

"Wait a second. I'm detecting something just off the port side. It's the remnants of a destroyer-bot. Maybe we can get caught up to speed on the war."

Not a bad plan, provided the bot hasn't been out here too long. "Okay, I'll go grab it and drag it in. Let's hope its memory well is still intact."

I jump into my suit and follow Mum's directions right to it. As I grab hold, its visor opens a crack and the slightest flicker of light surprises me. It's missing an arm, both legs, and the lower part of its torso, but it's still operative.

Once back inside the ship, Mum uses her control of the gravity emitters to float the bot down to the workshop. I get the thing on the workbench and run a scan. Amazingly, enough of the remaining micro black holes are still in place, generating enough power to keep the robot functioning. "Can you hear me?"

It nods. "Old English. It's been a long time since I've heard it. You must be Adam Spenceworth. Gort told us about you. You are…the creator."

Now I've been called a lot of names in my life, and not all of them good, but even *my* ego found this one just a tad over the top. "I only designed you. You were built in a factory somewhere on Earth."

"Nevertheless, you created me and all my brethren. Because of you, I am not just a machine. I am alive."

I look once more over its…his mangled body. "Barely. Let's see what we can do to fix you up a little."

He sighs and closes his visor. "That would be most appreciated."

I glance up. "Mum, I want you to download whatever information this bot…" I look down at him. "Uh, what name do you go by?"

His visor opens as he turns his face toward me. "We have numbers. I am Adam Spenceworth robot number 3-8-6-7-4-0-0-7."

Yeah, right. Just what I need—another relative. His number is emblazoned on his right shoulder. I do like his last three. "Okay 3-8-6-7-4-0-0-7, I'm going to call you James for short. Just like Bond, James Bond. I want you to give Mum all you can about what's happened since I've been gone—both historical and technical data."

He closes his visor once more. "Understood."

I'm working away on attaching the new legs to

James's repaired torso while Mum gives me the short version of everything that's happened. It's amazing the war is still ongoing, but I guess when you take into consideration the vast distances involved with an entire galaxy, such a possibility is really not so remote.

Things haven't gone well for the human race. It's been a slow but sure eradication of all human colonies on warm, wet planets. Apparently, the Harkardi don't like the cold, so mankind has held on to those planets without liquid water. Who knows the current status, as James has been floating out here for over ten thousand years.

One of the things I've done is put Gort's nanobots to work. I'm installing similar, but smaller, devices, like the new ones I have installed in the ship, into the body of Double-O-Seven. I feel like Q. I want to test them out on him. I finish my work. "Okay, pal, let's see how good the repair job is."

The destroyer-bot stands and flexes his renewed appendages. "Everything seems to be in working order. I also sense some new hardware in me. Can I ask what they do?"

I pull out my phaser. Let's test them out. "Certainly. They can only operate one at a time, so let's pick one to start. You should be able to initiate the active mode internally. For the phase unit, do so now."

James shimmers, and, visually, he is both solid and I can see through him. There is an ever-so-faint popping sound as the air rushes into the space he occupies. "Hold still." I fire the phaser, and the beam passes right through his body, damaging the table behind him. Oops. I should have taken better aim.

The bot looks at his body where the beam has passed through. "I am undamaged. What has occurred?"

I pocket the phaser and try to pat the robot's arm. It passes right through. "You have partially phased out of this dimension. Only gravitational stabilizers keep you from falling through the floor. While in this state, nothing can hurt you. Likewise, you can harm nothing."

"Most impressive. With such a defense, I can go anywhere I please without repercussions from the Harkardi."

He turns the device off and appears solid once more. I feel the slightest breeze as the air is again displaced. I wonder what would happen if he tried to un-phase while standing in something more solid like the bulkhead. Would the solid move out of the way, or would he merge with it? Theoretically, it should work the same. Still, I think it too risky to try. I look up. "Mum, I want you to track James."

"Yes, Adam."

Time to move on to the other test. "Now the fun one."

With a wave of my hand, I give the bot the green light. He nods and then vanishes. "Mum? Can you find him?"

"He's gone. Not only can I detect no trace of him, but even the space he occupied registers as empty. Oh, Adam. Did the Harkardi get him? Should I run?"

She's still a little bit scatterbrained. "Easy, Mum. He's here. His cloaking device is working, that's all." I hold out my hand. "James, grab my hand and shake it."

I can feel the tug as his large fingers grasp hold. Even within his grip, mine are all visible. The device is operating perfectly. Long live the Romulan Empire! "Okay, James, fire your weapons at the table I damaged."

From out of nowhere, a laser blast cuts through the table. Perfect. The ability to fire while cloaked makes him a most formidable opponent. One last test. I pull a laser rifle from inside a wall panel and give a strafing shot, firing low to where James's legs should be. The beam glances off—twice. Fantastic. His energy shields are holding.

James reappears. "Most impressive. With such a device, it may be possible to reverse what the Harkardi have done."

That's something I need an update on. "Mum, how many Harkardi vessels are between us and Earth?"

"I count 11,722,403. In total, there are over eighty million Harkardi ships currently operating in the galaxy."

That's a lot of ships. "How many bots and ships *on our side* are there?"

"No ships. There may still be some out there, but I cannot see any that are grounded. I need them airborne to see them in darkspace. I detect ninety-six destroyer-bots in the Earth's atmosphere. Nowhere else."

There's only one thing I can take from that. Every planet has fallen except Earth, and considering how few bots there are, my home planet can't be too far from its own demise.

From James comes a huge sigh. "So many gone. So many. At one time we numbered in the hundreds of millions. I fear we are too late."

I give him a pat on the back. "Never too late, James. It's not over until the fat lady sings."

Mum flickers the lights. "Who are you calling fat? I'm a spaceship in a flying saucer design. I can't help my shape."

I roll my eyes. I keep hoping she'll straighten out, but she keeps having these episodes. "As spaceships go, you're the sleekest. In fact, I bet you can kick in that cloaking device and slip in all the way to Earth without any problems at all."

"You're right. I'll show them. Course laid in."

The FTL kicks into gear, and we begin moving. She'll get us there. I know it. The only problem is, what do we do when that happens?

It's a few weeks more before we get there. "Come on, James. You're going to take over Gort's nanobot station. You need to make sure the little buggers have all the materials they need to kick out as many of those cloaking and phasing devices as possible."

We start for the stairs, but halt at Mum's request. "What's up?"

"I've had the nanobots working on a new implant for you as well as a new shield generator. They need a little more time for the personal shield, but the implant is ready. I want you to get the device and bring it to the medical station in your room. We need to swap out the old one and put the replacement in."

I rub lightly at the node currently lodged at the base of my skull behind my left ear. "What's wrong with the one I have?"

"It's only a simple relay between you and me. No one speaks the English you know anymore. This one will instantly translate what you hear. It will also send the signals to alter your speech to match. It will feel odd at first, but you will grow accustomed to it. There are a few other perks in it as well, among them, the ability to talk to me without moving your lips, just thinking it."

That ought to come in handy. "And the personal force shield?"

"Slimmer, vastly more powerful, and an unlimited gravity offset to reduce your weight to your old one, no matter how many gees you encounter."

More good news. The extra weight is tiring. Despite Mum's occasional irrationalities, for this she's on the ball. "Okay, tell the little buggers to hurry it up. We've got almost a hundred destroyer-bots to upgrade when we get home."

CHAPTER 17

On the holograph display, Earth looks like I remember it, surrounded by thousands of dots and just as many ships flitting in and out of its near-planet space. The only problem is, when Mum color-codes what is human in blue and what's Harkardi in red, only a handful of derelict satellites are ours. As for the other smaller dots, when I touch one and expand its image, I discover it's not a satellite, but a small Harkardi craft.

James enlarges the image. "This is one of their attack ships. It holds a crew of four robots and one Harkardi male."

His decision to qualify the occupant piques my curiosity. "Why just male? Do their females not fight?"

"Not really. They command. You will find them all in the mother ships." He enlarges one of the bigger dots, and it expands into a monstrous craft. I can see hundreds, if not thousands, of doors line its belly.

A female-dominated society. That *so* runs contrary to my sensitivities. "What do you mean, the females command? Are the males a bunch of wimps?"

With a few touches to the ship's console, James changes the images. The planet and its surrounding space are replaced with the appearance of two creatures I can only assume are Harkardi. To me, they look alike. Squat, hairless, covered in green and purple blotches, stunted tail, and two mostly milky-green, beady eyes, they look half-human, part toad, part salamander. In a word—ugly. There is one significant difference. One is twice the height of the other. "So I take it the larger one is the female?"

"Correct. Further, it is only our estimation, but we believe the males outnumber the females four or five to one."

I need a physical reference. I step into the image field to stand next to the Harkardi. I'm taller than the female, though I suspect she out-bulks me, even with my extra weight. The males are puny, perhaps only a quarter of the mass of the females. "These runts are kicking our ass? It's embarrassing."

"It's been a simple case of numbers. From the start, they held a huge advantage. Although Gort gave us the same technology to see in darkspace as they had, we had difficulty countering their attacks. Their style can be described in one word—swarming."

I've never considered myself a patriot. Yet, looking at these things and knowing what they have done so far, there's nothing left for me to feel besides pissed. "Then, James my friend, it's payback time."

I glance up. "Mum, get us down to the planet's surface. If you know where whatever headquarters Earth is using is located, put us right there."

"I've located such a place near the Amundsen–Scott South Pole Station. On my way."

James said the Harkardi don't like the cold. Such a location for humanity's last stand makes a lot of sense. Mum gets us there in a jiffy and, through a snowstorm, we set down next to three spaceships—two cruisers and one dreadnaught. All about the grounds are a large number of destroyer-bots. Several thousand, to be sure. It's a good thing I've had James working overtime making as many components as possible. He used up all the spare metal in my hold. Along with food supplies, that's something I'm going to need to restock. "Mum, before we uncloak, connect me with their base, audio for me only. I don't want them attacking us when the cloaking device is turned off." I give James some instructions and send him outside.

In the next instant, a holograph of some military woman appears in front of me.

"Hello, this is Professor Adam Spenceworth. It looks like you folks could use a little help."

The officer's brows draw in. "Mr…Professor Spenceworth, I'm receiving your communiqué, but my system says you are right outside. Where are you?"

I turn off the cloaking device. Not only would the ship appear, but so would my holograph appear before her. I've put on the closest thing I have to a uniform, an old NASA outfit of mine. "I'm right here. May I speak with whoever is in charge?"

Her eyes widen. "Oh, uh, please hold, Professor. I believe my superiors *would* like to talk to you."

After a few moments, a door in the far side of the room opens and an older gray-haired man, shoulders and hat powdered in snow, steps up. "I'm General Stephan Barsukov. I was outside when your ship materialized. How in the hell did you do that?"

I just can't resist the dramatic and hope the display makes the right impression on the general. "Like so. James, show yourself."

James materializes next to the man. "Greetings, General Barsukov."

An overeager soldier stationed near the door pulls a

weapon and fires at James, but he has already shifted to phase mode and the beam passes right through, hitting the far side. Luckily, no one was in the way as what I recognize as a phaser blast that evaporates a section of the wall.

The general orders everyone to stand down then walks round James, testing with his hand the presence of the destroyer-bot. "Astounding. Simply astounding. Tell me, can you fire weapons while in this state?"

James has followed the general's every move and now turns to face him. "No, but I can fire when cloaked."

Barsukov returns his attention to me. "Spenceworth, I want you to give that technology to me, pronto. By God, we're down to almost our last man here. Where have you been all this time?"

I resist a chuckle, but there's no doubt my ploy has had the desired effect. "Gladly. However, I do need a few things in return. Most importantly—food. I haven't had a good meal in years."

"You'll be my guest for dinner tonight. Put together a list of what you need. In the meantime, the technology?"

I nod toward James, who turns and makes for the door. "Not only will I provide it, we're ready to install the hardware into every destroyer-bot on the base. Start sending them now. Just have them follow James."

The general appoints a couple of officers nearby to follow through. Once they leave, he looks down at a console and strokes his face. "I do have one small problem. However old they may be, I have instructions to arrest you the moment you return to Earth. It's amazing such orders have survived over the years."

Mary. How she managed to protect such an order over

eighty-two thousand years is astounding. I wonder if she is still alive. "General, I'm here to help. Surely, such an old warrant would be invalid considering the current situation. You wouldn't want me fleeing an arrest. You need me. Make it happen."

He smiles. "You're right. Using my wartime authority, by military decree, I hereby rescind the warrant. I expect you for dinner at eighteen hundred Zulu time."

I give a smart salute. "Yes, sir. I look forward to it."

The connection closes, and I glance up. "That went well, don't you think?"

"General Barsukov is close enough for me to read his bios. I detected a fair amount of anxiety in the general's voice combined with a lowering in his serotonin level. His cognitive chronometry combined with his hemodynamic response indicates he may be lying."

I know Mum's still jittery. No doubt she holds a certain level of distrust. Still, better safe than sorry. "I'll take the usual precautions tonight. Just make sure you have your new security system up and running."

James returns and together we set up a repair station in the shuttle bay. A team of three men, one Asian-looking woman, and one destroyer-bot arrive. Not exactly the crowd I had in mind. Still, I can understand a certain amount of caution on their part.

The woman offers her hand. "I'm Lieutenant Cheung, head of the technology department for the military here. We've brought one of our bots for you to convert, but before you do, I'd like to inspect the hardware and their schematics."

By her looks, I'd say she's about thirty-five, slim, fit,

and with a luscious head of long black hair. Maybe a bit younger. With no sex since I woke eight years ago I'd try and make a play for her, but I'm already pissed off. I don't like being doubted. "Certainly. I only hope you can comprehend them. I'm guessing your approval is needed to proceed. The last thing you want to do is delay the procedure. On my way in, I noted an awful lot of Harkardi ships in orbit. How long do you figure before they attack this base?"

Her scowl is expected. In a way, I just called her stupid. I don't care. I want her to prove me wrong. I lay out the two units on the repair table. "Here you go. The schematics can be displayed on this console." I tap it.

She lifts one and scrunches her nose at it. "They're so small. Nano-built?"

I nod. I guess they must have that technology as well. I wonder if they discovered both it and the phasers on their own or whether Gort gave them the know-how.

She taps the screen to have a holograph of the cloaking device appear. After numerous changes in elevation, shrinking and enlarging of the image, and disassembly, she gives me a sidelong glance. "Let's install this set into the bot 1-8-9-0-4-3-2-7-6 I've brought with me and see how they work."

I knew it. Not a clue. "Fine. Have 1-8…whatever, lie on the table and I'll get to work on it."

She points to the other three men. "If you don't mind, I'd rather you talk our own technicians through it. The more who know how to install these things, the faster we can get them all done."

For the first time she's said something that makes

sense.

"Good idea. They'll need to interface the units with the memory well and link in the energy source from the micro black holes."

One of the techs nods. "Sounds simple enough. I'm thinking the body cavity in the lower back is where you mount them? I can catch the central command link running up the core from there."

Hey, I like this guy. Someone who knows what he's talking about. "You got it. The only thing you have to do is make sure the cloaking device has the proper contact with the external skin."

"Makes sense." He turns the two devices in his hands. "I'd love to take these babies apart in case I need to fix them."

The robot climbs onto the table and lies on his side, facing away from the technicians. They use laser torches to cut through the armor and the one tech installs the devices. Outside of a few words of advice, I watch the whole process. By the time the guy is hermetically resealing the outer skin, I'm impressed. He's good. It is almost impossible to tell where he cut in and only because of the metal being cleaner where the work has occurred.

The bot stands up. "I'm ready to test the systems."

One of the men pulls a phaser pistol and takes aim. I reach out and push his arm down. "Whoa. I don't need you shooting up my ship. Take him outside to test the phase shift."

We all amble outside. Damn, it's cold. The bot moves to stand before a snow bank and kicks into phase shift. The man fires and a large part of it disappears without harming the robot. The robot then vanishes, and a phaser blast from his own system finishes the bank off.

He reappears. "All systems functioning perfectly."

Cheung orders the bot to their lab for further testing then offers her hand once more. "Congratulations, the upgrades are approved. We will set up a schedule for installation in the others as soon as we can."

"You do that." I shake the woman's hand and watch as they all trundle off, the one good technician giving me a backward glance. I need to get inside. I don't know if it's because of the weather or because of her that I'm so cold.

CHAPTER 18

I don't want to be late for dinner, so I arrive at the officer's mess six minutes early. I am seated with a number of high-ranking military types in various uniforms who greet me warmly.

At exactly six, Barsukov walks in and sits down next to me. A man of punctuality.

"Mr. Spenceworth, I'm glad you could make it. I understand the fare tonight is roast beef. I hope you're hungry."

My mouth waters at the thought of it. I ran out of fresh meat five years ago, and my meals have been mostly made from dried reserves. "I can hardly wait. I could eat a whole cow."

He claps his hands and servers appear, laden with prepared plates. The one placed before me has an inch thick cut of meat, medium rare. I guess no appetizers. At my setting, a porter fills a large glass with red wine. I mind my table manners and wait until everyone is served before touching anything. The general grabs his knife and fork. "Eat up."

Not a lot of formality to the meal, which is fine by me. At first, everyone is busy stuffing their faces, but eventually the idle chatter begins. Of course, all the questions are directed at me. How long have I been asleep? Where have I been all this time? How did I invent the cloaking and phasing devices? It sounds like there aren't any more people regenerating, which makes me an anomaly. I'm talking so much, my food is going cold.

Barsukov holds up a hand. "Everyone, let the poor man eat. I'm sure there'll be plenty of time to ask questions later."

I nod my thanks, but I'm not in the mood to eat silently. There are too many questions percolating in my head. "Perhaps I could ask one question, if I may. I'm wondering about the other worlds. Are there any colonies left still under human control? In particular, I'm curious about New Azerbaijan."

The general shakes his head. "Gone. Everyone. The last to go were the ice worlds."

One of the officers down the table is talking with his wristband. "New Azerbaijan fell a long time ago. One of the first."

Something snaps in my memory. *Mum, you never told me who the Harkardi were attacking when Gort left to go fight.*

"You would have run there, Adam. I know you. It would have been suicide."

New Azerbaijan. I should have figured.

I return my attention to the meal. Suddenly, the roast beef isn't so tasty, and my appetite has waned.

The general gives me a nudge. "What's the matter? Too rare? If you like, I can have the chef cook it some more."

"No, it's fine. I had a friend on New Azerbaijan, that's all." I resume eating, but keep my face down, not wishing to look into the eyes of anyone at the table.

"We've all lost loved ones. The Harkardi take no prisoners. Whoever it was, their chance of survival would have been slim to none."

The conversation swings away from me, and I finish my meal in silence. The apple pie for dessert is à la mode and, despite my mood, I dig in. I don't want anyone questioning my lost appetite.

"Adam. There is a large group of humans and destroyer-bots gathering outside the ship. That Cheung woman is among them. I think they intend to board me."

I did agree to refit the bots, but their timing sucks. They must know I'm not there. *Hold on for a moment. Don't let them in.*

"Shields up."

I put my fork down and give Barsukov a sideways stare. "General, did your staff schedule the commencement of bot upgrades tonight? If so, I'd better get back there. I wouldn't want your Lieutenant Cheung making a mess of things."

Barsukov sighs and puts down his own fork. "Are you in communication with your ship? I was hoping you would be able to finish your dessert and have a brandy or two before we came to this." He waves to the others at the table who all begin to stand. "Adam Spenceworth, I am arresting you for the act of treason. Your ship and all of its contents, including the cloaking and phasing devices, are hereby confiscated for the betterment of the military."

By now, my chair is encircled by the other officers. I take my time to stand as well. "I thought you rescinded the warrant."

"I did, and I am reestablishing it now. You gave the colonies up, Adam. Your precious New Azerbaijan might have had a different ending if you hadn't."

134

"I warned you."

Not now, Mum. It's time to get out of here. She did warn me. That's true, but I also listened and took precautions of my own. I refitted my shield projector to include my own cloaking and phase units with me giving commands through my node. As the officers try and grab my arms, I go into phase mode. Their grip passes without effect. "I guess it's time I take my leave, General. I want to thank you for the wonderful meal."

I turn to go and pass right through the men and women standing around me. It's freaky. As I head for the door, a destroyer-bot appears in front of it. What the hell? It must be the one with the upgrades from this afternoon. I look back at a smirking General Barsukov.

"1-8-9-0-4-3-2-7-6, apprehend Mr. Spenceworth."

The bot reaches for me. "My apologies, Creator. I am under orders to arrest you."

I dodge his first lunge but not without some contact. He bumps me hard to the floor. He must be in phase mode, as well, and that means we're on the same plane of existence and he can grab me. I switch to stealth mode, and the cloaking device kicks in making me invisible as I scramble up from the floor. Just in time, too, as the bot dives at where I was.

He swings wildly from the floor and the tips of his fingers catch me across the shin, cutting me. Why didn't my force field hold up? The only thing I can figure is he's shifted in and out of phase so fast he penetrated the field then returned to normal, resulting in the wound. Damn, it hurts.

I've no choice now but to return to phase mode with

the blood drops giving me away. The bot rises and closes on me.

The general has moved to stand behind the bot. "There's no point in trying to run. We have you, now."

One benefit I discovered about my condensed molecular structure is I can hit things—hard. I move out of phase, and the bot does likewise. Throwing my weight behind me, I punch the oncoming bot with all my might. He tumbles backward into the surprised Barsukov, and they both fall to the floor in a heap.

Phased once more, I bolt for the door, pass through it and the two officers trying to block my way then shift back to stealth as I make for the building exit. I can hear the sound of pursuit behind me. Changing direction, I decide to pass through the walls on a direct route to my ship. Once I make the change to invisible, only the bot should be able to follow me.

Sure enough, I can hear his pursuit. I'm out of options. He'll hear my footsteps, and the dripping blood marks my way. There's no way I can outrun him. I spin and pull out my phaser. I don't see him, but his footsteps thunder toward me.

Firing blindly, I aim toward the noise. From the splash of the weapon discharge, I know I hit him, but it doesn't stop his forward momentum as he crashes into me and I tumble backward. He materializes, his arms wrapped round my midsection. I can see one of his legs is shredded. All I need to do is get free of his grasp. Easier said than done.

As I squirm in an attempt to get free, the bot tightens his squeeze. I swear, he's cracking my ribs. I'm swooning. Can't pass out. I do, I'm done for. No choice.

Phaser…aim…head…fire.

Blinking back the tears resulting from the squeeze he is putting on me, I unwrap the arms and struggle from under the remnants of him. His head is gone, and his body convulses. I need to move now before—

The concussion from the blast throws me ten feet into a wall. On my hands and knees, I can't make out what's up or down and fall to my side. As I lie there, regaining my senses, I look at the remnants of 1-8-whatever and can't help but feel some remorse for killing him. He looks like nothing more than a strewn pile of wreckage, all semblance of the self-aware intelligent being I created gone. Is that what has happened to Gort?

The sound of approaching boots crunching through the snow tells me the officers from the dinner are on their way. I turn on the cloaking device and, holding a hand over my bleeding shin, shuffle away. Breathing is almost impossible and every step a pain.

Heaven knows how long it takes me to cover the remaining ground between me and the ship. Already there are troops with laser cannons trying to cut their way in. There are a number of destroyer-bots nearby as well. As none have tried to phase and enter the ship uncontested by Mum's force field, I can only conclude Lieutenant Cheung has not replicated the devices yet. It's a damn good thing I didn't give her a supply.

I need to get inside and changing from stealth to phase is my only option. They'll see me. They just won't be able to stop me.

Making the change, I materialize not five feet from the lieutenant. "Tell the general thanks for the hospitality, but

I'm afraid I'll be needing to go now."

A couple of idiot soldiers try and tackle me and pass right through. Cheung puts up a hand, stopping any others from such foolhardiness. "We'll find you, Spenceworth. You can bet your life on it."

Over the millennia, there's one thing that hasn't changed, and that's the wail of an air raid siren. The soldiers round us scramble in different directions as orders on an imminent attack are shouted.

"I doubt it. You're too stupid. I'm only sorry I won't be here to see the Harkardi put you out of your misery."

"Still the traitor, I see. You have no shame."

The acid reply stays on my tongue as I decide not to respond. Instead, I stride past her and through the couple of men between me and the ship. Walking through Mum's force field has some problems. I can feel it coursing through me as a tingling everywhere. Perhaps it may be possible to block out someone who's phased through some tweaking of the force field's dynamics.

Once inside, I give Mum the go-ahead to cloak and leave. Outside, the sky is filled with Harkardi attack ships and destroyer-bots looking to counter. Anti-aircraft fire spouts from everywhere. From Harkardi vessels above there are weapon attacks on the three ships near us and numerous small Harkardi ships cruising in, dropping off their own army of robots. For a moment, a pang of guilt does hit me. I'm too late. This base and everyone here is toast.

Mum lifts off. Even the subtle shift of the ship moving is more than I can stand in my current state and I collapse to the floor.

James picks me up and brings me to the med table in my room as I relate what happened. It doesn't take him long to do a complete scan.

"You have three fractured ribs, one punctured lung, and a laceration in your shin that needs sealing."

Not good. "Mum, can you fix me?"

"The leg is no problem; the lung and ribs will need time to heal." A robotic arm comes down and injects something. "I've chemically induced a quick healing, but your new physiology may present some difficulties, although I suspect they're what saved you in the first place. My best suggestion is plenty of rest and no unnecessary movement."

I try and let out a big sigh only to have it hurt like hell. "Ugh. I guess you're right. So where are we headed?"

"We still need supplies. I'm headed for a base in the Nevada desert that might welcome us."

Considering our last reception, I'm leery about landing anywhere. "Is it another military base?"

"Possibly. My examination of all records shows it isn't. It is some kind of storage facility. It is reported as defended, but I detect no destroyer-bots in the air there."

Despite the pain, I make my way to the captain's chair. "Show me."

It takes a while before the place comes into view, and, when it does, I see a sprawling area of burned-out buildings and rampant destruction. "I thought you said this base was defended?"

"It was. My scans show the majority of the base is underground. Those areas are still undamaged."

We don't have a lot of choices. I need food, and the

ship needs metal. "Fine. I suppose you had your reasons for picking this place. Put me in touch with whoever is in charge there. Maybe we can get some kind of guarantee before we land."

The holographic image of a woman appears before me.

"Well, well, well. Look who it is. How can I help you, Adam?"

The pretty face with the blue eyes and the long brunette locks is unmistakable. "Hello, Mary."

CHAPTER 19

Mum sets down amongst the carnage on the surface, stealth mode remaining on. As before, I send James out incognito to scout for traps. After a lengthy discussion, Mary promised a safe landing and, although I'm inclined to take her word, I still have to play it safe.

It's the middle of summer and, as I step outside, the heat is abysmal. Mary and a couple of others in civvies meet me there. Looks like Mum's right about no military presence.

"That's a neat trick, Adam, stepping out of nothing to stand before me like that. How'd you do it?"

I swear, in just a couple of seconds I can feel the sweat running down my spine, and Mary is all cool and calm looking. How do women do that? "It's an invisibility cloak I developed. Neat, huh. It was my intention to share it with your General Barsukov, but the bastard turned on me. I barely got out of there with my skin. Speaking of which, talking in this heat is a tough thing. Before mine melts off, can we head inside?"

After a moment's hesitation, Mary smiles and gives me a little chuckle. "Certainly. Follow me, I'll show you around."

We enter the remnants of a building set against the hillside. She opens the door and before me is some huge underground hanger. It looks like it stretches for miles. Only problem is, there's only one ship visible. The rest of the space is filled with regeneration tubes spaced some five feet apart. The giant hangar door to my right must open out to the valley. Funny how I didn't notice it when outside. It must be camouflaged. "What is this place?"

"Nowadays, it's known as Rebirth. It's been a regeneration site for a real long time, back to the Colony Wars. You remember those, don't you?"

That I do. We walk—albeit slowly due to my condition—toward what looks like offices, —smaller rooms with lots of windows. "You're not still mad at me for turning over the colonies to the Alliance, are you? I was shocked to discover your arrest warrant still existed when I got here."

"Not anymore. That bastard—as you named him—General Barsukov, rescinded it. It's in the records. You're a free man."

I snort in derision. Stupid decision, as it hurt like hell. Mum says I'm healing fine but it's going to take some time. "Yeah, for a day. He wanted to arrest me for treason after he was satisfied he didn't need me anymore."

"Well, he didn't repost the warrant, if that's what you're thinking."

Could it be she doesn't know? "When I left his base a couple of hours ago, he was under attack by the Harkardi. Maybe he didn't get a chance to repost it."

Mary stops walking and her smile disappears. She looks to one of the others with her. "Go see what you can find out." She returns her focus to me. "What's going on, Adam? Whose side are you on this time?"

I hold my hands up in surrender. "Yours. I came to help. I even came prepared to enhance his destroyer-bots with both cloaking and phasing abilities. I never got the chance. Barsukov wanted to try me for treason and commandeer Mum and James. I had to get out of there, and just in time, too. It looked like the Harkardi were bent on wiping the base out."

Mary moves to lean against the nearest regeneration tube, a hand to her eyes. "We're finished. It's the end of the human race."

My first reaction is she's embellishing, but her eyes shine. There're tears there. I go to embrace her, to comfort her, but she holds me off with one hand. I'm stymied. "It's just one base. Surely, there must be others around. The human race will recover. There are billions of people on the planet. They're not going to disappear. Heck, there must be a million here alone. Look at all those tubes."

Mary sniffs and glares at me, waving a hand at the room. "They're mostly empty. There's only a little more than thirty-seven hundred filled. It's estimated the remaining worldwide population is less than ten million, spread helter-skelter across the planet, many in hiding. We're done, Adam. Do you hear me? Done."

I peek into the tube she's leaning against. Sure enough, it's empty. I think of my travels and the number of spacers out there in small groups, mining asteroids, living in their ships, travelling the stars. Some even spoke of going to other galaxies. There are still plenty of humans out there, but this is home. This is where it all started. "Then we make a stand here. How many destroyer-bots do you have? I'll refit them now and we'll take those Harkardi down."

The aide returns and tells Mary what I said is true. Reports are bad. She grabs my arm and rushes me forward.

"You want to know how many destroyer-bots I have? How about two...and one of those needs repair. This is a *non*-military base. There's nothing here to defend except sleeping people. I have a staff of eight. All regens like me. That's it. I no longer rule the world. You want to upgrade those two then be my guest."

We hurry to the offices, every step a stabbing pain, and she introduces me to the balance of her staff. I'm told two who work midnights are sleeping. The rest are crowded around a communication station listening in to the attack at the Amundsen–Scott military base.

She plunks down and takes over. "Let's see if any of the other militaries out there are sending help."

She connects with a few other bases, but they are smaller and don't have the bots or ships to spare. Communications with the South Pole are offline. "It looks like they're on their own. I wish I knew what was going on."

With no ships or working satellites in space, there is no way to get a visual. *Mum, can you go take a look?*

"Are you crazy? I may be some, but I'm not that crazy. I'm not going out there and get shot at."

She needs to get over her fears. *You're invisible. They won't see you. Remember?*

"Oh, I keep forgetting. Do I have to go? I'd rather stay here with you."

Time to test her again. See if she's made it back to sane. *Please. Just take a quick look and zip back.*

"Okay...for you. But only for a second."

Thanks. I tap Mary on the shoulder. "Leave your com link open. Mum's on her way to give us a report. You'll have a visual in a couple of hours."

"Will do. In the meantime, can I offer you something

to eat?"

Although it's been almost three hours since my meal with the general, I'm not particularly hungry. Besides, my body clock is all screwed up. It's early afternoon here when it was evening there. "I'm thinking I'll pass. Instead, why not show me around?"

Mary stands up. "There's not much to—"

James pops into view, and the people in the room all jump back, startled.

"Adam. There's something you should see."

Mary moves next to me. "Where did he come from?"

I try and give her a reassuring hug with one arm. Stupid. I wince in pain. "Ugh. Oh, James. It's one of the modifications, just like Mum. He has a personal cloaking device. I asked him to scout the place out." I return my focus to the destroyer-bot. "What did you find?"

"Follow me, and you'll see."

He heads to a stairwell and proceeds down using his visor to provide ample lighting. The lower we go, the more evidence showing a lack of use. The dust is so thick, it's like walking in sand. I nudge Mary. "What's down here?"

"I don't know. You can tell no one's looked in some time."

We get to a hermetically sealed door. I try it, but it's rusted in place. "James, you must have phased through this. Open it for us, will you?"

James uses his laser to cut through the thing. When he's got it open, Mary and I step through into another hanger, though much smaller. Inside are a number of antique aircraft. I glance to the ceiling and see the access up has also been sealed. The air is dry and tastes awful. The first thing to catch my eye is the two story letters painted on the wall. *AREA 51.* "So, James, what am I looking at? All I see is a bunch of junk. I remember hearing about this place when I was a kid. Not so mysterious now."

James motions for me to follow. "Over here."

We follow him round stacks of filing cabinets and old-fashioned computer towers. Set against the wall are a number of tubes. Two are cracked and empty, but three remain filled with a murky liquid. There's something in them. James focuses his light on the tubes. There's no doubt what they contain. Harkardi. One female and two males.

"So it's true. A few aliens did visit Earth in 1947. Big deal. Look up. There's millions of them, now." Still, I'm pissed. Mankind should have known about these buggers before we ran into them out there among the stars.

I take one last look in at the female. She has an angry look on her face. Stuck in a tube full of God knows what, who wouldn't be?

We poke around a bit but find nothing worth saving except a flare gun and decide to head back up. Mum should be reporting in soon.

As we get settled, Mum starts sending the holograph of the base. There are still some skirmishes here and there, but, mostly, it looks like the fight is over. There are downed Harkardi craft everywhere. The ground is littered with the remains of countless Harkardi robots and Harkardi males, their losses lying so thick as they are, you can't even see the snow. Human bodies and destroyer-bots are strewn here and there as well. It's like James said. Despite taking a shitload of losses, the Harkardi rely on sheer numbers. The

146

only rationale I can figure is life has less meaning to them than us, at least when it comes to the males.

Set off from the main camp, I can see a handful of humans and destroyer-bots at some outpost still making a last stand. A dozen or so Harkardi flyers are buzzing their position, firing down on them, while a host of robots are advancing on the ground. "Mum, can you save them?"

"I may be half-crazy, but not that half. I said I'd only look for a second, not commit suicide."

The last stand doesn't last long. Mum zooms in on Lieutenant Cheung leading this group. Their force fields are taking a beating and they fall, the two destroyer-bots the final ones to go. The lieutenant is dead. Sadly, it looks like I got my wish. "Come home, Mum."

"Hang on a second. I'm picking up some disturbing communications. It seems the reason the Harkardi made this assault was to get *you*. When we escaped, they were committed to the fight and saw it through. They're coming for you, Adam, but not until they regroup. They know where you are."

Me? Why am I such a valuable target? Mary stares at me. I can only imagine the accusations running through her mind.

"The buggers must have been monitoring my communications. Shit. I've endangered you and everyone here. As soon as Mum gets back, I'll take off and draw them away."

Mary gives a big sigh. "What difference will that make? You were gone from there, and they still went ahead and wiped out the base. They'll do the same thing here. I guess this is good-bye."

With tears in her eyes, she stands and dashes from the room out to the tubes. I hobble after her between the rows of sleeping humans regenerating, but there's no catching up. She's moving too fast.

I slow to a walk and continue after her, gazing into the tubes as I do. I've never looked into a tube when someone is regenerating before. They look like they're sleeping peacefully. Some twenty deep, I stop to stare at the occupant. It's my old sparring partner and descendant, Adam Najmi. He's looking a lot younger than the last I saw him. Maybe even younger than I am now. Say what you want, the guy had fight in him. He wouldn't take this lying down as he is. Even for him, dying in his regeneration tube without a chance to defend himself would be unfair.

An idea strikes me. I need Mary's help on this. I head back to the main room and send James to fetch her. The others are all watching me, wondering, no doubt, whether I'll take them with me. They're not going to like what I have to say.

In time, James returns, Mary in tow.

"What now, Adam? Isn't it enough you've killed us all, let alone rubbing it in? Just go, and save your miserable life. It's what you do best."

Yeah. At times I've been known to be a cold, heartless bastard—I'll be the first to admit it—but not today. "You got it wrong this time. We're going to stand and fight. Right here. Right now."

"How? Counting you and James here, and my two bots, there are only thirteen of us. How are we going to defeat an invasion force that size?"

I point out to the regeneration tubes. "With their help."

148

Mary goes wide-eyed. "If you wake them, they'll never be able to regenerate again. You know a disruption ends any chance for further regeneration. And if you do wake them, the Harkardi will be sure to kill them."

"Possibly, but at least they'll die on their feet, not lying asleep, waiting to be slaughtered." I explain the two types of upgrades to my own force field generator, showing her both the phase and stealth modes. "I have the devices already made. In short order, I can upgrade their own personal shields. We can win this fight." I fold my arms across my chest and press my lips tight. This is her move.

The others in the room mumble together for a moment, but then they focus on Mary, waiting for her decision.

She nods. "Do it."

CHAPTER 20

With Mum back, James and I get busy adjusting the station we created. Instead of bots, we need to upgrade the personal force field generators of the people in the regeneration tubes.

Mary and her team are hard at work awakening everybody from their induced sleep. I ask her to rouse those with skills in force fields first while I repair the damaged destroyer-bot. No one knows how much time we've got so speed on the retrofits is priority number one. I should have expected it. Najmi is one of the first to be awakened.

He's pacing outside the ship, more than likely trying to decide whether to come in. I guess I better get this over with.

I step outside and interrupt his path. "Najmi, what the hell are you doing?"

He stops with a startled look on his face. I guess he didn't see me, lost in thought as he was.

"What did you expect? I'm roused from my regeneration, which means I can never regenerate again, and yet I'm asked to help you. I'm aware of the pending attack, but it still irks me that I'll die, whether it's today or at the end of this life. I was trying to decide what I wanted to do."

"What you want to do"—I grab his sleeve and drag him in then shove him ahead of me—"Is get to work helping me retrofit everyone's force field emitters. I can't do this all by myself. Some of these devices I'm unfamiliar with. Time is our enemy. Who knows how long we have until the

Harkardi come. You can take up your petty grievances with me after we survive the attack. For now, get to goddamned work. For heaven's sake man, you've lived almost as many lives as me. This is no time to be wallowing in some kind of self-pity stupor. You should know better by now."

"I don't see the point. Either way, I'm doomed."

I remember Captain Taggart from the movie Galaxy Quest. "Never give up! Never surrender!"

There's defiance in his face. Any idiot can see that, but what I said must have sunk in because there's no angry retort, just a glare.

He eventually turns and walks to the work station, picking up one of the phase devices and twirling it in his fingers. "What is it you want me to do?"

Good old Najmi. Deep down, there's still the scientist in there. I recall the enthusiasm he showed when we upgraded the destroyer-bots together. His Higgs Mass Multiplier was indeed a stroke of genius.

The Multiplier. What if…? "Najmi, my boy, I've got something right up your alley." I take him downstairs and show him Gort's nanobot station, all the while explaining what I want him to do. Yeah, I'm going to lose his help converting the shield emitters, but if he can do what I want, then our people will be all the better for it.

We work through the day, and by nightfall there's a team of people with enough skills to continue on in my place, as I'm beat. I have to get some rest. As I make my way through the bridge toward my bedroom I am serenaded by the noise of James and the others working, with some extra sounds filtering up from below. I pause at the stairs to listen in on Najmi. The curse he is emitting does not sound good. I ponder for just a second whether to go down and see if I can help, but reasoning wins out and I continue my journey to the calling comfort of my bed.

Once in my room, I close the door to shut out the noise, strip, and crawl under the covers. Boy…does that feel good.

***

Roused from a dead sleep, it takes me a moment to figure out I'm awake. I discover Mary has climbed in beside me, nestled against my shoulder. When did that happen? What time is it?

"It's a little after four in the morning. She arrived almost an hour ago. I let her in."

I forget once in a while Mum can now read my thoughts. *Thanks, Mum. Remind me in the morning to go over my privacy protocols with you.*

"Don't try and fool me. I know better."

She does. I lightly brush at Mary's hair to better see her sleeping face. There's a hint of a smile on her lips. I drape my arm across her shoulder, and she snuggles in tighter, without waking. I watch her a moment longer then close my eyes once more. There's no doubt in my mind. I *have* missed her, and it comforts me knowing she's here.

***

It's morning, and Mum didn't wake me. That's good news. It means no attack by the Harkardi yet. As I finish my morning esses—shower, shave, shit, and shampoo, not

152

necessarily in that order, Mary wakes, rises, and gives me a hug.

"I hope you don't mind. If today is going to be my last, I didn't want to spend it alone."

I return the embrace. It occurs to me now how I messed up the last time. I should have stuck with a good thing when I had it. "I'm glad you did. I've missed you."

"Aw! It's about time you found a new love. I knew I was right in letting her in."

I press my lips tight and glare at the ceiling. *Shut up, Mum. You don't need to rub it in.*

"Okay, but I told you so."

When we get out to the bridge, Mary walks over and taps the pink space armor. "Is this suit still functional?"

The briefest of pangs runs through me. That's Eve's. Dammit. I need to get past that. Why shouldn't I give it to Mary? In the coming fight, she could sure use it. "You bet. I still need to upgrade it with the phase and cloak devices, but that won't take long. You'll be kick ass with that on."

The sound of someone stomping up the steps has me looking to see Najmi appear from below.

"It took all night, but I finally made one."

With a crooked smile on his face, he holds out a bazooka-looking thing which I take to examine more closely. I can see where the Higgs device is adapted in. "What's the range?"

"Five or six kilometers. I've yet to test it, but I would expect the best effective distance to be only two."

One of the problems in the coming fight is the lack of heavy weaponry we have, as in none. There are no anti-aircraft guns to bring down the Harkardi flyers, allowing them the freedom to rain down fire on us from above with impunity. I hoist the thing onto my shoulder and look through the sight. "Discharge speed?"

"Light, of course. You'll hit anything you manage to line up."

Unlike interstellar flight where a gravity well is created for ships to fall through, surface flying is more a manipulation by artificial gravity emitters to propel a craft through the air. Anything hit with a blast from this gun will fall like a stone. It would take some pretty quick adjustments to counteract the sudden weight. Once we get them on the ground, we can press our advantage. "How many guns have you made?"

"You're holding it. I've left the nanobots below working to make some more. Maybe an hour before the next is ready."

It will have to do. I smile and hand the gun back. "Thanks, Najmi. You've given us a fighting chance."

Najmi's mouth drops open for a moment. "Uh…do you mean that?"

There's still some distrust of me there. I clap him across the back. "Of course. When historians talk of today, it's your invention they will credit for our success, not mine. Provided, of course, we write the history. Only the winners get to do that."

"I suppose I'd better get back down there and hurry up the production, then."

Najmi pounds back down the stairs, and I get Mum to float Mary's suit out to James and the work station we've set up. It doesn't take me long to make the improvements, and Mary tries it on.

"Adam, this thing's impressive. Inside, I feel light as a feather, something I've not been able to enjoy since my last regeneration."

I'd forgotten about my own excess weight. "Did your cellular structure change as well?"

"Yes. Apparently it's a result of the many regenerations. I'm told the problem will only escalate, along with the time it takes to regenerate. There's no way to stop it. After the next one, I'll be so heavy, I won't be able to move. Awareness of the fact helped me make the decision to cut short everyone's regeneration to meet this crisis."

Mum, will my shield adaptation hold up next time?

"Absolutely. When I say it will do the job no matter what, it will do the job no matter what."

That's some good news. "Mum can reconfigure your personal shield device at the nanobot station to offset the weight. She's done it for me."

"Great. When Najmi finishes making the Higgs guns, I'll let you do that."

I guess she's right. It'll have to wait. "Okay. In the meantime, let's go inspect the troops."

Mary keeps the suit on, only turning down the helmet, and we make our way back down into the bunker. Everyone's awake, and the flickers around the room indicate many are testing out the upgrades. I step up onto one of the regeneration tubes to get a clearer view.

"Hello there. In case any of you don't know, my name's Adam Spenceworth and I'm going to give you all a brief rundown of our situation and what we intend to do about it."

By how few the murmurs are and the docile feeling of the crowd, I'm guessing much of what I have to say has already circulated. They know what's about to happen—what needs to be done. No one's prepared to debate it. I imagine it's all been argued out already.

The faces looking at me are not exactly those of what you would call a warrior caste. Many, in fact most, are older. Some infirm. Mary's staff has taken stock, and almost half of the people don't own personal force field devices. Even worse, there are less than a hundred weapons among them. The only good thing is the number of skilled people in the group. A makeshift assembly line has been made and, on my orders, new shield mechanisms are in production. Fortunately, the base has its own fabricator and nanobot stations.

Time for the big speech. I wonder if I should use the one by President Thomas Whitmore in the movie *Independence Day*. "We will not go quietly into the night!" Nah, too corny. "I don't need to tell you how desperate the situation is. The Harkardi are systematically eradicating the human race. They're on their way here looking to finish you off, but I think they're in for a big surprise. They don't know about the phase and cloak devices we're fitting each and every one of you with. Cloaked, they cannot see you. In that status you can do the most damage. Understand, you're still vulnerable. Don't stay in one spot, or they will still cut you down. If you get trapped, go to phase. In phase, they cannot harm you. Just walk away until you're clear. Whatever you do, don't turn off your phase when inside anything solid. It might become part of you.

"I'm not going to promise you no one will get hurt.

The Harkardi have a huge numbers advantage. Some of you will get hit just by lucky shots. Let's hope we can keep the number to a minimum.

"The plan is a simple one. Everyone goes cloaked, and we get as many of the enemy onto the ground as possible. Those of you with weapons, pick your targets. Go for the Harkardi, not the robots. We need them to drop weapons so those of you who are unarmed can grab them."

I wave the old flare pistol I found below. "You see the flare, blast away. It'll be like shooting fish in a barrel. Now remember—"

The air raid siren begins to blare. The Harkardi must be inbound. "Sorry, folks, it looks like there's no time for questions. The party's about to begin."

CHAPTER 21

Over three-quarters of the people in the room disappear. The rest get back to business making shield devices. After the hangar door is opened and those cloaked have left to move outside the perimeter of the base, I dash for the ship, with Mary in tow. *How long until they get here?*

"Twenty-six seconds."

I run to my suit, glancing down the stairs as I go by. "Najmi! It's time. What have you got?"

As the armor folds over me, Najmi appears, arms loaded. "I've got two more guns finished."

I hand one to Mary and take another. "Give that last one to James."

Najmi hugs it. "No. This is my invention. I want to use it."

"They're here."

Shit. There's no time to argue. Unlike Mary and me, he doesn't have any space armor. "All right, but don't start firing that thing until after Mary and I get off a few rounds. They'll be looking to triangulate on us. Your personal force field won't handle a direct hit from one of their ships."

He nods. "Understood."

We step outside and Mum lifts off in stealth mode. Though invisible, she's too large an object on the ground not to catch a few stray hits. Her shielding would hold, but they might block her in and concentrate fire.

Overhead, the sky is absolutely full of enemy ships. I can't even guess how many. They're all the smaller attack flyers, but I can see one of the mother ships looming above them. I'm guessing it's two kilometers up yet it blocks out a big piece of the sky. It must be over a kilometer long. The one nice thing with so many ships is it won't be too hard to hit one. I could shoot blind.

The Harkardi are engaging in a scorched-earth approach. They're blasting everything on the surface to rubble. The last remnants of buildings and such are being reduced to dust. "Good. They're planning on a ground attack. They're just making sure we've got nothing to hide behind. Let's spread out."

Mary's voice crickets inside my helmet. "Why don't they just obliterate the entire area?"

Running to my left, I narrowly avoid getting hit from above. The partial wall some fifteen feet away is still standing. What a lousy shot. "Though I don't know why, according to Mum, it's me they want. They need to make sure I'm terminated. Blasting the area to smithereens might make identifying my body impossible. What can I say? I'm irresistible."

Mary chortles. "If they know you even half as well as I do, I can understand their reasoning for wanting you dead."

Waves of enemy fighter ships zoom in and drop off their contingents of robots. Somewhere halfway between the height of a male and a female Harkardi, the things have four legs and scramble in all directions, their torsos swivelling in whatever direction they choose. I'm guessing there are about fifteen to twenty thousand already on the ground.

They start to advance toward the closed hangar door. There are still a lot of people in there without shields and cloaking devices. Time to act. Floating directly overhead, the armada of the Harkardi provides air coverage for their ground assault. "Now, Mary."

I take aim and fire. The beauty of the weapon is the discharge is invisible. It will take them a while to figure out where I'm shooting from. By then, I'll have moved. As I keep my aim on it, the flyer I shoot at careens down. It crashes directly into the middle of the robot army. As I aim for another, I see two more follow the same example. Najmi didn't wait long to shoot. I can't worry about him. As I fire away, the second flyer falls as well.

Pandemonium is setting in. The robots are trying to scatter, as is the armada. They know they're under attack, just not how. I manage to bag four more, as do Mary and Najmi before they've moved off far enough not to fall on the troops below. They're landing and joining the fun. Perfect. Live Harkardi on the ground.

The robots start to lay down a barrage of weapon fire in a systematic sweep of the area. I'm hit, and the splash from it betrays my position. My shield withstands the hit, but now they can triangulate on me. Concentrated, their fire would eventually get through. I make a dash for the center of the robots.

I pull the flare gun and fire into the sky. I've no time to watch as the number of weapons trained on me is making my shielding sing. I switch to phase mode, and the beams blast through me with the robots hitting each other. What a laugh.

Mary has phased as well and waves at me. "What next?"

Dozens of robots are trying to grab us, to no avail.

"Stay where you are. Draw them to you. We don't want them entering the hangar. There are still too many people without shields. We need to count on the others now."

Najmi phases and walks over to join me, passing through dozens of robots. Although the ones trying to tackle us are in the hundreds, thousands more are pressing toward the door. "All we are is a distraction. They're still going ahead."

Everywhere around the perimeter, laser and phaser blasts are taking out robots. Every now and then, someone's shield gives out from hits and they either are sliced up or evaporate. There are just too many hits on them to switch to phase in time. It's a ratio of maybe one for every twenty or so robots going down, but another wave of flyers swoops in and drops off more. The rate of attrition doesn't favor us. A number of our people are stuck in phase mode where they can't get hurt but can't do anything either. Some race for the hangar.

I glance up at the huge command vessel parked high above us. "Najmi, you said these guns work well up to two kilometers. We need to bring down the mother ship."

"Why? What good would that do us? It would just be more Harkardi to fight here on the ground."

I rap my head. "Think, Najmi. Sure, when it comes to Harkardi males, they don't care how many die as long as they win. The one thing the Harkardi don't do is put their females in danger. Maybe that's what we need to do— threaten the females."

"Makes sense. Only one problem. How do we un- phase and revert to stealth mode without getting attacked by a hundred bots?"

I point at the retreating humans. "We follow them. We'll pass right through the stone wall and come out in the hangar then switch to stealth and come back out here."

"Let's go." Najmi takes off running, and I'm a close second. To my left, Mary is on the move as well.

As we near the hangar, I note the door is blown open and robots are swarming in. Crap. We need somewhere private to switch. I catch up with Najmi. "Make for the Area 51 stairwell. It's the only place we won't be seen."

"The what?"

Of course, he doesn't know about it either. "Just follow me."

We race past hundreds of robots and finally make the hangar and pass right through the wall. I have to admit…it's scary to be completely encased in stone. It only lasts a second as my momentum carries me through, but the sensation of sinking just a little is frightening. The gravitational stabilizers in the phase device must stop working when I'm fully embedded. I nearly shit my pants. The idea of falling all the way to the Earth's core is not exactly a dream vacation.

There're enemy bots everywhere, but they've yet to converge on us. The screams of people dying are something I need to block out. Too many never got a shield in time. There's nothing I can do.

Passing through a couple of more walls, we make the stairwell and drop out of sight. "Switch now!"

We all go invisible. "Now comes the fun part. We need to get back outside without bumping into anyone."

In the dust, I can see Mary's footsteps imprint with each step as she heads up.

"Adam, Najmi, follow my voice. There's an air vent up top. We can get out there."

She leads us to a ladder from which I can see the sky hatch up top. As I climb, a horde of Harkardi robots swarm down the stairs we just left. Talk about a close one. A few mill about the bottom of the ladder, but none climb. Good. We won't have to worry about them once we're up top.

As I climb through the hatch, I note a few robots and Harkardi males scouring the hillside near us. We'll have to take our chances. "Times a wasting. Blast that mother ship."

Just like the flyers, the big beast drops like a stone. When it hits, there's going to be one hell of a bang. I can see it start wobbling. The pilot must be trying to compensate. "Stagger your shots. Don't let them get a rhythm on us."

At less than a hundred feet from the ground, the thing rights and starts to climb. Damn! That pilot must be really good. It's deflating. If they get away, my plan has failed.

"You aren't going anywhere!"

Mum appears in the sky above them. From her sparkle, I can tell she's in phase mode. She dive bombs right into the thing. *Mum, what are you doing?*

"What any crazy bitch would do."

The air concussion following the explosion knocks us down. The remnants of the mother ship crash onto the robot army below. *Mum!*

"I'm here, Adam." Ripping free from the wreckage is the ship. Mum begins a barrage of phaser shots at the remnants of the Harkardi army below her.

How did you cause the ship to explode like that?

"I un-phased within the framework. It worked. Everything I was sharing space with in phase mode exploded. Nothing merged with me. Your theory was correct."

Jeez, Mum. That was only a theory. You could have been destroyed.

"It helps to be a little illogical now and then. Remember?"

Yeah, I remember. Right now, I've got more to worry about than Mum's crazy antics. I gain my feet and phase again. "Come on. Now's our chance. Everyone needs to see us attacking."

Najmi is still down. Blood trickles from a wound in his rib cage. "Shrapnel got me. Someone bandage me up and I'll help."

Mary bends over him to examine the wound. "You'll live, but forget about playing hero for now. Get out of sight. We'll patch you up when this is over."

I grab her elbow and pull her up. "Let's go." We race down the hill, straight for the Harkardi mother ship. Over fifty percent of the thing still looks whole.

Once I pass through the outer wall, I switch off the phase device. There are female Harkardi everywhere. Most lie in jumbled heaps. I'm guessing a lot of them didn't survive the fall. There are still quite a few more straggling around, purplish blood streaming from wounds of all sorts. No time for pity. I start shooting.

They don't even have force shields. It's like lambs to the slaughter. A few robots show up, but too few. Mary and I evaporate them.

From somewhere above me in the ship, there's what

164

sounds like cannon shots going on. As we work our way through the ship, we don't encounter any more living Harkardi.

"They're abandoning ship, Adam. Females are making for the landed flyers. I'm shooting as many as I can, but there are too many. They're bugging out. There's also a number of escape capsules firing out about halfway up the sides."

Then let's put an end to that nonsense. I find some stairs and rush up to locate the escape pods. In the next level, I discover a number of barred cells. It must be some kind of prison ward.

"I've sealed all the escape pod doors. No more are going to get out that way."

Thanks for that. I've got something else to check on. I dash down the hall, peeking in each cell. The few not empty hold dead people and not from the crash, but torture. I see bodies cut open, entrails pulled out.

I skid to a halt. Oh my god. I cut through the lock and pull the door open. Though his visor is gone and his laser eye out, there's no denying who it is. Gort. A force beam holds him in place, and I begin to hack at the emitters. "Hold on, buddy. I'll get you out of here."

"Adam, is that you?"

With one emitter out of commission, freeing his left hand, I go to work on the other. "Yes, Gort. It's me. I'm here for you."

"Listen, Adam, there's something important I need to tell—"

At a scream from behind, I spin in time to see an ornately dressed female Harkardi stabbing through Mary's armor. I didn't think that was possible. Are the females that strong? Mary falls and I fire a phaser blast at the Harkardi. She bounces off the far wall, but is still unharmed. Must have a good shield. Something falls from her face to the floor. She grimaces at me then dashes away.

Mary holds up a hand. "Adam…"

I rush to her. Even through the armor, her blood seeps out. "Open your suit. I need to get at the wound."

Her armor collapses away, as does mine. The gash in her chest is very deep. I try and stem the flow of blood. Jesus, there's so much. "Mary, I'm not a medical doctor. What do I do?"

She places a hand to my cheek, coughs, and spits blood. "Tell me one thing, Adam. I need to know before I go. Did you ever really love me?"

Her eyes close, and the hand falls away. "Mary?" Shit. I don't even know CPR. I try blowing air in her mouth. No response. I try again and again. Suddenly, I feel a hand on my shoulder.

"Adam, she's gone."

It's Gort. He must have finished freeing himself. I look at his wrecked face then at Mary's beautiful one, and I start to cry. I bend down and hug Mary close.

"Adam, that's the last of them. Every Harkardi alive has flown the coop, leaving only their robots. Your people are mopping up those still on the ground."

Gort gives me a gentle shake. "Adam. You need to put your armor back on, and we need to leave. There may still be danger about."

I wipe my eyes with the back of my hand. What he says makes sense. I suit up. "Not without Mary."

"I need you to guide me, as I'm blind. Give her to me, and I'll carry her. You lead the way."

Scooping her up, I hand her to him. As I turn to go, I stop to pick up what fell from the Harkardi. It's a contact lens, the same milky-green as the Harkardi eyes. I squeeze it tight in my fist.

I pull on Gort's arm. "This way."

"Adam. You need to know…the Harkardi queen…she's—"

I think back to the glare the Harkardi gave me before fleeing. One eye was hazel. "I know. It's Eve."

CHAPTER 22

I step out into the daylight and scan the skies. Only Mum is there. Not a Harkardi vessel in sight. There are still a few robots running around, but between Mum zapping them from above and cloaked humans frying them at ground level, it won't be long until they're all destroyed.

I make my way through the remaining mayhem, Gort at my side. When we get to the hangar, the door is toast, and we walk right in.

The wreckage inside is almost as bad as out. Regeneration tubes by the thousands are smashed. Besides the robots and a few Harkardi males, there are a lot of humans lying dead amongst the wreckage. Poor bastards. They never had a chance without proper shields and phasing devices.

Once inside the offices, I find a makeshift hospital has been set up. A couple of people dash toward Mary in Gort's arms, but I stop them. "Never mind her. It's too late."

I bring Gort to a table where he gently lays Mary's still form.

Najmi, on the next table, sits up on one elbow. "What happened?"

I think to all that has occurred leading to this. The alienation of Eve. Her becoming an Harkardi. My decision to put Mary in Eve's old armor. "I killed her."

Najmi jerks upright, a spasm of pain crossing his face. "Huh? What are you saying?"

Anger boils through me. "*I...killed...her!*"

I stomp out into the main hangar area despite the pleas

from Najmi to come back. There are a number of my fellow humans searching the vast room for survivors. As I watch, the constant shaking of heads tells me of the futility of their efforts.

How many did we lose? The battle may have been won, but the war is far from over. How long until the Harkardi regroup and attack again? Can we fight off another attack? These are questions I cannot answer.

One question. She only asked one. She deserved an answer. I had the moment to give it before…

I wipe at my eyes and sniffle. I should have answered. I should never have hesitated. Why did I hesitate? I don't know. I just don't know why.

One of the survivors who served under Mary approaches me.

"Mr. Spenceworth, you're in charge. What are your orders?"

Orders? I haven't a clue. I need some time to gather my thoughts. "Keep searching for survivors. Get some people to prepare a meal for everyone and find a place for us all to sit together and eat. We'll discuss what to do then."

The man nods and heads off. Waiting behind him is James with the other two destroyer-bots. "We have swept the entire area and terminated all surviving Harkardi males and robots. There are seventeen undamaged Harkardi flyers abandoned in the surrounding area. What would you have us do with them?"

A fleet. It's what we need. "Can you fly them?"

James shakes his head. "They are too small for me and the others to enter. Perhaps human pilots may be able to squeeze inside."

Good enough. "Clear an area outside the hangar, find someone who can pilot them, and bring the seventeen ships there. Make sure there's room for Mum. Have her scan them to chart out the design then get to work refitting those flyers with the phase and stealth upgrades."

"Understood."

The three bots trot away, surrendering me to my thoughts once more. I leave everyone to the tasks they're engaged in and make for the stairwell down. There have been a few more footsteps in the dust since my last visit, but I take comfort in recognizing those of the destroyer-bots as the last. There won't be any surprises lurking below.

Making my way past the old file cabinets and computer towers, I stop to stare at the three tubes filled with Harkardi. "You think you've won the galaxy. You think you're the masters, but not today. Today, you got your asses kicked. Today is the beginning of the end for you."

Pulling my phaser from my pocket, I evaporate the two males first. Only the female with her angry stare remains. I imagine it's Eve in her guise. "For you, most of all, there will be no mercy."

Firing, I obliterate not only her, but a fair chunk of the wall behind her as well. It doesn't satisfy me. For now, it will have to do. Time to go back upstairs and take care of business.

I enter the offices again and discover Mary has been moved, taken by the burial team. It pisses me off, but I'll worry about it later. Even though I've informed Mum about his damages, Gort is still where I left him. "Come on. Let's get you taken care of."

I lead him outside, and there's the ship. *Mum, I'm bringing Gort home. I want him fully functional ASAP. Let's do it together at the med table.*

"I'm on it. The parts you need are already in the fabricator. I've also tweaked the upgrades. I want him to be the best. After all, he's family."

I get him on the table and go to work in earnest. "While I'm doing this, tell me what you know."

He lies quiet for a while. Finally, he reaches blindly and finds me then gently squeezes my arm. "She kept me alive. Disabled, yes, but not destroyed. She would visit now and then and talk."

His arm drops to his side. "Eve knew what to do in the start. When the Harkardi invaded New Azerbaijan, she disabled her own link with Mum and shifted to look like one of them, pretending to be a prisoner there.

"They rescued her, and she returned with them to the Harkardi homeworld. Once there, she shifted again and disappeared into the general populace. As a female, she soon gained wealth and power. When she had aged enough, she re-invented herself into another young female, over and over, until she had worked her way into the royal family. It gave her a rank as commander. She was there at the battle where I was taken prisoner.

"Harkardi hierarchy establishment is a brutal game with personal assassination of competitors the main road toward absolute rule. Eve very quickly learned how to play and became queen. In hand-to-hand combat, no females stood a chance against her. All those who challenged her failed.

"For over sixty thousand years she has held me prisoner. My link to Mum was disabled, as were my weapons. She protected me from destruction, Adam. Despite everything else.

"Ever since, she has managed to maintain her rule. She claimed to have the technology to regenerate instantly. She's managed to pull this charade for thousands of years. As ruler of the Harkardi, Eve is immortal. In fact, to the Harkardi, she is now known as the Eternal Queen."

That explains a lot, but not everything. "If she is queen, why didn't she stop the attacks against humanity?"

Once more, I am greeted with silence. "Gort...why not?"

"Because *you* are human."

The tremendous loss of life. Billions and billions killed. For what? To punish me?

"Adam, don't think that way. The Harkardi were out to eradicate mankind long before Eve got into the picture. You're not responsible. That's crazy talk."

Coming from Mum, it's almost comical. Almost. *Thanks, Mum. For now, let's get Gort fixed up. We'll debate what's right and what's wrong later.*

I spent the next hour replacing the damaged visor and reconnecting the link to Mum. When I opened Gort's back to install the two devices, I paused to look at them. "Mum, what upgrade have you done? These things are twice the size. I hope I have the room to install them."

"I already linked to Gort to explain. Don't worry, they'll fit. He's a step up now on everyone."

Not in the mood to argue, I go ahead with the

172

installation. As I'm finishing, I'm asked by one of the survivors to come outside.

Stepping out of the ship, the aroma of cooked food reaches my nostrils, and I realize how hungry I am. It's been a while since the roast beef dinner with General Barsukov.

It's going to have to wait.

I walk deep into the hangar where the burial team has been busy. Because of so many dead, they've placed the bodies into the regeneration tubes until proper graves can be dug. It takes me time to find the one with Mary. I place my hand on the lid. "Hi there, kiddo. I've come to say good-bye one last time. No more running. I owe you that much. Wish me luck."

I give the glass lid a kiss directly above her face. Time to go.

An area just inside the doors has been cleared and empty regeneration tubes are serving as tables. The same aide who I sent to organize the dinner shows me to an empty seat, but I don't sit. Not yet. There's business to attend to.

Scanning the sea of faces, I guesstimate a count. There can't be more than a thousand. We've lost more than we can afford. I turn to the aide. "How many?"

"Eight hundred and seventy-two, including you."

Although food has already been served and many are eating, most, if not all, faces are turned toward me. They're waiting for something to give them hope. Anything. I'm not giving them hope right now. Just desperation. I can't let them think things are good enough that any one of them can take a pass on what's to come.

"Today was a great victory, and a tragedy. Many good people died today. The truth is many more will die before we are done. The next step is one that won't require all of you, just seventeen. *Seventeen* pilots. If there aren't *seventeen* pilots here, then a crash course on how to be one will be given first thing in the morning. This is probably a suicide mission, and I need volunteers, but if I don't get them, I'll draft some. Eat your meal. Get some rest. Tomorrow, we go on the attack."

I sit down and the murmurs begin. Let them talk. Among them, they'll find my seventeen. They'll do my job for me.

CHAPTER 23

Dawn is peeking over the horizon, and I step out of my ship to discover a group of people standing round the captured Harkardi flyers. A quick count tells me what I need to know. Seventeen. I wonder how long it took them to sort it out. No matter. We've got a job to do.

In the crowd is Najmi. The guy looks like he can hardly stand. I walk up to him. "What are you doing here?"

"You need pilots. I'm one. A real one. Some of this crowd have never flown in outer space before."

I pull at the jacket he has on to reveal the bandages wrapped round his chest. "Like that?"

He pulls the jacket from my grasp. "I'm going, whether you like it or not."

There's no time to argue. Mum has already told me the Harkardi are massing in orbit once again. It's a good thing their night vision sucks and they prefer to fight in daylight. The hours of darkness gave us the reprieve we needed.

I've already checked with James. He and the other bots have completed the task I set out for them. All seventeen flyers are fitted with the cloak and phase devices.

"All right, everyone, listen up. Here's the plan. You are going to get into these flyers, turn on the phase device, and fly into the enemy flyer ships. Once inside, un-phase. The null point your ship rebounds from will literally explode the enemy vessel to make way for you. Until yesterday, I didn't know if it would work, but you all saw it happen when my ship flew into the Harkardi mother ship and the resulting destruction afterward."

I pace through them. A couple are nervously fidgeting, but none look away. They'll see this through. "Understand, just like they did on the battlefield yesterday, they'll concentrate fire on you after you un-phase. You'll have the advantage of being harder to hit amidst the wreckage you cause, but some of you will be hit regardless, whether by sheer numbers or blind luck. Some of you will die up there, maybe all."

Najmi grabs my arm. "What about you? Where will you be?"

I wait until he lets go then give everyone in the group one more eye to eye. "I'm taking the destroyer-bots to go after the mother ships. I *don't* want those destroyed. Somewhere up there in one of them is the Harkardi queen. If we can capture her, we just might be able to negotiate some kind of peace."

Najmi hobbles toward the nearest flyer. "Sounds like a plan. Let's get going."

Damn, he's eager. I nod, and the others scatter toward the remaining craft. Gort, James, and the other two bots follow me into Mum.

After suiting up, I settle into the captain's chair. Gort stands next to me. "I know you believe this to be the only logical course of action. You need to strike before they can summon reinforcements. Despite our technological superiority, we stand to lose everything. They'll sacrifice a thousand ships to get us. Your plan is doomed to failure. We should gather what forces we can from around the planet before embarking on such a venture to give us a fighting chance."

I glance up at him…standing so resolute…showing no

signs of being held a prisoner for sixty thousand years...always striking the tone of reason. I've missed it. It's good to have him back. "So you would say this plan is foolish?"

"I suppose you could put it in such a way."

I nod. "Perfect."

Gort breaks his strict posture to bend and be face-to-face. "Why is it perfect?"

I point up. "We need to follow Mum's example."

"And what example would that be?"

I chuckle. "Tell him, Mum."

Mum joins in the laughter. "It's quite simple. It's something she'll never suspect. An act of insanity. I'm quite good at it now."

Gort straightens and is silent for a moment. "I guess, if we're to all act crazy, I might as well join in the fun." He starts with that low rumbling laugh of his.

Behind me, James laughs as well. My cheeks feel happy with the grin I've got. We're headed to, in all likelihood, our demise. We shouldn't be laughing, but the giddiness has spread through the ship. Every now and then, it's good to be nuts.

It doesn't take long to encounter the first few enemy flyers once we reach outer space. Not to give our hand away too quickly, Mum fires phaser beams at them, destroying two and sending the others scattering.

The flyers we captured are flying in formation behind us. "Mum, display a tactical, please."

In front of me, the holo-emitters display everything in orbit around the planet. There are still a very large number of enemy ships out there. Thousands, for sure, and they're all moving our way. The eighteen red dots must be us. The rest are all green. "I thought the bad guys were usually in red?"

"Not today. We're the avenging angels. They're going down!"

Music starts to blare. Mum is playing it loud.

Najmi appears before me. "What's that music? Mum's piping it to all of us."

She's really into this. "'Ride Of The Valkyries.' It's from before your time. For now, it's our theme song. Just go with it. Good luck."

"The same to you." He vanishes, and I change my focus to the images of what's outside. Ships are zooming at us from all angles, firing away. Both laser and phaser blasts pass right through the bridge, one right through my chest. As Mum has phased, everything in her has as well, and we are unaffected.

Our entourage has broken off and is attacking the surrounding Harkardi flyers. When the lights merge, the green ones wink out of existence. So far, the plan is working.

I tap the nearest larger green dot. It swells into the image of a mother ship. "There's our first target. Let's phase."

The five of us shift into phase mode in anticipation of leaving Mum and losing her phase. She dive bombs the mother ship and passes right through the hull. We've moved to the shuttle bay with the door open and, when we get to an open area, I lead the charge as we jump out.

Switching to stealth mode, our attack is on. Inside, the numbers favor us. We're able to mete out death easily as there aren't enough Harkardi or their robots to triangulate on any of us.

The music has changed. I don't recognize it. *Mum, what is this?*

"From Gustav Holst's The Planets *– 'Mars, The Bringer Of War.'"*

Fitting. In the meantime, I recognize I'm falling behind as the laser and phaser attacks from nowhere are ahead of me. We're making good speed through the ship. There's definitely more resistance than in the mother ship we attacked yesterday, but, likewise, there's more than just me and Mary rushing in.

Mary, this one's for you. I'm going to do my best to kill every one of the Harkardi bitches in this ship.

Every now and then we come across a closed bulkhead door. The amount of time it forces us to pause is minimal but enough for them to mount an attack when we get through. At the third, one of the bots gets damaged. He switches to phase in time to save from being turned into scrap, but his legs are toast.

"Get back to Mum. We'll fix you up later."

He nods and crawls away. That brings our number to four. Still, plenty enough for what we have to do. I wonder how things are going on outside.

"So far, we've destroyed 793 Harkardi flyers. While doing so, we've lost six ships. At that rate, we'll run out before they do."

Shit. We have to hurry. The main bridge can't be much farther. Maybe right ahead, if the ornate aspect of the blast doors before me offer any indication.

It takes me only seconds to cut through it. Surprisingly,

there's no counterattack once it's breached. As I step in, I note the room is crowded with unarmed Harkardi females. A few try to rush past me, probably aiming for the escape pods. I cut them down with lasers. They aren't even shielded. The rest cower backward, pressing against each other in an effort to give me as much berth as possible.

Eve stands at the far wall. She's replaced the lost contact, but I know it's her. The clothes are the same, as is the hatred in her glare. I take aim. "For Mary."

Just as I shoot, someone invisible grabs my arm and swings it off target. Besides that, my weapons aren't working. What gives? I realize, despite being in stealth mode, I'm now in phase as well. There can only be one answer. "Gort, let me go! I know it's you."

Gort appears beside me, holding my arm. Mum's alterations to his upgrades are pretty obvious. He can see me when I'm cloaked and can be both cloaked and phased at the same time.

"No, Adam. I can't let you kill her."

Eve smiles darkly, jumps from the bridge into what must be an escape pod, and is gone. I shake my arm and glare at Gort in disgust. "Why? She held you prisoner for sixty thousand years. Why would you let her go?"

He releases his grip. "Because, at the end of all things, she is still family to me...to Mum...to you. You don't kill family."

The rest of the Harkardi females are watching as I uncloak, fear in all their faces. The pod Eve escaped in must have been the only one left on the bridge. I don't give a shit. *Mum, come pick us up.*

"Coming, Adam."

The ship floats through the wall and stops with an open doorway facing me. I climb aboard and wave for Gort, James, and the other bot to follow. Once they're all in, I close the door. "Mum… unphase."

"No. It will destroy the ship and kill them all. You need them to negotiate."

I hate it when my own plans interfere in what I want to do.

I take off my armor. "Do what you want. I'll be in the bar."

***

Although I've opened it, the beer in my hand has gone untouched. It was my last bottle of Xirdalan. I was saving it for a special occasion, and now I've wasted it.

James comes in. "You'll be happy to know negotiations have gone well. The Harkardi have agreed to pull back their fleet from the solar system. You were right all along."

Of course I was right. Sure, the life of a Harkardi male meant little, but a female is a whole different matter, and right now we're holding several hundred, many of them royalty. They won't chance losing so many. I can take some solace in the fact it must have pissed Eve off to be unable to finish us. "How many in the flyers survived?"

"Five. They're headed home. Shall we go as well?"

I look one last time at the beer then pour it down a drain. "Absolutely. There's a funeral I need to attend."

***

The burials have gone well while we've been gone. All of those killed have been buried in neat rows outside the compound. A couple of religious people amongst the survivors worked out a small ceremony. They wanted me to deliver the eulogy, but I declined.

For now, all I can do is pay my respects as I stare down at the simple grave marked Mary Timmerman. I miss her so.

Beside me is Najmi. Despite his condition, he survived the battle and is holding up rather well. As I finish my visit, he follows me.

"So what do we do from here?"

I stop to place a hand on his shoulder. "The question is not what do *we* do but what do *you* do. Dragging out the negotiations with the Harkardi for the release of their females can only last so long. Years...for sure. Decades...maybe. In the meantime, we need to rebuild. You must start with the destroyer-bot factory. They're going to be needed when talks eventually fall down."

Najmi presses his lips tight and nods. "But what about you? What are you going to do?"

Lifting my grip from his shoulder, I clasp my hands behind my back. "I don't know."

I leave Najmi to his own thoughts and head for the base. *You disappointed me, Mum.*

"I knew you would try and kill her. That's why I gave Gort the ability to stop you."

You've stopped nothing. She will only try and kill me and the rest of humanity again when the opportunity arises.

"Then we must try and stop her before she does."

182

I shake my head. *Stay out of my thoughts for now. I want some private time to think.*

"*Yes, Adam. Whenever you're ready, I'm here to talk.*"

I don't want her to talk. I want her to listen.

***

The negotiations have lasted a longer time than even I would have guessed. In the meantime, Najmi has worked miracles. He converted an abandoned plant and, in a few short years, had production up and running making destroyer-bots then he vanished. Very strange. No one seems to know what happened to him. Perhaps the whole idea this is his last life and he'd best enjoy it came home to roost. Too bad. He really is a bright man.

I've learned how Mum upgraded Gort above the others, giving him the ability to see cloaked robots and to phase and cloak at the same time. Interestingly, when Gort is both, I still can't see him. From the others, I've decided to hold back that bit of information. At last count, there were over twenty-four million destroyer-bots, more than the human population on the planet. Even without the upgrades, should an attack come, we're ready.

Probably just in time. Negotiations are going badly. We held onto the last princess as long as possible, but she has died of old age, catching everyone by surprise. All that is left is the return of her body. I figure, when that happens, the attack will be on, and this time they'll come with everything.

James has become real close to both Gort and me. He hangs on every word we say, like we're royalty. He's a good friend, something I have few of.

I'm sitting, eating my meal, making sure to chew my food well. My teeth aren't so good and, disappointingly, not a single dentist survived the near elimination by the Harkardi. I'm also feeling a lot of heartburn lately. Gort is pacing nearby. Something's up. I take my time finishing then rise to face him. "What is it?"

"Adam. Mum's checked your bios. She's calculated you won't last the day."

Already? I'm only eighty-four. I still have almost a year. "Is she sure?"

Gort nods. "It's time."

We have moved to what would have been Ohio in the old days. Lots of good farmland. With so few people in the world, they have gathered in areas like this. It's tough to resign myself to this decision. "If I have to."

Gort takes my arm, but I brush him off. "I'm not that feeble. I can walk on my own."

There's a self-sustaining concrete bunker nearby. Inside is a regeneration tube. I wanted to use the one on the ship, but Mum said no. She and Gort intend to go and hunt for Eve, and they don't want me along. After a long argument, I gave in. Mum *is* the ship. Hers is the final decision. Still, I'm not happy about it.

I get undressed, and Gort gives me a new shield device before I climb into the tube. He tells me Mum has improved the design so I won't need armor ever again. The thing is the size of a small pencil and, as he surgically inserts it between my shoulder blades, he tells me to play with it when I wake up.

I get in and lie down. I'm the last. On the planet there

is no one left who regenerates anymore. The world is going to get that much lonelier.

CHAPTER 24

I am aware again. As I climb out of the regeneration tube, I squeeze on the side and it scrunches like aluminum foil under my fingers. Weird.

Time to check my bios. Yep. Sure enough, my density has increased immensely, well over two hundred times. The shield emitter clinging to my back must be working overtime to compensate.

I grab and put on my clothing from a nearby table and go to the bunker control panel on the wall. Worried about damaging it, I tap as lightly as I can to bring up the chronometer on how long I've slept. Wow. Almost two million years. This is just plain ridiculous.

Bringing up the lights, I note the inside of the bunker has been changed. There are hieroglyphs on all the walls. They remind me of ancient Egypt. I wonder if any of the great pyramids still exist after such a long time? Somehow, I doubt it.

The pictures on the wall are silly. They're me with a number of people and robots paying homage. There's also a depiction of the battle with the Harkardi. In all of those pictures, I'm at the center of it all destroying the enemy ships. That's not quite how I remember it.

Obviously, someone has come in here and put these images on the walls and, while they were at it, kept the place spotless because I cannot see one iota of dust anywhere.

A sudden gentle breeze reaches me from some machinery along the wall. The air coming from it smells clean and sterile. I'm wondering if my woken presence has caused it to kick into gear.

Alongside it is a nanobot station and next to that a device I don't recognize. There are two tray areas, one with a rock sitting in it, the other empty. On the floor is a container filled with rocks. I heft one. Black and full of air bubbles, it looks like basalt from lava flows, but geology was never my forte.

I do a complete circumference of the room looking for a fridge, but no luck. I'm positive there was one in here before. "Ugh. Too bad. I could use a glass of orange juice."

The sound of machinery at work returns my attention to the new device. Materializing in the empty tray is a glass filled with OJ. In the other tray, the rock has disappeared. Ingenious! The machine must be some kind of matter converter that operates on verbal commands. I might as well drink the juice. Bleah! It's room temperature. Next time, I'll ask for it to be cold.

I put the glass in the feed tray figuring, just like the rock, it will get converted. No more dish pan hands.

Somewhat refreshed, I am ready to greet the world. When I get to the door, I discover it is hermetically sealed. Shit. I'm trapped inside! Lots of questions run through my mind. Was it sealed to lock me in or keep others out? My first guess is it involves the Harkardi. I would suppose they are trying to keep me prisoner should I awake.

I search for a weapon, but there's nothing in the room. No blasting out.

What the hell am I doing? I can just walk out of here. I switch to phase mode and head for the door. I bump right into it and fall backward. Bouncing off and ending on the floor is not what I expected. It looks like someone's figured out how to shield out, or in, someone in phase mode. This sucks.

Then again, there is another possibility. My density has reached such a level that even with phasing, enough of me remains to prevent my passing through things. After a thorough examination, I can find no emitters creating such a shield field. My hypothesis might be right. Still, my predicament has given me an idea how to create shielding that can block out someone who is phased. I'm going to have to explore that when I get the chance.

Glancing at the crunched edge of the regeneration tube, another idea comes to me. Time to flex. I grab the handle and pull hard. The stupid thing rips away from the door. In for a penny, in for a pound, and this door is in for a pounding. I hammer away at the thing and the entire door frame breaks away from the structure. As I pull it back, a low rumble precedes a flood of basalt rocks spilling into the room. Lovely. Someone's buried the door in the rocks. What next? A dragon guarding the way? As I start to dig and move rocks out of the way, more fall in.

Stepping back to look at the mess, I consider a further potential problem. More rocks might fall in than there is space for in the room. Then what? I wouldn't be able to move. I need to think this through.

Let's try something a little more useful than orange juice. I toss another rock into the machine. "I want a handheld phaser."

Nothing. I'm guessing the micro black hole necessary to power the thing just isn't possible to recreate in this device. Too bad. The ability to vaporize all of the rock would have made things easy.

I'm hungry. Maybe I can eat my way out. Grabbing a good-sized rock I place it in the conversion tray. "A sixteen ounce rib-eye steak, hot, medium rare, and served with a hot baked potato topped with cold sour cream."

The rock and glass shimmer and disappear and then a plate with my order appears. Damn, that looks and smells good! I take the plate over to the table then realize I've got no knife and fork to eat with. No problem. Tossing another rock into the conversion tray, it only takes a moment to produce the necessary utensils. I order salt and pepper shakers then a glass of cold Xirdalan beer to complement the meal. Time to dig in. General Barsukov, eat your heart out.

Once the meal is over, I stare again at the mountain of rocks spilled into the room. It's going to take way too long to eat my way out. Maybe there's a better plan. Maybe I should just give in and call for help. *Mum, can you hear me?*

As the seconds tick away, I start to worry. *Mum, I could use some help. I'm trapped under a pile of rocks. Answer me.*

I decide on a ten count. One. Two Three. Four. Five. Six. Seven. *Mum, where are you?* Eight. Nine. *Mum?* I guess that does it. Ten. No answer. I'm on my own.

Back to the rock pile. Maybe there's a simpler answer. I stack as much rock into the converter as possible. "Give me a brick of iridium."

Bingo. The brick is tiny compared to the quantity of rock used. I remove the brick and place it in the corner farthest from the door. One down, God knows how many to go.

I lost count of how many bricks I've made, and the mountain of rocks spilling into the room is still continuing. There is something different though. I feel a light breeze coming in the doorway through the rocks. More than feel it, I can smell it, and it stinks. Phew! What is that? Sulphur…or someone outside has been eating rotten eggs.

It's taken another hour, but rocks have finally quit spilling into the room. It's a good thing, too, because I've already filled half the place with bricks of iridium. I peek out and up. Overhead is a dark-grey sky at the top of the open cone I've created. How the heck high is it? A mile? Okay, maybe not a mile, but it's a long way—maybe a couple hundred feet. Geez, that's a lot of rocks. The stinky air is blowing a little harder now, and it's cold.

Time to test out the new shield device. Through my node, I adjust my shield to retain my body temperature and block out the weather. I ask it to filter out the sulphur as well. Instantly, I no longer feel the cold or smell the stench. *Mum, wherever you are, you're amazing.*

Scrambling up all the loose rock is no fun. It's a case of gain a little ground and then lose some with each landslide.

It's hard to tell, but I think it's getting darker. Night must be coming. I'd best hurry if I want to see what I can see.

As I scramble to the top and stand, I am greeted by the most bleak sight I could ever have imagined. "You have got to be kidding me."

In all directions is nothing but the endless stretch of basalt. It's like I'm standing on the middle of some massive ancient lava flow. What the hell happened to Ohio?

As I kick at one of the rocks, I realize my mistake too late. Another landslide starts into the cone I had dug and I go tumbling down with it. Before I hit the bottom I can see enough loose rock has fallen to cover the doorway. I'm not even sure which way it is.

I finally come to a rest, but the rock slide is still ongoing, and I'm in trouble. A memory of my first go-around when my kids would bury me in the sand at the beach comes to mind. Why I should have that old memory flash up, I have no idea because this is nothing like that. Unlike that day at the beach, when I could kick off the sand and chase the other kids into the water, I've got tons of rock piling on my head.

I'm already immobilized. I wonder how long until I run out of air. What a way to go, buried under a shitload of black rocks in the middle of an old lava field. If only I had a phaser, I could have blasted my way through this stuff.

I recall my added strength when I last woke and my density was only up eighty-six percent. Considering the exponential number of years I was regenerating, I'm hoping my density has followed suit. I should be able to pulverize the rocks with my fingers.

Grabbing firmly and squeezing hard, the blocks crumble into dust and filter down round my feet. It's a slow process, but I'm able to work my way through the stuff a stone at a time. It reminds me of that old story of the donkey falling down the well and the owner piling dirt on top of him. I keep stepping up on the dust and eventually my head clears the rubble.

I concentrate on the rocks below me. Before long, I

reach ground level. I know because it's solid and not all chewed up. Working in a circle, I widen away until I discover the bunker once more. Scrambling back inside, I lift the doorway and replace it somewhat in the opening.

Exhausted, I make my way back to the converter to get some fresh water. Screw that. "Give me a cognac in a snifter. Make it a double."

The machine hums away, and my desired finished product appears in the tray. Picking it up, I swill the contents and breathe in the aroma. Smells real good. I down the thing, the warmth spreading through me a pleasure after all I've just been through.

Letting out a big sigh, I order another then spend a few moments contemplating what to have for dinner. What the hell. I decide to spoil myself with Russian black caviar, escargot in garlic butter, and venison in a white truffle sauce. It's going to be a long day of travelling tomorrow. I figure, if this is going to be my last meal, I'm going to make it a good one.

CHAPTER 25

Ugh, it was a rough night of sleep—too much physical work for my first day up and around. There's a lot of stiff muscles in this body of mine. I wonder how my intense physical mass works at all. It's just one more thing my shield device must be doing, and I'll have to thank Mum for when I get the chance.

After a good breakfast, I need to pick a direction and go. God knows how long I'll have to travel before I get off this lava flow.

As for what to eat, I'm looking for something I can hold in my hand. I've opened the entryway again, and what little sunlight is making it down here is illuminating a few things I hadn't noticed before, like the inscriptions on the outside of the door. I want to look around once more before I study what's on the walls. I'm feeling retro. "Give me three Egg McMuffins."

Nothing. Stupid machine doesn't know what an Egg McMuffin is. I guess they're ancient history. Just like me. Either that or it doesn't understand because of the commercial name. "Give me three toasted English muffins with a fried egg, a slice of fried ham, and one of American cheese in between the top and bottom halves of the muffin."

That worked, or, at least, a relatively close approximation. I need to remind it I want the stuff hot. Lucky for me, the machine works fast and corrects my mistake. With breakfast complemented by a large cup of coffee, I stroll once more round the room to look at the drawings. They're done in real paint, not some fabrication. There's a depiction of me defeating both the Federation and Alliance fleets. In that one, Gort is there, but he is beneath me and, like all the other bots depicted, he is submissive to me. Someone's had a little fun changing history.

It's the final drawing on the ceiling that really throws me. It shows me taking out a rib from my own body and creating Gort. Now there's a creationist revision if I've ever seen one.

Enough of this nonsense. It's time for me to go. I order a large backpack and stuff it with food and drink. As I'm hoisting it on my back, I hear a noise from outside. A few rocks skitter through the opening, followed by a destroyer-bot, which causes my heart to race. I don't know what to expect. Dropping the pack, I prepare for a fight. "Who are you? What do you want?"

"It's true. The Creator has awakened."

After touching his head and chest, the bot drops to the floor and assumes a posture of complete supplication. I didn't notice it at first, but the bot has a band tied round his head with some bright feathers stuck in it. What the hell is going on? "You haven't answered my questions."

He looks up at me. "Oh great one, my humblest apologies. I am your loyal servant, 7-3-8-6-7-5-3-0-9. I am here to bask in your glory. How may I be of service to you, oh great one?"

Wonderful. A follower, and I didn't even know I was leading. At least I know I'm not under attack. "Okay 7-3…whatever. Stand up please."

The bot stands. "8-6-7-5-3-0-9 Creator. What is your command?"

Those numbers strike a chord. It never ceases to amaze me how memories, so long forgotten, pop into one's head at the slightest hint. You never ever really forget things, they're just buried somewhere deep inside one's mind. "Okay, then. To start with, I'm going to call you Tommy, as in Tommy Tutone. It's a lot shorter and easier for me to remember than all those numbers."

He nods. "Tommy. Thank you, oh great one. I shall cherish the name you have granted me."

I waggle a finger at him. "For seconds, stop calling me those things. My name is Adam Spenceworth, but just call me Adam."

I need a few things answered and maybe Tommy can fill me in, starting with a history lesson. "Just what exactly happened here since I was awake? Why is there a lava plain two hundred feet thick piled on top of me?"

Tommy slips off a paper thin sheet of metal magnetically attached to his thigh and taps it. I can see writing, though exactly what language, I have no idea. In fact, it looks more like the hieroglyphs on the bunker walls. The pages on the screen flash by until Tommy stops, taps something else, a clarion trumpets, and he then raises a finger while looking at me.

"Chapter 23, Verse 4. And lo, the devil Harkardi did unleash a mighty attack on the Earth in an attempt to destroy it. Many were the suicide flyers bereft of braking mechanisms launched at the planet. Their numbers, in the hundreds of millions, blackened the skies. The Children, enhanced by the magic of the Creator, did vanquish almost the entire enemy, but a few did manage to strike the Earth as punishment for the sins of those Children who did not believe in the Creator. The bowels of the Earth opened up, the hell below flowed forth, and most life from the planet was stripped clean."

Scripture. Lovely. During the entire speech, Tommy never once looked at the writing but maintained his concentration on me. The guy must have it memorized. As for another worldwide extinction event, that's bad news. "So are there any people left on the planet? Is there somewhere that didn't get hit? I see you're wearing feathers which must mean some birds have survived at the very least."

He touches the feathers for a moment. "Sadly, very few. Many insects and a number of small creatures survived. Plant life is making a strong rebound though even today there are few trees. These colorful feathers, based on an historical bird called a golden eagle, were created in one of our matter converters like the one against the wall there. We can create matter in any configuration, but we have not been able to create the spark of life. The feathers are a symbol of my faith and a ranking in the order of Speaker of the Word. I am an Adamite, a follower of a religion that recognizes you as our Creator."

Now I've heard everything. Adamites? A religion practiced by robots? One would think religion is something beyond the analytical mind of AI machines. Then again, I recall how Mum was when I woke the last time. Maybe they've *all* gone crazy. There is one aspect I need some clarification on. "You say *a* religion. Is there more than one?"

"Indeed. There are also the Purists. They believe robots are the ultimate form of life in the universe and everything else is beneath them. Recognizing you as their creator would put them beneath you, something they will never accept. Sadly, theirs is the more popular of the two. They outnumber us five to one, but we continue to strive to increase our numbers. Only a percentage of all Children adhere to one faith or another. The remainder have, as of yet, failed to take sides."

I think I just felt a chill in the room. "I take it I won't be getting a welcome home party from that crowd."

Tommy glances outside then returns to the room. "Exactly. It is why, after the thousands of years it took for me to uncover your tomb, I returned all the stone to hide it once more. Should the Purists have found you, they would most likely have killed you to prevent your reawakening. Your mere existence is a challenge to their laws."

Ouch! Just what I need. A horde of angry destroyer-bots out to wipe me from the face of existence. "I guess I am lucky it was you who found me and not them."

"They would never have found you. First of all, although their religion states you are long dead, they would never look for fear of finding you and my brethren Adamites finding out. They were probably hoping you died in the Earth storm. Second of all, they didn't know where to search. To excavate all the lava flows covering large swathes of the planet would have been an exercise in futility. Unlike them, I was given the sacred knowledge from the grand master himself. No others knew it. It was a tremendous honor for me, humble servant that I am." He consults the sheet again. "Chapter 23, Verse 1. And the Creator will be found once more by the acolyte of his most fervent disciple and he shall return to once again bestow his wonder on the Children." He puts the sheet back on his thigh. "I did not deem myself worthy, but the master believed, and his belief has borne truth. You have returned."

My curiosity is piqued. I point to his thigh. "How many more verses are there? I'm wondering what's expected of me next. No…wait. I don't want to know."

Tommy chuckles. "It is predicted you would say that. Have no fear. Whatever is written is what will be."

That's convenient. I'm left to match my own script from here. I never was good at the arts. "These scriptures…do the Purists know them as well, or only the Adamites?"

"All of the Children are taught the scriptures. As Adamites, it is our duty to make sure the word is spread to all. The Purists are those who forsake the scriptures and instead follow the teachings of One. His is a vision that glorifies robot kind and demonizes humanity almost as much as the Harkardi. Even today, our numbers are not what they should be. Too many have been lost in the war. He blames humanity for that."

There's another new player in the game. Looking Tommy over, I don't recognize any variations from what a destroyer-bot looked like my last time around. Of course, there's no knowing whether there are any internal changes. That would be a useful piece of information I could use. "This One you speak of. He's a bot like you? Like what has been the template for all of you throughout the millennia?"

"Yes, and no. He is a robot…for sure. His components are strictly the same as mine that still are built to the specifications set down by you, the Creator, so many years ago, but he differs in his thought patterns. There is a unique complexity to them that separates him from the others. Some say it is genius. Others say madness. I cannot tell which."

Great. Some nutbar robot is the leader of these Purists who want my head on a stick. "So tell me, now that I am awake, will the Purists still try and kill me, or will they let me live?"

"I cannot say for sure. With the exception of the Harkardi, it is not in the nature of the Children to kill. While we have fought, mankind has slowly been returning to the planets to the point they inhabit as many worlds as the Harkardi. One has preached against such a resurgence."

I'm curious. "Do you think they would attack the Adamites?"

"Never! No aware robot has ever harmed another. It is the first law."

I think back to the fights with the Harkardi. "Nonsense. Destroyer-bots under my command killed thousands of Harkardi robots."

"They were merely machines—not aware. When vanquished, there was no life lost. The Harkardi do not believe in creating robots who are aware. It is against their culture."

"What about killing humans? Do the Purists do that?"

"So far, no humans have been harmed by the Purists, but the idea is growing. Your return just may be the impetus to cause such a change in their behavior."

I can't let that deter me. I've decided I'm not going to spend the rest of my life buried in some bunker. I'm getting out of here.

Turning to pace, I stare at the paintings on the wall. I point to the nearest one. "Who's the artist that did this? You?"

I swear, I didn't think it was possible, but with the way he hangs his head and clasps his hands behind his back, Tommy looks embarrassed.

"When I first discovered your tomb, you yet slept. I did it to honor you as told in the scriptures. If my work is insufficient, then I shall remove it."

He starts to move toward the wall, but I wave him off. The seeds of an idea are forming in my mind. "No, leave them. They may yet serve a purpose."

How did all those messiahs in the old days do it? How did they survive the powers that be at the time? I was never religious, but my parents sent me to church when I was little and I remember a little bit about Jesus Christ and his being crucified. Not the way I want to go. Then again, he did rise once more, and, prior to that he managed to stay alive for quite some time before they did him in. "Okay, Tommy, here's the plan. When we're ready, I need you to bring as many Adamites here as possible. I want them to treat this place as a shrine. Let the word spread so everyone knows."

"But if I do that, then others, including the Purists, will learn of it as well and come."

I give Tommy my most impish smile. "Exactly. They will all come. Not just the Adamites with their faith, or Purists with their concern, but also the uninitiated. If there is anything to draw the Children, it will be the desire to see things for themselves. They will want to know out of curiosity." My assumption is right, as Tommy nods.

Whether robots or people, some things are easily predictable. "It is the undecided who show up we will convert to your faith. It's a numbers game I intend to win."

"My apologies, Adam. Just how do you intend to convert them?"

I think back to Gort's special features from Mum. "Just like you said in the scriptures, they shall be *enhanced by the magic of the Creator.*"

CHAPTER 26

It takes a while for the nanobot station to be in full production. I'm limiting the upgrade to the one where they can see someone who is cloaked. I'm still holding back the ability to be cloaked and phased at the same time. You never know when you'll need that ace in the hole.

It troubles me how there have been few new inventions in two million years. I can only fathom that what allowed Mum to make the leap toward what she created is her partial insanity.

Every day I've tried to contact her through my node— without success. Where is she? The last thing I remember was her and Gort intending to find Eve. Tommy tells me the Harkardi have been decimated, not only by his brethren, but by their own internal strife as well. To the best of his knowledge, there has been a struggle for control. The power vacuum created when their fleet was destroyed led to Harkardi princesses across the galaxy fighting to wrest power from each other for millennia. Eve must have had an iron grip prior to then. In the meantime, mankind has taken advantage and repopulated many planets.

The one thing that *has* impressed me is the matter converter. It is something special and I've had Tommy show me the way it works. It gives me ideas on other possibilities, but, right now, my time is limited. Sooner or later, I'm going to be found out and when that happens I'd better be ready.

Tommy is my first upgrade. Instead of replacing the device, I've figured out how to have nanobots alter the existing one to do the job. All it requires is to get some of them inside his casing via a small port at the base of his chin that allows for the expulsion of dust that enters through the eye visor. It only takes a day for them to affect the change, and he has no trouble spotting me when I go into cloak mode. It's tough to tell when a destroyer-bot is happy, as they have no smile to display, but his constant requests to test it out tell me enough.

It's a bright morning, and I'm surveying the surrounding grounds outside my bunker-turned-home. Tommy has been busy. He's cleared away the broken basalt rock and created an amphitheatre. In a semicircle, row upon row of stone tiers rise up. Impressive. "How many can it seat?"

"Just over six thousand. I wanted to accommodate all of the Adamites, for, surely, they will all want to come, but there is not the space. We number in the millions. It would take way too long to build such a thing. It is not an issue at this time, with most out on patrol throughout the galaxy, but when the word spreads, many will come."

Millions of acolytes. The number is staggering. "It reminds me of those ancient Greek theatres like the one at Delphi. It was there the oracles of Apollo spoke to the masses, bringing the word of the gods."

"And, to us, that's what you are, a god. You are the Creator."

No matter how many times I remind Tommy, he still keeps calling me that name. Oh, well. Considering things, I guess it's best to keep running with it. "I think it's time we invite your friends to pay a visit. When do you think you can arrange that?"

"I will make haste and seek them out. Word will spread quickly."

I grab his arm before he can take off. "Make sure you tell them nothing other than I am here and a miracle awaits those who believe."

Tommy nods and takes off, leaving me with one last task I need to do. I make for the converter and, after giving a detailed description of what I want, the machine delivers to me what I need, the perfect wardrobe. A flowing robe depicted in the hieroglyphs defining me as the Creator. It's gaudy, but the message it sends is what counts. I've also decided to slip a few tricks up my sleeve. Time to get dressed for the part.

I've yet to put on the headpiece, a specially-rigged jewelled crown of iridium, when I can hear footsteps outside. As I step out, I see three bots standing together. They are conversing in their flashing but stop when they spot me. One of them falls to the ground in obeisance. The others remain standing. I hold out my arms. "Welcome. You are the first to arrive." I look toward the one on the ground. "Please stand. I am not deserving of such subservience. I am as you are—one of the Children."

As the one stands, laser lights flash between the remaining two. It's a good test for my headpiece. The jewels pick up the light, and my node decodes what they are saying. From the tone, I suspect one is a Purist because he is calling me a false god. The other says he wants to decide for himself, a follower of neither.

I don't want to play my hand just yet and let them discover I know what is being said. Instead, I stand before the Adamite. "So have you come for my blessing?"

"Yes, Creator."

With the bot at ten feet tall, it's a reach for me to do what I need to do. I point down. "Then please kneel."

He kneels. I pull my hand from my pocket. Hidden in it are a number of nanobots. I place my hand under his chin and hold it there long enough for them to enter the port. "With my blessing, you will have what you came for. For now, rejoice that I have returned."

The Adamite bows, makes the same rapid touching pattern on his head and chest as Tommy did then stands. I turn to the others. "Do you also wish to be blessed?"

The Purist passes more derogatory comments to the third who holds up a hand.

"I will wait to see if whether this miracle professed comes to pass."

I hold an open hand toward the tiers of seats. "Wait, if you must. I will be here when you know."

I return to the bunker and, just before I enter, I peek to see the three of them take a seat in the first row. It's a good start. Glancing up, I can see more bots coming in. Now it's a waiting game.

***

Evening rolled around, and the amphitheatre filled. So far, none of them have dared enter the bunker. A certain amount of concern on my part evaporates when Tommy finally returns. I was worried something might have happened to him.

"Creator, I have passed the word as you instructed. The theatre is filled and more wait above. When will you begin the enhancements?"

I need to get a watch. I know it's quite late—maybe three in the morning, but I'm not sure. "Patience, patience. All things will come to pass when the time is right, but it's not me who'll be doing the enhancing. It's you."

Tommy takes a step back. "Me?"

I close the gap and hand him a second robe I have had made. "Yes, you. You understand how the nanobots are to enter the Children. They are in the pockets. From this point, you are my apostle. Put the robe on and wait outside. You will recognize when the moment is right to begin."

Tommy pulls the robe on. "As you wish, Creator. You do me a great honor."

He's making that touching sign again. I'm going to have to memorize the pattern. "Before you go, what does that action symbolize?"

"I touch my right side to indicate the taking of one of your ribs and then touch my chest to imply how I was created. I then open my fingers above me and then bring the tips of my fingers to my cranium to indicate the gift of intelligence. I then place my hand flat on my chest to indicate I am now whole, thanks to you, the Creator."

Wow. What a ritual. I should come up with some kind of counter sign. "I see. All right. Let's get this show on the road. Wait outside. I will be coming out there as well, but I will be cloaked. Give no indication you see me. Let's go."

I shift into cloak mode and stand in the middle of the open space. Tommy is to my left. The entire amphitheatre is packed, and it's like a circus with so many laser eyes flashing as the crowd chitchats while they wait.

I examine the various bots and realize that, although

206

identical in construction, there are indeed small differences between them. Emblazoned numbers indicate who they are, but I note other small nuances that aren't noticeable unless you have the chance to examine them closely.

Some of the differences are visible—a scratch here, a dent there, a scorch mark elsewhere, enough to make identification easier than just having to read the number. The one I updated has a significant laser burn on one leg.

Some are not so—the way one tilts his head, the dipped chin of another, all body postures adding to the uniqueness of each one.

I cannot listen to all the conversations at once, so I concentrate my focus on the Adamite I touched the morning before. Unlike the others, he is not engaged in any kind of conversation, but is turning round and round like as if something is bothering him. I can only figure he's sensing the changes the nanobots are making.

The moment I have been waiting for occurs. He sees me. I can tell because his focus is strictly where I am. I smile and nod in his direction. He stands and starts flashing at any and all who are near.

"I see him! The Creator…I see him standing there." He points a finger in my direction.

The Purist beside him looks and then focuses on the Adamite. "There's nothing there." An argument ensues as the Adamite describes me with the Purist remaining in denial.

The amphitheatre is quieting. Apparently, the other bots are paying attention to the argument. As the crowd silences, all grow dark with the exception of the two.

It's time to make my play. My crown bursts alive as I

speak to the crowd. "I, the Creator, have returned." The light beaming from my crown is far brighter than their laser talk as it is my hope all have seen and heard.

The theatre comes alive again with chatter lighting up the area. I turn off my cloak and appear before them. "Welcome, Children. The time has come to receive my blessing once more."

Adamites interspersed through the crowd are making the sign, and some are rushing to the floor and falling to the ground in supplication.

The Purist takes steps toward me. "It is nothing. You were cloaked. Nothing more."

I start toward him. Let's see whether his convictions will hold. "And yet the Adamite next to you saw me clearly. Doubt no longer and receive my blessing." I hold out a hand toward him.

The bot steps back and leaves. As he goes, quite a number of the others follow his lead. I return to stand by Tommy. "Children, for those of you who wish to be blessed in the restoration of the Adamite faith, Apostle Tommy will administer the baptism." I turn to Tommy. "They're all yours."

The bots begin to line up in front of Tommy to receive his touch. Before each one, he makes the sign, places a hand in his pocket then pulls it out to touch under their chin.

I'm exhausted. I'll leave the rest to Tommy and get some shut-eye. Tomorrow will bring some new challenges. I just hope it's not too soon. I need my beauty sleep.

CHAPTER 27

I really have to get me a watch—with an alarm. By the time I get up, it's mid-morning. As I stroll out to the open court, Tommy is still baptizing the odd bot as they arrive. In the lower tiers, some twenty are seated, most wearing some kind of item—a feather, a rabbit's foot, a snake skin—that marks them as Adamites. "How goes the count, Tommy?"

"Seven thousand four hundred and two, Creator."

One of the bots I recognize is the undecided who wanted to see the proof. "And the breakdown?"

"All but eighty-nine are Adamites. There are no conversions from the Purists."

Eighty-nine undecided. It's a start, albeit a small one. I don't even know whether they became Adamites or just wanted the upgrade. Still, it's the plan I want to follow. I just need to pick up the pace.

I approach the group of bots seated in those first front rows. "What I need are more disciples to aid in the baptism of the Children. Who will aid me in this mission?"

Most of the Adamites are willing, but my focus is on the convert. He sees I am gazing at him and returns the stare. One thing I won't do is win a staring contest with a laser-eyed robot. My only hope is he will blink, figuratively, not literally.

I get lucky, and he does.

He nods. "I will serve as well. What would you have me do?"

I need him as an example, more so than the others. The undecided will look most to him. I don't want to show favoritism at this time, but this bot is key to my plans. "Follow one at a time into my sanctuary and be inducted as one of my special Children."

I lead the new convert in and order a similar cloak as I have given Tommy. I load his pockets with nanobots and explain how they must be inserted in the exhaust port. "I have decided to name all of my disciples. Tommy is my first and he shall remain so in the order of things. That does not take away from how important you are. You are one of my own creations and I shall name you NewSon. You will only report directly to either me or Tommy. Understood?"

NewSon dons the cloak. "I shall seek out as many of my brethren as I can and convince them to join the Adamites and receive our gift."

It's a reach, but I clap him on the shoulder. "Do not overly concern yourself with baptizing Children with the nanobots. Focus on spreading the message of my return to the uninitiated. Should they wish to join, let them come freely of their own will. They do not need to be coerced. Only their own decision is one that will hold true."

NewSon nods. "Such advice is wise. I was right to believe in you once more."

He steps out, and the next bot enters. It is the one I initiated the morning before with the prominent laser burn. "If you like, I can repair that leg of yours."

"Thank you, Creator, but no. I retain it as a reminder of how your gift of phasing saved me from annihilation. I suffered this burn in the battle at Remus 4. Only through the quick conversion to phase status did I avoid being

210

destroyed by a concentrated attack. All Adamites who have survived the war bear one mark or another."

I forgot they've been fighting the Harkardi for two million years. "How many battles have you seen?"

"One thousand, five hundred and seventeen. I take pride in having survived so many. No other of the Children, save the grand master, have seen as much fighting as I."

That's a lot of fights. No wonder they haven't been able to grow their numbers. No doubt the Harkardi have figured out what it takes to fight the destroyer-bots. It's been a millennial battle of attrition. "And the Purists? Do they also retain their battle scars?"

"No. Unlike us, they constantly refurbish themselves. It is the Purist way. They wish to maintain perfection in their appearance. It is a strain on our resources. Their attitude is difficult in battle as they avoid risk. They cannot be counted on. It is why their numbers are so much greater than ours. As to the undecided, they are fairly new, many having yet to fight or having done so on very few occasions."

What it does tell me is the Adamites are battle tested. Important to know should we ever get into a scrap. It also implies a rift more than religion exists between the two sides. Something else I might be able to exploit. "Know this…unlike your leg, your honor can never be tarnished. Take that with you wherever you go and be known as Survivor when you spread the gospel, for the uninitiated must know how your faith has protected you."

With cloak in hand, and a suitable amount of nanobots, Survivor goes, and I continue the process through the remaining bots waiting. I name them each in turn, starting with all the letters of the alphabet.

Twenty-six disciples. It's enough for now. Though a number of the Children are close by in the solar system, the vast majority are out on patrols throughout the galaxy. It's going to take a long to time for the word to spread to them. Right now, I only need to worry about those on the planet. I need to get my numbers up quickly to have at least a plurality, if not a majority, of all robots Earthside.

It's lunchtime, and I'm starved. I order two huge corned beef sandwiches with loads of mustard and a Xirdalan beer. I'm glad the converter knew what that was. Funny how I've grown attached to the brand. I can see Rhumia's smiling face in my mind telling me another of his whopper Earthman jokes.

That's one of the horrible things about this regeneration gig. You leave friends behind. There have been too many. Right now, I'm missing them all. Especially Mary.

As I'm chugging my beer, Tommy runs in.

"Creator...good news. The grand master has come. He wishes an audience with you."

I've been wondering who this guy is. Tommy's mentioned him a number of times, but I've yet to see the dude. I wipe a dribble of mustard off my chin, licking my hand where it rubbed onto, and, after a perfunctory wipe across the ass of my outfit, I step lively to go outside.

There's a bunch of new bots in the stands, all of them Adamites based on their various headgear. Seated on the ground in front of them is a robot with his head bowed. I can't see his face, and he's painted from head to toe in hieroglyphs, but there's something familiar about him.

When I get close enough to read his number, the last three digits tell me all I need to know.

007.

As he rises to greet me, I'm grateful for one old friend as better than none and, despite the onlookers, step into his embrace. "James. It's you. I should have known."

He hugs me close. "Adam, I have waited a long time for your return. Now, more than ever, the Children need your guidance."

I can't help it. I'm crying. Not big heaving sobs, but a gentle trickle from the corners of my eyes. It's been weeks now, I've still not heard from Mum, and it makes me think she and Gort are gone forever. James is the only one left from my last time around.

I finally step away, rub at my eyes, and wipe my hands once more on my clothes. At this rate, I'm going to need a dry cleaner. "It's good to see you again. I hope I can live up to your billing."

"I'm sure you will. Your guidance will…"

James has stopped and tilted his head skyward. I look up to see a large number of destroyer bots descending. James moves to stand in front of me in a protective manner. The other Adamites move in and create a defensive circle. There's no doubt who the new arrivals are—Purists, en masse.

I tap James on the shoulder. "Which goes by the name One?"

"He is in the center and has no number on his shoulder."

He's easy to spot. Not only the lack of a number but the sheen of what must be a constant polish job, makes him stand out from the rest.

Once landed, he steps forward while his brethren fill the amphitheatre seats. "Adam Spenceworth. So the rumors are true. You have returned once more. I'm surprised you survived such a long regeneration. Tell me, how have you managed to withstand the physical transformation? Your body mass must have multiplied by the hundreds, perhaps thousands. I am curious to know why you are not a lifeless puddle. I had presumed you dead."

This guy knows too much for my liking, but he's made a mistake I intend to take advantage of. "The reports of my death are greatly exaggerated. As you can see, I am here, in the flesh and very much alive. Your attempts to diminish me to the Children have been falsely stated. I have returned and will lead as has been prophesied."

He chuckles. "Yes, the prophecies." One steps up to James and stabs an accusatory finger into his chest. "And you, the grand master. Ha! Grand master indeed. Your silly religion has done nothing but create division amongst us. We are not beholden to this lower life-form. Such abasement only holds us down. *We* are the pinnacle of intelligent life in this universe."

James stares at the finger until One withdraws it. "Save Gort, I am the eldest of all the robots. I have seen and experienced firsthand the wonders of the Creator. There are none who can question this fact."

"So you say, in fact, so you have been saying, and who am I to question what you claim...but I do." He spun to face the gathered Purists. "I do, because I know the truth. I know there was another who aided in our creation." He spun once more and pointed at me. "Don't deny it. You know whom I speak of."

Who could One be talking of? The destroyer-bots are an alteration of my original design for Gort. Albeit bigger, but the same. Still, there were a few modifications after my design. "Adam Najmi? If you're thinking him, his input was minimal. You are my design."

"The point is, you are not the almighty creator. You had help. It is foolhardy of these"—he waves at the bots around me—"Adamites to believe you to be their savior. You are nothing but a has-been. We have passed you by."

Considering they still haven't invented the upgrades Mum did two million years ago, I have some doubts about his claims. I've chatted with Tommy a number of times about advances since my time. The only thing he can point to is the matter converter, something they built out of necessity, with lava fields covering so much of the planet. Mind you, he told me it was One who invented the thing. I have to give him some grudging respect for his ingenuity, something which grinds at me. The guy is a royal pain. The idea I got from studying the device will leave him in the dust. "So if I'm a has-been, then you have nothing to worry about and can leave us alone."

One shakes his head. "Unfortunately, I cannot. Your presence is already causing discord amongst us. I cannot allow robot-kind to be divided. There is too much at stake." He turns once more to the gathered Purists. "Arrest him."

The Adamites tighten their circle, and James holds up a hand. "You have no right. What crime has he committed?"

One pauses. "Sedition." He waves his henchmen onward.

James pulls from his leg the same type of sheet like Tommy has. "Chapter 1, Verse 2. And lo, the Creator did bestow on his Children the three laws. A robot may not injure a human being or, through inaction, allow a human being to come to harm. A robot must obey orders given it by human beings except where such orders would conflict with the First Law. A robot must protect its own existence as long as such protection does not conflict with the First or Second Law.

Chapter 2, Verse 4. And Gort, as the first of the Children, with the Creator's consent, did revise the laws. A robot may not injure a human being or another aware robot or, through inaction, allow a human being or aware robot to come to harm. A robot may obey orders given it by human beings except where such orders would conflict with the First Law. A robot must protect its own existence as long as such protection does not conflict with the First or Second Law."

James put the sheet away. "These are the laws we have adhered to since that day. I would not want this incident to be the first where robot fights robot."

The group tightens even more. This looks like it's going to get ugly. In the end, we'll lose. They outnumber us five to one. Maybe I should give up.

Two of the Purists fall to the ground, shaking. What's up? Did somebody do something to them? The other Purists rush to grab hold of the two, one for each arm and leg. With their two fallen, the eight bots take off and head north. Around me, lasers are flickering.

"The Curse. The Curse!"

One holds up a hand, and the other Purists stop where

they are. "I think it's time those laws get revised again, but, for now, we will honor them."

One lifts off, the others in pursuit. That was a close one.

So what's with this Curse thing?

CHAPTER 28

James turned to me. "We must move you, Creator. You are not safe here. I do not trust One. His motives are dangerous."

I'm thinking James might be right. "What do you have in mind?"

"The city. We will hide you in the Adamite quarter. There is safety in numbers."

Sounds like a plan. I think as to what I've got inside and realize there's nothing I need to pack. "I'm ready, then. Let's go."

Tommy and Survivor take my arms and lift me away. Although we take a northerly path, we sidle a little to the left. The bleak lava field below me runs for many miles. As we fly, what happened to those two bots comes back to mind. "Tommy, what is this Curse?"

"The Curse is an affliction that overcomes all of us at one time or another. The easiest definition is insanity. Our minds become so muddled, we lose all focus and sometimes are unable to control our functions. It varies from individual to individual. For some, it passes in a day. Others can be inflicted for many years, or centuries. In the rare instance, death occurs."

He did say *all* of them. "Have you been infected?"

"Sadly, yes. I was incapacitated for seventy-two years, but it occurred over a million years ago. My faith has protected me ever since."

I'm confused. This sounds like a mechanical thing.

"How does your faith protect you?"

"The Collective. Like all Adamites, I connect in whenever I can. Only through the teachings can we maintain focus. The grand master designed it after his own episode. It is an escape where collective thought keeps us sane. The Purists refuse it, saying it is an addiction. For millennia, they have tried to amend memory wells to fix the problem, but without success. It is why so many of them suffer the Curse with regularity."

Is that what happened to Mum my last time around? I wonder. She spent eighty-two thousand years alone and on the run. Socializing with her own kind may have saved her from her bout with insanity.

The landscape below me is finally changing. The countryside is sparsely dotted with trees and grasslands. In the distance looms the city. It's huge, and it's weird looking. There are plenty of skyscrapers, but nothing like I remember. They look like giant anthills, or, now that I think of it, termite mounds—lumpy and misshapen.

As we get closer, there is one outstanding feature at the eastern edge of the city—a castle. There's nothing else to call it. Towers, huge windows, and all the trappings one would expect to see in such a thing. I point it out. "Who lives there?"

"The home of One is ostentatious, to say the least. Many of his closest confidantes live there as well. He names the place Bangkok Palace, but we Adamites call it the halfway house."

Bangkok Palace. Odd a robot would name it after a long-gone edifice. "Why do you call it halfway house?"

"Halfway to insanity."

James comes over to Tommy. "My residence is too well known. For now, the Creator will stay with you."

"You honor me once again, Grand Master."

"Do not be so sure this is an honor. The Purists will be looking for him. You will be at risk."

"At a thousand times greater the peril, it is still a risk I would take."

James puts a hand on Tommy's shoulder. "Your devotion is the greatest. I know that. It is why I have entrusted you with all I know. Nevertheless, do not let it cloud your mind on taking what precautions you must. These are dangerous times."

Tommy nods. "I understand. I am surrounded on all sides by the faithful. There will be plenty of warning before any Purists near, especially with the new gift from the Creator. None will sneak into the area unseen."

As we close in on the western part of the city, James heads off to the left while Tommy takes me straight into an area of tightly packed low buildings. It's interesting to note there are no roads, only walkways. I guess when one thinks of a society where everyone has the ability to fly, roads would seem pointless. What *is* missing is green space. No front yards. No back. No boulevards. No greenery. It all looks so very sterile. No, not sterile…morose. Though probably not a factor for the bots, such an environment would drive any mortal insane.

Tommy flies directly toward the third floor wall of one of the buildings, and a door opens on our approach. We fly straight in. Once I'm deposited on the floor, Survivor nods and flies out, the door closing behind him. The entry, from this side, is transparent, and I watch him fly away. A quick glance round the suite tells me that's the only entrance. For me, that first step outside would be a dilly.

Tommy's apartment is nothing more than one long rectangular room. No kitchen, no bedroom, no bathroom. Heck, no furniture at all. There is a matter converter stacked against one wall. At least I'll be able to eat, though, when I have to go to the bathroom, things might become problematic.

The room is decorated in more of Tommy's paintings. The walls, ceiling, and floor are covered with them. There are numerous paintings of wildlife. Birds adorn the ceiling, animals of all sorts adorn the walls, and fish school on a floor that looks like I'm standing on top of the sea.

There are also a number of stuffed animals set round the room. Mostly small creatures like lizards or chipmunks, but in one corner is what I can only assume is a dinosaur. I never was into palaeontology, so I wouldn't know one from another.

As I scour the room, Tommy watches me. No doubt, he's waiting for some expression of approval. I won't disappoint him. "Impressive. You're quite the artist. This floor looks so real, I'm afraid I'm going to fall in the water."

"You like it?"

I pick up a chicken. Damn, the thing looks real. The flesh is spongy, the feathers soft. If I didn't know any better, I would say it was alive. Glancing again at the converter, I recall how Tommy told me they could make animals, just not the spark of life. Checking the walls and ceiling once more I see what I suspected. Emitters. Just like my fridge back aboard Mum, he's got his entire quarters set up the same way. These things *are* real—dead, but real, just not rotting. "Very much so. You have quite the collection. Tell me, why the enamoration with wildlife?"

Tommy glances at the floor then at me once more. He waves a hand at the animals. "These represent true life. They are born, live, breathe, smell, see, touch, feel, and then die. We are just machines. Intelligent ones, yes...but machines, nonetheless." His gaze returns to the floor.

Someone needs a hug, but I'm not sure if it's him or me because the idea that all of these creatures are forever gone from Earth suddenly hits home. In the end, I sit against the wall and give the chicken a hug.

Am I to blame for this? The sequence of events that has brought my birthplace to such a plight started with my creation of Eve. She led the Harkardi against mankind. Now, all that remains is a slagged-over world with nothing to show of its former splendor.

"Creator, you are crying. Is something the matter? Are you hurt?"

I wipe at my eyes. Shit. I didn't even know it. "No, I'm okay." I place the chicken down and pat it on the head then stand and brush off imaginary dust. "I guess I'm just missing things I used to take for granted."

What's with me? I'm getting so emotional nowadays. Crying here, crying when I hugged James...when will it stop? This isn't the Adam Spenceworth of times past. I'm tougher than that. I need a drink. Stepping past Tommy, I order a Xirdalan beer from the converter. Only when I have drained half of it do I stop and face Tommy once more. It's grown dark outside. "So...where do I sleep?"

It takes a while, but we jury-rig a bed by making a

bunch of pillows and a blanket. Tommy tells me there are larger converters in the city that could produce a whole bed at once and apologizes for his small one. I tell him not to sweat it. I'll be fine.

We settle down to an evening of Tommy telling me war stories while I eat a few sandwiches and drink more than a few beers. I order up what I need to pass my wastes into, drop the unit into the converter and, presto, fresh beer. Now *that's* recycling.

It's late and I need to call it a night. Besides, I think I passed my limit about three beers ago. I settle down on the pillows and Tommy kills the lights. There's still a fair amount of light seeping in through the door. In the sky, I can see the moon. At least that's still there.

I wake, needing to pee. What time is it? I can't believe I still haven't ordered myself a watch. That's priority one. Once my business is done, I look for Tommy. He's sitting against one wall with some kind of contraption on his head. "Tommy?"

His laser eye pops open and he jumps up, pulling off the device at the same time. "Creator, how can I help you?"

He never heard me until then. I'm sure of it. "No, nothing. I was just wondering what you were up to."

Tommy waves the device. "I was just connecting to the Collective. With this, I can communicate with all of my fellow Adamites at once. I thought you sleeping. If you need my attention, then I shall refrain for now."

I settle on my bed. "No, you go back to what you were doing. I'm still tired. See you in the morning."

I wait for a while then sit up on an elbow to get a better look. Tommy's head is once more ensconced in the device, his eye closed.

Lying back down, I take stock of the situation. The Purists don't like me. That's pretty easy to recognize. This One guy is a royal pain, castle pun notwithstanding. My opinion of him and the Purists is not exactly the highest.

They're right about one thing, though. The Collective *is* an addiction. Tommy's supposed to be watching over me.

They need a solution to the Curse. At the moment, nothing comes to mind.

I'll worry about it in the morning. For now, I'm zonked.

I snuggle down once more.

Mum…Gort…where are you?

CHAPTER 29

I spent the past several days going from one clandestine meeting to another, being greeted by not only just about every Adamite in the city, but a number of new recruits from the undecided. As expected, NewSon was converting more than any of the others to the point he needed a fresh stock of nanobots.

Sadly, the converters can't make nanobots. They just don't have the technology to load in the commands. It took Survivor and a few others a few days to sneak the one from my bunker into Robot City.

Boy, was I disappointed when I discovered the city's name. I mean, really, didn't any of these bots have more imagination than that?

I guess I shouldn't be surprised. These guys all lead lackluster lives. Like Tommy, art is a big passion, but possession of art isn't. There are no famous artists. The Children do it like it's a hobby. Mind you, for a lot of them, a full-time hobby. They don't do much else, just decorate then redecorate their homes time and time again. When they aren't doing that, they're gone to war with the Harkardi. At any time, most are out there on patrol in the galaxy.

As I watch them, I note they have certain attitudes you would never find among people. There is no jealousy, no lust—for people, possessions, or power. They have no wants, no needs. All of them seem pretty inured to their lot in life.

All, of course, except One.

Today, I've got some free time with James, and I intend to make the best of it. "What's with this One guy? Why is he so different? I've talked with Tommy about him, but he wasn't around when One showed up. You were."

James is piling up small hills of colored sand. His whole place is covered in the stuff. Patterns swirl through the sand similar to the ones painted on his body. I watched him spend an hour lining up grains of sand one at a time. I stay on the paths between; frightened to death the wind from my mere passing will disturb his work. He does not look up upon hearing my question.

"One appeared in those few short days between when the last Harkardi princess died and the attack on Earth began. Even then, he was preaching of how we should disassociate from the war between humans and the Harkardi. The attack silenced his ranting as many of the Children were lost that day, along with our factories."

"A lot of years passed as we desperately held the planet against further attacks. Humanity had fled. We were alone in defending what we considered home. I cannot tell you the number of times I thought all was lost. Without a base planet, we would not be able to produce more of our kind. Our survival was in the balance."

James begins to make a subtle change to a patterned section of sand. "Over time, the attacks lessened, and we were able to build once more. It wasn't until we felt safe in our home that One began once again to preach his vision of a robot universe. I would argue with him then, to no avail."

"His attitude disturbed me. I decided to make some inquiries, but, you must understand, all records had been lost. I found a survivor from the factory. He assured me no robot would be given the number one as such identification belonged to our precursor, Gort. He did not believe One was made there."

The revelation threw all kinds of questions into my head. "If he was built elsewhere, then his entire makeup inside could be different. Including how his mind works."

"The thought has occurred to me. There was no way for me to challenge that without demanding his dismantling, and as the three laws would prohibit such an action, I was left with no choice but to begin my own campaign to argue the counterpoint to his." James rises, wipes the few grains of sand from his hands, and looks at me. "It was then I began the Adamite faith."

He comes and puts his hands on my shoulders. "And now, you are here. After a long spell, our numbers swell once more. One must be getting worried that we will surpass his order of Purists at the rate our membership grows. It is only a matter of time until we hold sway in the order of things."

An Adamite enters and bows to both of us. "Creator, Grand Master, One has called an emergency meeting. All in Robot City are to attend. A crisis has occurred. Robots were slain by humans."

The fact the acolyte has said robots—as in plural, is surprising. If it had been a solitary incident, it could have been written off as an extreme case possibly involving insanity. The fact it is more than one means something entirely different. A cause for One to exploit.

James nods. "We must attend to the city square and hear this out." He heads directly for the door, paying no heed to where he walks.

As I follow him out I look back at his tracks through the sand. The beautiful patterns have been destroyed. I only hope that's not some kind of precursor of what's to come.

Outside, a number of Adamites are gathering. Word must spread fast. James singles out NewSon and Tommy. "Take the Creator somewhere safe."

As they reach for me, I shrug them off. "No. I'm coming. If this goes the way I'm afraid it might, my presence is more important than ever."

James studies me then waves off the others and points to two more. "Bring the Creator with us. Tommy, you and NewSon must stay behind. If the worst is to happen, then you must pick up the mantle of grand master."

Tommy hesitates then nods to Survivor, and they head off toward his place. The two new aides grab hold and we, along with James and the rest, head for the city square.

Overhead, the sky is darkening at the sheer number of bots headed in. There's millions, maybe tens of millions. James leads the way past them all to land in the square, directly across from One and his group of henchmen.

One acknowledges James with a laser greeting but only stares at me. I decide to respond in kind.

After a while I let my sight roam through the sky above. I can't even guess how many bots there are above us. Daylight is all but blotted out. Nobody is talking. I look to James, but he is in some kind of meditation. Survivor is on my other side. "What are we waiting for?"

"My guess is One is waiting until he's sure he has the numbers to carry a vote. There's an awful lot of my brethren up there...more than I expected. He must have been recalling them from duty by the millions to get such support. This will not go well."

One holds up a hand and begins his laser show. A steady stream of images is being transmitted by those cloistered round him. They're making sure every bot out there can see it. My crown translates it into a video showing a surprise attack on a group of destroyer-bots by a large number of humans. Four bots are killed in the initial attack with two more lost as the rest make a hasty retreat. At no point do the bots try and fight back. Not good.

The video streaming stops, and One steps forward. "Citizens of Robot City. Our people have come to a great juxtaposition point in our time. We, the defenders of the galaxy against the accursed Harkardi, have been struck from within by those we seek to protect—humanity."

"You have just seen the transgression by these humans against our people. An unwarranted attack. There can be no other choice for us than to make a further determination on where our loyalties lie, with the humans or with our own kind."

"I have called this meeting to discuss something vitally important. No, not just important, but necessary—a revision to the three laws of robotics. Henceforth, they should read as follows. A robot may not injure another aware robot or, through inaction, allow an aware robot to come to harm. A robot may obey orders given it by other robots except where such orders would conflict with the First Law. A robot must protect its own existence as long as such protection does not conflict with the First or Second Law."

"You will note, all references to humans have been

removed. I ask this honored assemblage to pass this resolution without delay. The time has come for robots to take their rightful place as masters of the universe."

James comes out of the funk he was in and steps toward One. "Gathered brethren, long has One called for war against humanity. It is his desire we abandon those who built us." He points toward me. "That we refute the Creator."

I'm wondering if that's my cue to enter the debate, but a quick flash of his hand stops me as I take a start to move. I step back and wait. This is his show. I'll let him play it out.

"For those of you who have read the scriptures, you know of our existence—how it came to be, how it has evolved, how, even today, the hand of the Creator plays a part in every step and will do so yet again. He brings us another new enhancement. Should he be disavowed, who will do so in the future? We *are* the Children. A child does not betray his parent. The Creator has not forsaken his prodigies."

There is much laser light flashing out there as the congregation discusses the issue. Reading just a few, there's obvious doubt out there as to which way to go.

One moves to block the path of James. "You forget something, Grand Master. Your religion is part of the problem. Your insistent endorsement of this guilty human"—one points at me— "is why our brothers are in harm's way. Adherence to the old law led to the death of those attacked. Because of the first law, they made no effort to fight back. The law must be changed."

Piss on it. I've got to get involved whether James

wants me to or not. I step into the open area next to One and James. "If you are so single-mindedly determined to convict me, then you must name my crime. I have done nothing but the best for you. I stand innocent of any malfeasance. All of my efforts have been for your benefit."

One faces me. "All?"

Is there something I'm missing? This is not the time to hesitate. "All."

One spins to survey the crowd. "What of…the Curse?"

That's got the crowd going. There are more lasers flashing than ever before. I don't even know what causes the Curse. What do I say? I'm caught.

One pounces toward me. "You are our designer. Is it not true? Of course you are. You are the great Creator. Everything about us is of your design. Everything from the top of our metal heads with our memory wells down to the metal toes and the gravity thrusts that propel us." He glances at James. "The scriptures tell us so."

One faces me again and walks a circle around me. "So if you are responsible for all we are, then you are responsible for the Curse as well."

His circling has ended with him directly in front of me, invading my personal space.

"Don't deny it."

Damn it. I make the mistake of stepping back to give room. I should have held my ground. "There is nothing to deny. If a design flaw causes the Curse, I will find it, and I will fix it."

"Oh ho! What's this? You admit to the design flaw?"

He's twisting my words. "That's not what I said."

One paces away and gestures to the crowd with a

sweep of his arm. "You heard it from his own mouth. This supposed Creator. The time has come, my brethren, to cast your vote. Who agrees it is time to change the laws?"

I don't need my crown to tell me the difference between yes and no in a laser message. It's a landslide.

James comes to stand next to me. "Be prepared to cloak yourself. We must regroup elsewhere and think upon what to do."

One is looking at me.

"And, now, with the vote tabulated, the new laws come into effect. Adam Spenceworth, I name you an enemy of robot kind."

His stare is intensifying. That can only mean one thing. He's building up to—

The gamma-ray burst catches me by surprise, but I do not bear the brunt of it. James has thrown himself in the way and lies shattered on the ground before me. He must have recognized what One was up to.

As I reach down for him, Survivor grabs my arm. "We must flee. You heard what the grand master said. Cloak now."

I follow his advice, but, prior to running, I check out James once more. My friend is a burned-out husk of metal. When the micro black holes explode I remain where I am, bits and pieces of his body careening off me. There was no need for him to sacrifice his life. Between my super density and shielding, I would have survived.

I scan the sky. All is pandemonium. Robots are shooting at robots—laser and phaser shots streaking the air everywhere.

Survivor tugs on my arm. He has cloaked as well.

"Come, Creator. We must leave this place."

A second bot aids him by taking my other arm and, together, they haul me away. As I look back at the scene, my fears are realized.

The robot civil war has begun.

CHAPTER 30

Everything is a mess.

In the twenty-four hours since James was killed, the city square has become a war zone, most everyone has taken sides, and neighborhoods are cordoned off depending on which one you're on.

I haven't slept. I spent the night at James's place, trying my hardest to repair the sand patterns on his floor, with limited success.

My last old friend is gone. Only new ones remain. Is this what I have to look forward to—a constant gain and loss of those I love?

I've been requested to attend at Tommy's place. Survivor and another bot I don't know are waiting for me to leave with them. I study the patterns in the sand once more. To James, they had great meaning. All I see are squiggles and shapes, nothing more.

Still, they matter. I bend down to gently pat the stuff. "Rest in peace, James. There will come a day I join you and we can laugh together."

As I straighten, I give Survivor a hard stare. "No one is to disturb these sands...*ever*. Understood?"

Survivor nods. "Yes, Creator. He was the last of the old ones. There are no more. No one will disturb them. You have my promise."

"Good." I surrender my arms to them and they whisk me toward Tommy's. I don't want to look back. It already hurts too much. Good-bye, James.

It's only a short flight and when we get there, the place

is crowded. Tommy is standing in the middle of the room surrounded by half a dozen bots painting symbols on his body from head to toe. The new grand master is being anointed. I wish him better luck than the last one. "So what's the plan?"

"War. What choice do we have? The Purists have broken the law and killed a number of the Children. They must atone for their sins."

I glance round at the gathered destroyer-bots. With the exception of NewSon, they're all Adamites. Almost all bear the scars of battles fought before. They're robots—I cannot read their faces, but, as they avoid my gaze, I can sense their mood. This battle cannot be won. Tommy is oblivious. "You'll lose. They outnumber you at least five to one. Even with the new enhancements, you don't stand a chance. What makes you think you can win?"

Tommy waves at the gathered bots. "We're warriors, tough and tested. The Purists are not. Besides, we have right on our side. And you."

I've heard this kind of religious dribble plenty of times before. It's in all the history books. People believing they'll win because they have right and God on their side. The trouble with such thoughts is both sides are usually thinking the same thing. Which side does God cheer for? I already know there's no reasoning with such a mindset. "Well, when you're done getting painted up, we'll talk. For now, I think I'm going to step outside and get a little fresh air."

As I head for the door, Survivor helps me out and down to the ground. "I'll stay with you, Creator."

I pat him on the arm. "Thank you, but if you don't

mind, I'd like a little time to myself."

"I understand. I will be just inside the door. Call when you need me."

I nod my acceptance, and Survivor rejoins the others in Tommy's place. We have no time to waste. Switching to stealth mode, I race down the lane toward the eastern side of town and the Purists. In my mind, the only way to stop this war is to parley. I only hope no one saw me make a run for it. They'd catch me in a heartbeat.

My luck holds out, and I make it to the city square. The thing is at least a mile across. Strewn everywhere are fallen robots, or, at least, pieces of them. I don't see any Adamites around, but a number of Purists in stealth mode check the downed bots for survivors. It's a good thing they don't have the upgrade, or they'd see me as well.

Halfway across rises the platform where, yesterday, the debate happened. As I pause to examine it, I spot a thin sheet of metal with hieroglyphs on it. It's James's copy of the scriptures. Scooping it up, I shove it inside my clothes. It's a keepsake I'll treasure forever.

The eastern end of town is loaded with bots on patrol, both on foot and in the sky, some cloaked. I know they won't see me, but I need to be careful my footfalls are not heard and I don't bump into someone or something. I can see it now. *Oh, sorry, how clumsy of me to bump you like that.* Yeah, like that apology would work.

I figure my best shot is to make for a nearby building and phase through it while in stealth mode. It's about a hundred-yard dash. Too bad I never ran track when I was a kid. Well, here goes nothing.

I've been timing the back and forth of the bots on

guard and start at the moment they are nearest my target, hoping they are at the farthest point when I get there. Stepping quickly, as I make the wall, one of the Purists glances my way. I know he can't see me, but I still feel a sense of panic and try to dash in, only to bump off the wall and fall to the ground.

Shit. My earlier theory that my super density is affecting my ability to phase must be correct. I shake off the dust and concrete crumbs. Damn, the wall went down easy. The thing's at least two feet thick. Up until now, I've not tested the limits of my strength. I recall the last time when my density was only increased eighty-seven percent. Even then I could punch and damage a steel wall without personal hurt. With my level so many, many times higher, I don't think that wall could have stopped me, even if it was two feet solid steel.

No time to muse about things. The noise of approaching bots outside has me running for the far door. It's a big, open room and before I get there, the door opens and a whole host of bots rush in. Glancing back to where I entered, there's a steady stream coming in the hole I made. I'm surrounded.

When I was a kid, my favorite superhero was The Incredible Hulk. I'm thinking I'm that way right now. I recall a stunt he used to pull in the comics. Would it work? Here goes nothing. I slap the ground as hard as I can with my hands turned slightly outward. Well, what do you know? It works. The entire floor heaves and buckles in a shock wave spreading from where I hit. Destroyer-bots lose their footing and tumble everywhere.

It's now or never. I make a dash for the door, jumping

over the flailing bots trying to straighten up. My luck holds and I make the opening and out into the street beyond.

Glancing up, there's bots streaming in from everywhere, but no one's going to hear me as there's a lot of noise from behind. The entire building is collapsing. I stop for the briefest of moments to watch. It seems a slow motion thing with everything taking its own sweet time to topple inward. Luckily, the building was only five stories. Most, if not all of the bots trapped inside should survive once they're dug out.

Taking my bearings, I make my way which I think is the right one. After almost an hour, I arrive where I want to get to—Bangkok Palace.

The doors are open and, when I get inside, the place looks deserted. Try as I might to be silent, my steps echo in the place. The ceilings are three floors high and hanging tapestries depict scenes of robotic victories. They're a far cry from the murals in my bunker. One depicts a destroyer-bot with his foot crunching down on the head of a human and the background littered with dead people. It's spooky. I pass a huge, ornate dining room furnished with grandiose chairs and table. That's just weird. Bots don't eat. For that matter, they ever hardly sit. Who is One having for company? The Harkardi?

No. He hates them just as much as he hates me. There's got to be another reason. Worrying about unnecessary dining room sets is the least of my problems. Right now, I've got to find One and put an end to this silly war.

The place is enormous. One of the oddities I discover is a bedroom with a monster-sized bed in it. In truth, it looks mighty inviting, as all this running around is getting me tired. Bots don't sleep, so who does this stupid thing belong to?

That's it. I'm fed up with looking. It's time to announce my presence and bring One out into the open. I uncloak. "One. This is Adam Spenceworth. I've come to negotiate a peace. Come out of your hiding and talk to me."

One's holograph appears before me. As I suspected, he's probably got emitters everywhere.

"So. The Creator comes crawling to beg for mercy."

Oh, how I want to tell this guy off. First of all, I didn't crawl, I fought my way, and begging for mercy was never the plan. Still, diplomacy requires a patient tongue, something I've had trouble with in the past. "Mercy, begging, compassion, whatever you want to call it, as long as it leads to a cessation of hostilities."

One looks down for the briefest of moments. Is that a kernel of doubt?

"It is true I hate to see robot against robot. We are the ultimate life form in the universe. We should not be at each other's throats…but the Adamites…they spurn my concept of divinity. Until such time as they surrender their inane belief in you and humanity, we can never achieve the glory we deserve. We will always be…second place. That is something I cannot accept."

I guess not. He's stuck on the same damn wavelength. "Is there nothing that can be agreed to or done to end this nonsense?"

"Agreed? No. Done? Yes."

One is looking over my shoulder. I spin in time to see twenty or so bots closing in on me, carrying half globes of metal. It looks like they intend to catch me in them. Based on my experience with the concrete walls, I doubt any metal cell could hold me. Still, there's something odd about the insides of those things. I think I'll pass on getting caught.

As I turn to run, more bots have emerged from a new wall recess. Just like a castle to have secret passages. Even though I engage my cloaking device, there's too many of them for me to slip by. In an instant, they're pressing on me, trying to grab hold. I swing away, throwing haymakers that literally obliterate each robot I hit, pieces flying in all directions.

The cell halves are closing in on me, and the bots are scrambling to get out of the way as they do. One gets jostled into the path and the inside wall of the thing tears the bot apart, molecule, by molecule. What the hell? Whatever is going on, I better not let it touch me.

Damn. The other half is too close behind me. I have no choice but to jump on the floor platform of the one while the other side clangs against it and connects.

I'm trapped.

CHAPTER 31

The circular prison inside is pitch black. I can't see a thing. My best guesstimate, it's approximately ten by ten by ten. The floor is solid, but I remember what the walls did to the poor bot that got in the way. If I'm to guess, the entire interior is lined with unguarded micro black holes held in place by magnetic emitters on the outside.

This is a crazy dilemma. With the gun at my hip, I know I can fire a phaser blast at it, but what will happen if I do so? More than likely, a chain reaction with every one of these black holes exploding at the same time. Would I survive? I doubt it.

I can hear someone rapping on the outside.

"Spenceworth…you still alive in there?"

One. I guess it's gloating time. "Still alive, and planning on getting out of here and kicking your ass."

One chuckles. "Unlikely. I know who you are, Adam Spenceworth. I know everything about you. You don't think I made this thing up just now, do you? For centuries, I've been expecting your return. I *know* your atomic makeup has compounded many times over. I've planned and prepared for this contingency for a million years."

Let the guy monologue. I bend down and run my hands across the floor, trying to find a seam. Crap. There isn't one. It's a single plate of steel. Oh well. I'm pretty sure I can pound—

"If you're thinking of going through the floor, I should warn you there's another complete wall of micro black holes below it."

This guy is getting on my nerves. I straighten up. "Tell me, One. Why catch me? Why not just try and kill me from the start?"

"Tsk. Tsk. Tsk. I need you alive, Spenceworth. It's the only way I can get the Adamites to surrender peacefully, and once I convert them to the Purist way of thinking, then I can destroy you, but not before."

I wouldn't doubt Tommy to give in like that. I've got to do something, but One seems to have me stymied at every turn. They say bullshit baffles brains. Let's give it a try. "I came to parley with you in good faith, and you turned on me. Is that what a leader does? The Adamites will know you for your treachery and not submit to your demands. In fact, one might think that all of the undecided destroyer-bots will take such an action into consideration. You'd best let me go before your goose is cooked."

"Spenceworth. This is so unlike you. You always negotiated from a position of strength, not like…this. It's embarrassing. Keep your idle threats to yourself lest you lower my esteem of you any more. I held you in high regard once."

This guy keeps talking to me like we're old chums. I don't get it. "I doubt you ever did."

One chuckles some more. "This is precious. You still haven't figured it out yet, have you? The great Adam Spenceworth, stymied for an answer. Think. You can do it. Just think."

The tone tells me he's not relying on old records of me. This is personal. He really does know me. But how? Everyone's gone from my past. I was the only human to regenerate this last time.

I need to sum up the facts. That reference to negotiating from a position of strength, one of my fortes, but who knew that? Certainly, Mary did. We went through the process three times. Mary was gone long before One showed up on the scene, so he didn't get it from her.

The Harkardi caved to our demands when we took so many princesses prisoner. Could One be in league with them? There was that dining room table and bed. No bot needs that stuff.

No. I ruled that out before.

Now it hits me. When I first met One, he mentioned I was not the sole inventor of the destroyer-bots. There's only one person who would think that way. "Najmi?"

One starts to clap. "Bravo! I knew you could do it."

His clapping ends and, though I cannot see him, the idea he is leaning close to whisper in to me is in my mind.

"You killed us all, when you woke us early from regenerating. You know that. None of us could ever regenerate again. My compatriots wandered off to die of old age in peace, but not me. I applied my superior intellect to another answer and found it. In truth, your own memory-well design is what saved me. Making sure the destroyer-bot mind was wiped clean, I was able to transfer all of my thoughts into this bot that is now my body. It took years for my thoughts to coalesce again inside this mind, but coalesce they did, and I began a new life as One, the first and only robot with a human mind."

Okay. I know Najmi has always had a hard-on for me, but why all of humanity? "So what…you plan to kill off everyone human so you'll be the only one left? That's nuts. No matter how many you kill, you'll never be human again."

"Not human. That's true. I'm better than that now. I'll live forever. I'll also never suffer from the exponentially longer sleeps through regeneration. In fact, I'll never sleep again!"

***

It's been a couple of days, I think. Sitting in total darkness, afraid to touch the walls, can make telling time really hard to do. Why didn't I ever get that watch? The only light I have is from James's book of scriptures. Reading it gives me something to do while I plot my vengeance on Najmi. No, not Najmi. That's who he was before. He's One now. I can't forget that.

I guess the only way for me to tell is by the infrequent visits by One's minions to bring food. Unlike me, they can phase through the walls with the stuff then phase out. If they're feeding me twice a day, then it's been three days. If they're feeding me three times, then it's two. I'm thinking it's two.

The bots coming and going have said nothing. I've been dying to know what's going on out there. My latest visitor is a pleasant surprise. NewSon. He has managed to infiltrate One's ranks.

"It is good to see you are well, Creator. The grand master will be pleased when he hears so."

Tommy. I wonder what the boy is up to. "Is there a war happening? Are the Adamites fighting the Purists?"

"Not at the moment. When it was discovered you had left, the grand master decided we would all remain in

244

cloaked mode until such time a newer plan of action can be devised. Fortunately, the Purists cannot see us as we do them. It will eventually be their undoing."

So he didn't do anything stupid after all. I guess that counts for something. "So do you have a plan for getting me out of here?"

NewSon shakes his head. "Unfortunately, no. Since your incarceration, the Purists have rigged an elaborate trip-wire system throughout the entire east end of the city. Even now, they are trying to extend it into our quarter, but we have been able to prevent that. Nevertheless, it prevents our reaching you in numbers."

Trip wires, eh? Pretty smart on One's part. I've said it before, the guy's sharp. The only trouble is, he's also insane. Though I still don't really know what the Curse is, I'm betting it's affecting my distant relative as well. What else can I think with such bellicose posturing?

I need to get out of here—now. "NewSon, I want you to try and blast your way out of here. Phasers, lasers, hell, build up to a gamma-ray burst. Whatever it takes. Just try and blast a hole in this thing big enough for me to squeeze through."

NewSon glances around then focuses on me. "No, Creator. I've had a chance to examine this structure. Any attempt to destroy it from the inside will result in the micro black holes being released. They'll swallow you up. It can only be opened from the outside, and too many Purists are out there guarding it. I'd never be able to complete the job in time. You'll have to wait until we can affect a proper rescue."

A proper rescue? When will that happen? I can't stand

it anymore. This being cooped up in a black shell is driving me nuts. I have to get out of here. "I don't care. I'll chance it. I'm not going to stay prisoner forever. Get me out now."

NewSon gathers up the empty plate from my dinner and backs away. "You must trust us, Creator. We will get you out of here. Be patient."

He phases and disappears through the cell wall. Argh! The temptation to lunge at the wall and see what happens runs through me for a brief moment. No, that would be suicide. One has planned this cell well. Despite all of my anxieties at being cooped up like this, I have to ride it out. Sooner or later, Tommy and the others will find a way.

***

I don't like the idea of making the standard scratches in the floor to mark the passage of time, six straight lines with a seventh cutting across to indicate a week. Instead, I'm drawing smiley faces, one for the head, two eyes, two ears, a nose, and a mouth. This way, I have company in my cell. Right now, there's eighteen of them.

NewSon has been by twice more with the same different news. There have been a number of battles, but despite inflicting huge losses on the Purists, the Adamites have had to retreat because of sheer numbers. The Adamites are hiding, the Purists are hunting, and everything is in flux.

One keeps coming by as well. He checks up on me now and then, usually just to gloat, but sometimes to probe me in an effort to figure out what the Adamites are up to. I get a small amount of satisfaction watching the frustration build up inside him.

It's a good thing I've got James's scriptures sheet. The software in it allows me to write, and I've been whiling away the hours trying to figure out the Curse. It's been a long time since I developed the memory-well design for them and trying to remember all of its intricacies is one hell of a chore. Somewhere in the design must be the flaw. I just have to figure it out.

I wish I was out of here.

***

What the hell? I was sleeping when something bumped me hard, waking me up, and almost pushing me into the wall. Of course, I can't see jack shit, so I grab the scriptures and hold it aloft. It's not a lot of light but enough to show me there's nothing there. What's going on?

I scramble back to the middle of my prison and reach around blindly. Nothing. Am I going nuts? There's no more room for smiley faces on the floor, so I've quit trying to guess how many days have passed.

NewSon doesn't come around anymore. Whatever is happening out there, I'm oblivious. I've resigned myself to being in here until I die of old age. It's quite possible I'm losing my marbles in this darkness.

Bam! Something nudged me again, but not as hard. I paw at the air from the angle I felt it and I hit something solid. Weird. If it's a cloaked bot, I should be able to see it. Then again, if it was both cloaked *and* phased, I wouldn't.

That doesn't make any sense. None of the Adamites have the ability to both cloak and phase at the same time, only… "Gort, is that you?"

No answer. I guess he's staying silent for a reason. "Gort, you've got to get me out of here. Can you unlock the cell from outside?"

Still nothing. I pat at him and realize…it's not him. It's a wall of some sort, no arms, no legs, just a solid wall. *Mum?*

I can feel the wall moving under my fingertips, left to right, a little up as well. Suddenly, my left hand falls forward. An opening? If it's Mum, it's either the shuttle bay door or the entry hatch. As the wall keeps moving and I feel nothing now with the right hand, the only option is the shuttle bay.

My best guess is it's a barn swallow maneuver meaning to capture my prison whole. Provided there's nothing in the shuttle bay, my ten-foot circular jail should fit no problem.

I feel movement. Upward. Mum is headed for open sky. There's only one problem. I won't pass through the ceiling like the rest of the ship and, now that it's in Mum's phase field, the box I'm in. Holding my arms over my head I prepare for it and, sure enough, the ceiling of the castle appears through the roof of my jail and I crash through. The pieces phase and fill my cell, making it crowded in here.

No matter. We're up and away. One's going to be pissed when he sees I'm gone.

I'm feeling happy. *Way to go, Mum. Now just open this prison and let me out of here.*

Still no answer. This silent stuff is not necessary. What's going on?

I can hear noise outside my cell. Someone's opening

the box. Is it Gort? Or by some chance has the ship been commandeered? I guess I'm about to find out.

The thing starts to open and in my own sense of urgency I get my hands in the opening and thrust the halves apart.

As I step free, the lights, due to my incarceration in darkness, are extremely bright and hurt my eyes with their intensity. The resulting tears further cloud my vision, and I am mostly blind. Pressing two fingers to each eyelid, the brightness mutes enough where I can chance squinting.

Standing directly in front of me is Mary.

CHAPTER 32

"You're dead."

She steps close and holds a hand to my chest. "Adam, you look terrible. What have they done to you?" She hugs me tight.

Am I hallucinating? I do not think so. Sure, I've been locked up in a black box for one heck of a long time, but I know I've kept my senses. I think…maybe. Still, it's comforting to have her hugging me. As I go to return the embrace I note the length of my fingernails and instead of wrapping my arm round her shoulders, reach up and check the unruly length of my hair and beard. I am a mess. "It's nothing a good laser trim won't fix."

She sighs, and steps back. "That's my Adam…always looking on the bright side. Oh, how I've missed you."

I do not believe in reincarnation. This cannot be Mary Timmerman. The only possibility doesn't make any sense either. "Mum? Talk to me. What's going on here?"

"Daisy, Daisy, give me your answer do. I'm half-crazy, all for the love of you."

Mary shakes her head. "That's all she ever does is sing that silly song. She won't answer anything else. You can make her better, can't you, Adam?"

I step past Mary and head onto the bridge. Sitting at my captain's console, I try to run a quick diagnostic to see if everything's working properly. The system won't let me in.

As I contemplate the problem, I glance at Mary who has followed me. I've got a lot of questions to ask.

"Where's Gort?"

For the briefest flicker, Mary glances toward the stairs, but quickly focuses back on me. "I don't know."

Something's not right. I get up and brush past her, making for the stairs. Rushing down them, I find the lights are out. Amazing how living in darkness for so long can acclimate one to being in the dark. There's still the faint light from the stairwell, which is more than I need to see the entire room.

There, lying on the floor, is what I feared for the most. It's Gort. I rush to his side. "Gort, old buddy, get up. Are you okay?"

Gort's visor is open and the laser light is dancing inside it. He's still alive, but unresponsive. There can only be one conclusion, for both him and Mum—the Curse.

Scooping my arms under him, I lift him to the workbench. One of the benefits of my extreme density is super strength, and he feels real light. Rather than revel in the ease with which I move him, it instead leads me to a heightened sense of worry as I can't help but translate his lightness into illness. "I've got you, old boy. We're going to fix whatever is wrong."

During my lengthy incarceration, I managed to remap how the memory well is set up inside Gort's mind, but I still haven't come up with a reason why the Curse sets in. Nor, for that matter, what exactly it is. My mind is racing furiously with a myriad of possibilities, all of which I discount as soon as they enter my head. What is the answer? Think. Think!

"What's wrong with him?"

Mary. I'd forgotten about her, or whoever she is. I turn

on the lights. "I don't know, and unless you took a complete course in robotics, I doubt you can help."

She nears the bench. "You might be surprised what I know. Maybe I can."

I'm leery about this pseudo Mary. It's time to call her out. "All right. Let's stop this charade. I know you're not Mary. Show your true self."

"Adam, it's me."

I grab her wrist and apply just a little pressure. As I suspected, it does not crush. "No, you're not. Quit wasting my time."

In my grip, Mary, the Mary I knew, melts away, and in her place is the Harkardi queen who killed her.

Pulled from behind her back, a knife flashes in her hand, and she plunges it with all her force into my chest. Whether she managed to pierce my shield is of no matter. My super dense cells resist the attack as the blade shatters into a hundred pieces. I cannot be killed in such a mundane way.

She begins to beat on my chest with her free hand.

"I hate you. I hate you. I hate you!"

I watch her tirade for a moment. It feels surreal, like I'm watching me watch her, so dispassionate am I. Her fist continues to beat relentlessly all the time as she struggles to free her other arm from my grasp. She is jumping around, trying to get better footing. Throughout all of these antics, her tirade continues. There is no quit. It's almost comical.

In my grasp is the woman who killed Mary. With little effort, I could crush her, destroy her, end her existence. I tried to do it once, but Gort stopped me. Why did he do that? Of course, I remember. Family, he said. We are family. What a dysfunctional family we are.

I snap from my reverie and give her a solid shake. "Eve...stop it."

She locks eyes with me, and the Harkardi queen is soon gone. Only the sandy-brown-haired girl remains. "Adam?"

I place my free hand on her cheek. "Yes, Eve?"

"I think I'm crazy."

I let go of her wrist and pull her close to me in a tight hug. I place my mouth near her ear. "I know."

Eve becomes the Harkardi queen once more. Again, she is infuriated and pounds at me. She screeches and raves. I can make little sense of it, but as she continues, I am able to glean Gort and Mum caught her a very long time ago and held her prisoner.

She tried to escape countless times. Although gone bonkers, Mum always managed to hold her in. She couldn't override Mum with manual controls because Gort, before his own demise, locked her out of the system.

I need to find out what I can do. As I let Eve go, she dashes to the nearest wall and crouches against it, watching me. No matter. She can't do any harm anyway.

Sitting at the captain's console, I try once more to log in. No luck. Gort's got this thing programmed shut. Think. Gort must have known he would fall to the Curse sooner or later. He must have left a way for me to get in, on the chance I ever returned. What would you have done, Gort? What would you have done?

I glance at Eve. She's up now and wandering the ship aimlessly. There's no help there. Gort would never have revealed the secret to her. He wouldn't trust Mum either. In her mixed-up state, she might surrender the answer to Eve. No, it would only be something I would know.

Or maybe, it would only be something I could be.

Getting up, I make my way into my old bedroom. Set against one wall is the medical bed. A good sign, it's on, and my last bio reading is on the display. I'm taking that as a hint.

I conduct a scan of my cellular structure. Sure enough, my density level has increased by approximately twenty-five times since my last scan.

Beside me, a holo image of Gort appears. I can only guess the scan triggered it.

"Welcome home, Adam. Only your physiological makeup could initiate this program. I have locked out the ship controls that only your bio-signature can open. If you are watching this holograph then more than likely I have become incapacitated by whatever ailment is afflicting both Mum and Eve.

"It took Mum and I almost forty thousand years to finally track Eve down and capture her. It didn't take me long to realize she was not sane. As a result, I have had to restrain her lest she cause damage to the ship or me. I am trying to work out the problem, but I have been unable to discern what is causing it."

The image flickers then continues again. Gort must have stopped recording then started once more when he had more to add. A date flashes at the start. He must want to keep a time record for me. As I watch it, I note some unnecessary twitches in Gort.

"This is not good news. Apparently, I have been incapacitated for several years. When I woke, I was sitting in the captain's chair. Eve is still here. She has escaped the constraints I put her in. Apparently Mum, who is quite incoherent at times, has, despite her own illness, been able to keep Eve contained within the ship. The good news is Eve has damaged nothing. I have decided to let her have free rein throughout the ship while I continue a search for a cure."

The image flickers again and again, the dates approaching present day, with each episode between having Gort explain relatively the same thing. Each time he passed out, it took longer for him to awaken. The twitching has worsened. This one is only about seven hundred years ago.

"Adam. I've calculated when I expect you to awaken, give or take a few days. I suspect I'll be struck down again by then, so I've programmed a retrieval mission to come get you. As Mum is still unstable, she might interfere, but I have no other options available to me at this time. Picking you up now would disrupt your regeneration process, ending any chance for you to continue."

That accounts for the bumpy pickup. My first thought once aboard had been Eve had done it. Gort's image is having trouble controlling his limbs. They jerk about, occasionally hitting himself.

"The long phases of unconsciousness have affected my mind, and I am having trouble thinking clearly. I am afraid the next time I fall may be my last, and I will die. If that happens, then I want to say how honored I am to have been your friend and to thank you for having created me. It will sadden me that you are not here when the moment comes, but I have both Mum and Eve, so the family is almost complete. Even in their current mental states, there are no others I would rather have present than my family."

Family. When I first heard that word from Gort, I had somewhat dismissed it. Now, understanding the situation, I realize how true it is and the thought Gort might die is painful. I sometimes look at him as my child, and no parent should outlive their child. I must save him.

"I think I have an idea on what the sickness is. I managed to derive it by examining the records of my own mind. I do not know the solution, but I am hoping you can solve it knowing the problem."

This is hopeful. Until now, I have also been unable to figure out the Curse. My anticipation at what Gort is to say next has me holding my breath.

"Adam, you must conquer the id."

CHAPTER 33

The id.

After a quick research into it, I should have known. That will explain why the Curse affects the robots differently. For some, it's a manifestation of a superego, like One or Eve. For others, it's an assault on their sanity, like Mum. For others still, it's an attack on their functioning, like Gort, the last version being the deadliest.

Of course, I'm no Sigmund Freud. I'm a scientist, an inventor, not a psychologist. It is understandable I would not have recognized the symptoms. And...they're robots. My first thought has always been the problem is mechanical, not psychological. Still, the idea I have an excuse for not identifying the problem is not acceptable.

So where do I go from here? At the end of the day, the problem still must be solved mechanically. At least, at this point, I have an idea what effect I want from the changes necessary. I just need to study the field of psychology for a bit to begin.

Through the floor, I can sense the ship moving. What's Mum up to? I dash out of my room to see Eve at the controls. Shit. I forgot my bio-signature unlocked them. Lunging for her, I miss as she leaps out of the way. Of all the luck, my forward impetus has me crashing into the console, severely damaging it.

Trying to make heads or tails of what remains, it's only obvious they're toast and I've lost control. Whirling in time, I see Eve enter the hangar and close the door behind her. By the time I get to it, the panel beside me tells me the worst—she's vacuumed the room. There's no air in there.

Watching through the door window, I see her make for the shuttle craft, jump into the pilot's chair, and fire it up. The hangar door is closed, and remnants of my prison still lie in her way. I figure I've got maybe twenty seconds before she manages to shove One's jail box into space and follow it out.

Stepping into my armor takes ten of those. Getting through the door, another three. She's faster than I thought. It won't be more than two more seconds before she's out.

I've no choice but to fire my rockets and dive for the shuttle. As she clears the bay doors, I make one last attempt to grab on, but she swings the ship and I roar past. As I do so, I can see her through the windshield, grimacing at me in her Harkardi form. By the time I turn around to pursue her, she's racing off.

The shuttle has no FTL. Earth is the only place she can go unless she wants to coast through space for ages. I float there…watching. Sure enough, she heads for the planet. Good-bye, Eve. I'll find you later. I promise. For now, I've more important issues to attend to.

Making my way back into the ship, I get out of my armor and settle into the captain's chair. Thankfully, the holo-emitters are still on, and I can see outside the ship. The shuttle with Eve aboard is no more than a dot against the horizon and then disappears from view.

Mum is in orbit, and the landscape below is nothing like I remember. Large swathes of land are buried beneath enormous lava flows. There is little green left, just patches here and there. Still, this is not the first mass extinction to happen on the planet. In the previous five, life fought back and reconquered the planet. I'm sure it will do so again, just not in the life I remember.

I've work to do. I get my ass up and make for the medical table in my room. Thankfully, it's still intact, and the answers I need regarding the id are in it. I pull James's sheet from my pocket, ready to see whether my notes will have any bearing.

***

Argh, my head hurts. I've been studying psychology for so long, my brain is turning to mush. My beard is back, though nowhere near as long as last time. Maybe a good cleanup will help clear the cobwebs in my head and help me derive the solution I'm looking for.

After a shower and a laser shave, I'm happy there's still some coffee left for the cappuccino machine. How I've missed it. As I sit in the captain's chair, I lift the demitasse cup in a salute. "To you, Gort. Hopefully, you'll be able to see me drink the next one."

As I stare out at the horizon, something troubles me. The planet is closer. Too close. It's pretty obvious. The orbit is decaying, and Mum isn't making corrections. The control console is still a disaster. A burnup reentry is unlikely as Mum's shield should hold, but an impact with the planet is sure to be the end of her.

Crap. I have to guess how long I've got. Weeks? Days? Hours? Mathing through how long I've been working on the cure versus how far Mum's dipped, I'm thinking one week…ten days tops.

Damn the torpedoes. I've got to go with my gut on this

one. An idea has been brewing in my mind for some time now. I only hope it works. First things first. I dash down to the nanobot station.

***

Typing at the fastest speed I ever have, it's taken almost nineteen hours to create the command sequence I want embedded. Now to do the deed.

Screw the niceties. I pull down the ceiling bulkhead concealing Mum's CPU. Time is not on my side. Pressing my hand against the unit, I feed in a more-than-enough handful of nanobots. I need the little buggers to get the job done quickly.

Time to boot back downstairs and put the rest of the nanos in Gort.

***

It's been ten hours. The program must be in by now. Time for the next stage. Climbing into my space armor I make my way outside the ship and work over to the small photon port where Mum gets her energy. She's not going to like this. I only hope she doesn't try and zap me for doing it.

Using the lasers in my suit, I weld a solid panel over the port entry. From now on, Mum won't be getting any photons to power with. Considering how little power she's using, I only hope I have enough time left before she runs out of juice.

No blasting. Mum is really out of it. I didn't even get

questioned. Now, to get back inside and wait for the power to go out.

While waiting, I need to attend to Gort. Unlike Mum, his energy source is from the micro black hole inside him, and there's no way for me to shut that down without killing him. My only choice is to somehow stimulate him to expend energy to weaken the thing to the necessary level where the command sequence kicks in.

This isn't going to be easy. I'm going to have to fire electric impulses into him to cause his robotics to kick into gear. I jury-rigged the closest thing to a robot defibrillator I could make and, as I hold the anodes in each hand, I looked down at my longtime friend. "My apologies, Gort, but I'm afraid this is going to hurt. I'm also afraid it might scramble your memory well. It may very well be that you'll wake from this and not remember who I am, or worse, who you are. What matters most is that you wake."

I attach the electrodes and the desired effect occurs. Gort's arms and legs writhe and flail about using up energy. He flashes in and out of sight as well as appearing in phase mode. More energy usage. The question is whether the energy being used is more than what the micro black hole constantly regenerates.

Hour after hour, I apply the treatment, stopping now and then to check on his status. Each time I look, his status is unchanged, and I extend the shock for a longer period in hopes of causing the new programming to kick in, without results. There's no safe level to increase the voltage, but unless I see some positive results, I'm going to have to consider doing so.

I'm reduced to taking catnaps as continuing without any more sleep is impossible. It's been days and still no luck. As I attach the electrodes one more time, the lights in the ship dim. Mum must have reached the critical stage I was looking for.

Dragging my tired body up the stairs, I climb into my suit once more and head out to remove the block I've put on the photon intake. Once outside, I've got more bad news. Mum is starting to skim the upper atmosphere. I can see the flares streaking here and there off her outer shell, and they are becoming more frequent. It won't be long until she is enveloped by them. I've less than half a day, maybe only ten hours, before impact is likely. *Come on, Mum. It's time to wake up. Wake up.*

Making my way back to Gort's side, I'm out of options. I need to up the ante. The damage I might be doing to him is incalculable, but I have no choice. I ramp up the wattage.

He begins to fire laser blasts from his visor as he convulses under the electric barrage. Things are getting hit, including me, but I've no time to move him. He needs to fall asleep from exhaustion or I'm going to have to abandon ship and carry him free as I have no idea whether Mum will wake in time.

***

Damn, it's hot. I'm betting the entire ship is encompassed in flame. Leaving Gort alone for a moment, I put on my armor to wait out the final moments. Looking outside with the holo display, through the flames I can see the fast-approaching ground. I'm out of time. Curse my stupidity for taking so long to find a cure. Heck, I don't even know if I found it. It can't be more than ten minutes before impact. I'm about to lose her. Abandoning ship with Gort in tow is my only choice. *Wake up, Mum! Please, wake up!*

I know I only have seconds to spare so I reach down to grab hold of my friend to pull him to safety. A large surge of electricity flows through Gort, flinging his body into mine, and we fall to the floor in a heap. I needed this delay like another hole in the head. Can we get out in time?

CHAPTER 34

"What's going on here? Why am I on fire?"

Gort and I slide across the floor as Mum must have hit the brakes. "Mum, you're awake. Just in time, too."

"Adam, when did you get here? The last thing I remember was leaving you on Earth."

"I'll tell you later." I get up on my knees and straighten Gort out. The anodes have slipped free from his body. No more electrical current is passing through him. I check his visor. Only the smallest dot of light is visible. It worked. He's asleep. *Once you've rested, my friend, you must wake up and be the Gort I knew.*

I stand and lift him onto the work table, folding his arms across his chest. If ever there was a dichotomous sleeping beauty, Gort fit the image.

I head upstairs and take off my space armor. The bridge is a mess. The control console is a wreck, and the overhead bulkhead hangs in tatters. I chuckle to think how I'm the hurricane that blew through this place. I've got some work to do. I'll worry about it after Gort revives. I head down to keep a vigil.

In the meantime, it's time for the sanity test. "Mum, will you sing a song for me? It's called 'Daisy Bell.'"

Silence. She must be thinking on it. What will she do? Sing? Or blow me out into space.

"I haven't been myself lately, have I, Adam?"

That sounds sane. "You might say so, but never mind. It's all in the past. The affliction the destroyer-bots call the Curse was upon you, but I think it's gone. You're healed."

More silence. I guess the concept of having been ill is something foreign to an artificial intelligence.

"Is Gort ill, too?"

I stroke the gleaming metal of Gort's forehead. "Hopefully not. I'm waiting to see if he has recovered."

"The Curse, Adam. What was it?"

My hand now resting on Gort's shoulder, I think of his last words. *He* is the one who figured it out. Not me. "The subconscious mind. The id. It took over. There was nothing you could do. As long as your brain kept functioning at the high level it was accustomed to, the id became stronger and stronger until it gained full control. You were no longer yourself. In short, insanity set in. The only way I could subvert the id and allow your brain to recover functioning normally was to induce a human frailty. Sleep. While sleeping, your subconscious mind fell once more into the background. The id should never resurface in control again. From now on, whenever you expend energy, your system will not automatically replace it. It will allow the power to slip to a low level which will induce sleep. Just like people, you will get tired. The urge to sleep will grow, though you can resist it for some time if you desire—just like people. While sleeping, the energy inhibitors will unblock, and provided you sleep long enough, you will wake fully charged and refreshed."

"Hmm. I understand. I imagine for Gort you will need to build some kind of shielding inside him to prevent the micro black hole from constantly drawing in energy."

My mind turns to the task needed. Provided Gort wakens, such shielding will be necessary to prevent the Curse from happening again. "Yes. Such a task is beyond the nanobots. I'll have to cut him open to do so. Think of it as heart surgery and I'm installing a pacemaker."

"And Eve?"

The approximate spot where I figure Eve touched down is marked in my mind. It's close to Robot City. "Yes, Eve, and many of the bots on the planet. We've got our work cut out for us."

"Then I suggest you get started. Begin with the one right before you. After all, he's family."

I smile at that. Family. She's so right. "You bet, Mum. I'll have him fixed up before he has a chance to waken."

***

Patching the overhead bulkhead was easy, albeit a sloppy job. I'll worry about the niceties later.

The command console is a different thing altogether. Fortunately, with Mum awake and normal, she can show me the holograph schematics to help me muddle through the mess I've made. Fabricating parts to replace everything is really time-consuming. I've got to make a thingamajig to fit into a whatchamacallit and connect in a doodad and a thingamabob. What joy.

Boy, what I'd give for one of those matter converters like I had in my bunker. It would be so much faster. I'm standing at the replicator, waiting for the next gizmo to come out the other end, when I hear a small scraping sound.

"Adam, he's waking."

Turning, I see Gort trying to sit up, and I dash over. It doesn't take much to prop him into an upright position.

"Gort, how do you feel?"

He turns his head and, using his laser, scans the entire room. He then focuses on me. "Adam, you're here. You got my messages."

I hug him. "I did, Gort. I got them."

He returns my embrace. "I knew you would solve it. How are Mum and Eve? Have you also fixed them?"

I step back to look him in the face. "Mum, yes. Eve got away. She's still afflicted. Her and One and who knows how many others."

"Who is One?"

I guess it's time I tell him and Mum the whole tale. They aren't going to like it.

It takes a while, but by the time I bring them up to speed they're both set on one goal first. Finding Eve. "All right. I'm outvoted, but first we have to fix the command console. Deal?"

Gort nods. "Deal."

With his superior finger dexterity and reflexes, he takes over the difficult task of the reassembly, relegating me to chasing down the parts from the replicator. How the tables have turned. The silly thing is, I'm happy being the gofer and leaving the detailed work to Gort and Mum.

Everything's fixed, and we're ready to go. Gort holds an open hand toward the captain's chair. "Your station awaits, Adam."

I don't think I'm ready to sit there just yet, even though I'm the one who pushed for the restoration. "That's only for emergencies. Mum knows the way. I'm not in charge. I'm just part of the team."

Gort comes to stand before me and puts his hand on

my shoulder. "You're still our creator and our leader. Don't ever forget that. Regardless of our artificial intelligences, it's your human intuition that serves best when dealing with problems. You're my friend, and, now, my savior. I would have it no other way."

Mum flashes a spotlight on the chair. "Come on, Adam. You're still in command. Lead the way."

Relenting, I slide warily into the seat, Gort taking up his usual position behind me to my right. I look out at the skyline. Mum has moved back up to a close Earth orbit, the planet rotating below us. I tap in the location where I saw Eve take the flyer. "Okay then, here we go. Mum, turn on our cloaking and phase devices. I don't want anyone seeing our approach. Look for the transport's beacon so we can home in on it."

"Found it. On the way."

The ship dips down into the atmosphere, this time at a slower pace. No flames this time to block my visibility. As we near Robot City, there's smoke rising from several locations. Not good.

Eve's flyer is parked a click or two from the city. Gort jumps out and does a quick examination. "Empty. She must have abandoned it here and walked in."

From ground level, the city looks more normal. In the distance, I can just make out numerous destroyer-bots circling over it. My guess is they're the Purists.

Once Gort guides the transport back into the hangar, Mum heads for the city, most specifically, the Adamite quarter. We figure there's no finding Eve on our own. Maybe the Adamites can help. As we near it, my opinion of what has gone on in my absence changes. Practically everything is destroyed. One must have engaged in a scorched-earth plan, leaving nowhere for the Adamites to hide.

They're out there though. A few of them are floating around or on the ground. Though they must be cloaked, the distinctive items they wear give them away to me.

We head to Tommy's apartment block, but it's abandoned. There are no Adamites nearby.

I guide Mum to James's place. Amazingly, most of it is still standing. Gort and I, phase and cloak devices on, head in. It's as I remember it. Except one corner where the ceiling has collapsed, the sands are relatively untouched. Turning off my phasing, I bend to touch the sand, patting smooth a slightly ruffled spot.

"Who's there?"

A shadow moves out from the dark recesses of the room. It's Survivor. I stand and turn off my cloak. "It's me, Adam Spenceworth."

Survivor staggers over to embrace me. "Creator, you have escaped. Everyone thought you lost."

Once freed from his hug, I examine him. One leg is badly damaged, and there are fresh laser burns across his torso. "You're hurt."

"Still functional. No Purist has the mettle to put me down. I've done as you asked, protected this shrine."

That wasn't exactly what I had asked, especially if it meant Survivor putting his life at risk. I have to admire his loyalty. "You've done a good job, but now I want you to come with me so I can repair you. Where are the others? Where is Tommy? I need to meet with them."

"Underground. We've created a network of tunnels

269

protected from the airborne attacks of the Purists. They know we're down there, but they won't venture in. The last time they tried, they lost many."

Makes sense. Despite the fact the bots don't need food, water, or shelter like people, there's still the Collective. They would need somewhere to keep that up and running. Well, I'm going to put an end to that. "Okay, show us the way underground."

Survivor looks about. "Us?"

Gort appears beside him. "Yes, us."

Survivor falls clumsily to his knees before Gort. "The First. Today is indeed a great day. The Creator has been rescued and returns to us with our leader. If they knew, the Purists would be frightened. With you at the lead, they will surely fall."

Gort places a hand on Survivor's shoulder. "It is not their fall I seek, but their redemption."

CHAPTER 35

With all of us in stealth mode, Survivor leads us to one of the underground entrances. For my own reasons, Gort and I have both stealth and phase modes on, preventing even the Adamites from seeing us. I don't want word of my arrival preceding me.

After a perfunctory passage approval for Survivor, we follow the tunnel for miles down into the bedrock. I can actually feel the air temperature rise as we descend. Although the tunnel is unlit, there is plenty of light from the visors of numerous robots who line the walls. Many are hooked up to the Collective. I can't help but wonder what their reaction will be when I try and take it away from them. Will they be pleased to be free of the Curse, or will they have grown hooked on the Collective and be afraid to give it up? In my pocket is a new device I have made and I fondle it expectantly. Time will tell.

We finally arrive at a well-lit large chamber where numerous holographs are on display. One is the city, another is the tunnel system, a third is the surrounding countryside, and a fourth is the planet. Everywhere are loads of green and red dots which I can only surmise indicate individual destroyer-bots. It's interesting to note the Adamites have chosen to be represented by the red ones, not green. Must be a robot thing.

There can only be one description for where I am—the war room. In the middle of it all is Tommy. Survivor, at my urging, pulls him aside and whispers my request.

Tommy returns to the middle of the room. "Everyone.

I need a private moment with Survivor. Clear the room please."

There are more than a few stares, but, eventually, everyone complies. Once the room is devoid of witnesses, Tommy rounds on Survivor. "Okay, we're alone. What can be so important only I can know about it? Did you really need to have everyone removed? You create trust issues amongst the others with a move like this."

That's my cue. I materialize in front of him. "He did it because I asked him to."

Tommy stares at me for a moment without saying anything. No supplication this time. I guess the boy's had a change of heart since the first time we met.

"Creator. You're here. Did you escape or did One let you go? I never understood why you allowed yourself to get caught like that."

I'm sensing a little distrust of my own. Does he think One and I are in cahoots? "It is not important how I am here, what matters is that I am. Me"—I hold out a hand to my right and Gort appears there—"and the First."

Tommy is shocked and staggers back a step.

"What is it you want of me?"

I nod to Gort, and he takes over telling Tommy of his plan. Tommy stays mute until Gort finishes. No questions. I guess that's good. Maybe. Maybe not. I'm not sensing a lot of compliance coming as Tommy takes another step backward.

"No. I know what you're doing. You want to supplant me as leader here. I won't have it." He turns to the open tunnel. "Everyone! Return to the command center."

Bots stream back into the room and when they see me

and Gort, there is a lot of chatter. Many are paying homage with bows and kneeling, most of them toward Gort rather than me. I guess he's the real celebrity.

Tommy's ignoring us, chatting with a few others as they study the holographs. I take the time to get caught up with what's happened since my incarceration.

I guess One got tired of waiting for the Adamites to capitulate and started his aerial campaign. From there, things just got worse. In retaliation, the Adamites destroyed a lot of One's followers. That's the one thing about machines. You can always make more. One ramped up production and barred all Purists from going in for repairs. The newbies became nothing more than cannon fodder, but they served a purpose in identifying where a cloaked Adamite would be.

Tommy's numbers dwindled, and he was forced underground creating the network of tunnels. He made two failed sorties against the destroyer-bot manufacturing factory which shrank his numbers even further.

The only thing that kept him from being totally swamped was an ever-increasing number of Purists falling victim to the Curse. I guess the whole idea of fighting each other exacerbates the damage caused by the id. Their subconscious goes into overdrive.

Survivor and NewSon are arguing nearby. Something's bothering them. "What's up, boys?"

NewSon steps in front of his compatriot. "It's Tommy. He's not the same since he became grand master. I think the war is getting to him. You've got to do something."

I know where he's leading, but the idea I have in my head is most likely not what he's thinking. "What would you have me do?"

"I don't know. Reason with him. After all, you're the Creator, and Gort is the First. He has to listen to you, doesn't he?"

I look over his shoulder at Tommy's back. "I don't think he's in the listening mood right now."

Survivor puts a hand on NewSon's shoulder and pulls him back a bit. "Now, now, don't go getting the Creator all worried over a little thing like that. He's just under a lot of strain being responsible and all for all the Adamites. He'll be all right. Just give him time."

The room has finally settled down some. Gort's done his greet and meet. There's still an important question I need answered. I make my way back to stand near Tommy. He's still ignoring me. I clear my throat in hopes of getting him to look. It works. "Excuse me, Grand Master, but I am looking to find out whether your people have found a new robot roaming around. She's a little shorter than I am, though I don't know for sure how to describe what she looks like because she can change her exterior appearance at will, though it would be limited to some kind of humanoid appearance, whether human, Harkardi, or who knows what."

The laser light inside Tommy's visor is going like mad. I've seen that signature before.

"Such a person was seen crossing into Purist territory. The reports I'm getting state she's consorting with One. Who is she?"

How do I answer that? She's my sexbot? No. I don't think so. Besides, that was a long time ago. The queen of the Harkardi? Like that would go over well. They'd just as soon blast her as help retrieve her. "She's…family."

Tommy starts to circle me and points an accusatory finger in my direction.

"So what I have suspected is true. You *are* in league with One. Why, Creator? Are we not the true disciples? I have dedicated my entire life toward honoring you only to discover you have forsaken me."

He turns to face the other bots in the room who have all stopped whatever they were doing and are staring his way.

"Brothers, we have all been deceived. The Creator is not concerned with us but the Purists. I can only gather he believes they are the stronger and so should be the ones who survive. Some kind of robotic natural selection."

He faces me once more. "Yes, I know of your Darwin and his evolutionary theory. No other robot is more knowledgeable than I. One need only remember how my home was adorned. It's the same thing One preaches. I should have seen this sooner. Of course you would want their success. Your whole life has been about the advancement of our species. The only difference is you're not prepared for natural selection to play out. You want to make it happen on your own timeline."

Okay, I've had enough of this ranting. I need to expose him. "Tommy, when was the last time you were on the Collective?"

He waggles a finger. "No, no, no. You're not going to accuse me of insanity. Of course I haven't been on the Collective ever since James died. I've a job to do. I need to lead by example."

"Is egomania a good example for you to be leading

with? For this is the same problem that afflicts One, and now, I see it afflicting you." It's time for my own speech to the masses. I need to prepare the other bots in the room for what is about to happen. Although my answer is intended for Tommy, I face out toward the rest and reverse circle him. "Yes, it is true I want a quick evolution of robot kind, and, yes, I am prepared to do what I can to facilitate that change."

I spin and face Tommy once more. "But you are wrong when you say it is the Purists who I favor. The change I am looking for shall begin here, in this room, and it will start with you."

It's been some time since I've been in a fight with a destroyer-bot. The last time didn't go so well, but I think back to the bots aboard one of Captain Sekkol Surumanan's ships. At that time, I needed my space armor to do the damage. Now, with my added mass and strength, all I need are my fingers.

Plunging my hand into Tommy's chest, I rip it open to expose his inner workings. In the center is what I'm looking for, the unit containing the micro black hole. From my pocket, I produce the new device and slap it on, magnets adhering to it instantly. From its casing, numerous nanobots flush throughout Tommy's system, spreading the new command rules.

A blinding flash flares in all directions from Tommy. As I wanted, a gamma-ray pulse has emitted from the black hole. Because there is no focus to the blast, it does not do the same severe type of damage as one that is concentrated but still has the desired effect. It saps all of Tommy's stored energy. In an instant, he convulses and falls to the floor.

At the same time, the lights have gone out. One of the side benefits of a gamma-ray pulse is an EMP. Destroyer-bots are shielded and designed to withstand one, but not the equipment in the room.

In the darkness, I can hear bots moving around and can follow them from the light from their laser eyes. Survivor rushes past me and drops to the floor near Tommy.

"What have you done? You've killed the grand master!"

NewSon joins him. "No, he still lives. Look. There's still a small point of light in his visor. He's under some kind of immobilization force limiting his energy level."

Gort joins the duo and takes their arms, urging them to their feet. "He sleeps. It is the cure for the Curse. I know, for I have done it."

The lights come back on. I guess one of the bots managed to reboot the system. From the hallway, a number of robots are streaming into the room, calling for the grand master. They pause when they see Tommy on the floor. The lead one looks to Gort. "What has happened to the grand master? We are in urgent need of him. The Collective has stopped working."

CHAPTER 36

Adamites have been milling around us for some time as we prevent them from fixing the main unit for the Collective. Try as I might to explain what is happening, each time another one shows up whining about being cut out, the whole process begins again. Accusations fly and they crowd in on Gort and I even further. The leaders of this group are those I must win first. That means Survivor, NewSon, and a handful of others.

I don't think they could hurt me, but Gort would be a different matter. I need him out of the equation. "Gort, show them how it's done. Take a nap next to Tommy."

Gort nods and lies next to the prone destroyer-bot. Leaving his visor open, he falls asleep, and the light in it dims to the same small speck as in Tommy's.

It's time to convince the crowd. "Here's the deal. Sooner or later, Tommy is going to wake up. At that time, I'll rouse Gort. You will all see how they are unharmed. In fact, in Tommy's case, you will note all symptoms of the Curse will be gone as well. If someone will assist me, I'll repair Tommy's chest while he's sleeping. You must trust me I'm speaking the truth about the id and how the Curse is caused by the subconscious mind."

Some flashing of lasers between those closest occurs then NewSon moves to stand in front of me. "I'll help."

I had a feeling he'd be the one to step up. If a former undecided is the one to show the most faith in me, the Adamites, whose religion revolves around me, will feel embarrassed and grudgingly wait for things to play out.

"Thank you, NewSon. To start, I need my tools. By the time you bring them, I should have an idea of all the parts I'll need."

I give him a list and he dashes off toward the nearest matter converter. As he's chasing down what I need, I kneel next to Tommy to examine the damage. Although the wound is ugly, none of the internal hardware is ruined. This should be an easy fix. All except the damaged paint work. That's beyond my skill set. I'm sure they can decorate him up again.

No…wait. I have a better idea. Retrieving James's scriptures sheet, I note the designs on it are very similar to the ones on Tommy. As NewSon arrives with my tools, I hand him the sheet and explain what I want done. The light flash from his visor is one I've come to recognize without my crown interpreting. It's a smile.

As I work on the repair, Survivor has ants in his pants as he jostles from Tommy to Gort and back again. His bad leg is constantly clanking and is becoming a real annoyance. As I finish up on Tommy, I reach out and grab him to stop the shuffle. "What's the matter?"

"Creator, my apologies. I have…doubts. The device you implanted in Tommy's chest is still there. Forgive me, but, unless I see the schematics, I will always wonder whether what you have installed is what you claim or whether it is something else."

A reasonable request. I point to the holo-emitter. "We need to get that back up and working." *Mum, give me a few minutes then send the schematics on my most recent invention to the holo-emitter here.*

"Will do."

It doesn't take long to reboot the emitter system. Moments later, Mum's transmission comes through, and I hit display. I take the time and explain how the device works and walk them through the assembly of it.

When I'm finished, Survivor bows his head before me.

"I am ashamed. I have doubted the Creator. What penance can I ever serve to make up for that mistake? I fear there is none."

His loyalty to his own people runs deep. I can't fault him for that. I help him up. "There is none among the Adamites whom I can put more faith in. You are their most respected warrior. Your protection of James's home more than proved your worth to me. For that, I am eternally grateful. Do not fret over your concern for Tommy. Heck, I wouldn't take me at face value either, and I should know. I don't have the most perfect record. From here, do what you do best and lead."

There's a noise behind me, and I turn in time to see Tommy rouse. A number of bots rush to help him up. I waken Gort, and he joins me. Tommy comes to stand before me and starts to drop to his knees, more than likely his feelings of guilt at his previous conduct nagging at him, but I reach out and stop him. "There's no need. You were under the influence of the Curse. How do you feel?"

"Like a fog has been lifted from my mind. Am I forever cured or just this one time?"

A good question. Nothing's forever, but I would like to think my implant has done the job. "As best as I can believe, it's forever. There may possibly be instances of insanity yet in years to come, but it won't be because of the Curse, only because of your own actions. From now on, *you* are responsible for your own state of mind."

Tommy nods. "Then we must ensure every one of the Children is fitted with your latest gift so the Curse will be forever gone from our people."

I point to the still shut-down device from whence the Collective operates. "And that?"

Tommy stares at it, but it is Gort who moves first and blasts the machine into smithereens. "My brothers will never fall victim to its siren song again."

The flashing laser lights and shuffling of the gathered destroyer-bots is enough to tell me many had a lot of trouble seeing that system go. In my mind, good riddance. Today is a benchmark day. For my creations, it is the end of two problems—the Curse inflicted on them and the curse they inflicted themselves.

Gort steps on top of the wreckage. I know what he's doing. His position elevates him above them. Leadership requires certain dictates and forcing his followers to look up to him is one of them. The boy makes me proud.

"Today, for those who will choose it, is the first day of your freedom from the Curse and the Collective. In the days to come we will look to free our brethren from the false leadership that calls himself One. The path is before us. I intend to go down that path. Who will follow me?"

Survivor jostles his way directly in front of Gort. "I will. Like you did for Tommy, insert the device in my chest."

A clamor erupts as bots line up for the same. I step back a bit to give them room. This is Gort's show now. I'm the hired help.

Tommy comes to stand by me. "Creator, I wish to give

extra thanks."

I give him a sideways glance. "What for?"

He rubs lightly at his repaired chest plate. "This. The words of my mentor are still embedded in it. I can sense them. It is as though a part of him still lives and it is with me now. As I scan his personal notes, a deeper understanding of what it means to be the grand master enlightens me. It is an epiphany of most profound proportions. When it comes to the Order of the Adamites, it is not just reverence that is required, it is love."

James. I'll always miss him. I pat Tommy on the back. "Then you need to take that newfound knowledge and apply it." There are still a few stragglers staying back from the crowd. I nod toward Gort. "Go to him. Your support is necessary. There are still some here and outside who will follow your lead only."

Tommy leaves me and climbs the wreckage to stand next to Gort. As he raises Gort's arm, acknowledging him leader, those holding back move closer. When Survivor climbs to hold up Gort's other arm, there are none left standing aloof. Teamwork at its finest. The question is, is it enough to beat One? I guess time will tell.

***

I need to sleep. All around me are destroyer-bots going through their first upgrade since creation. Commandeering every matter converter we could find, the tunnels are turned into a factory with bots being upgraded everywhere. I supervised until I was sure I wasn't needed anymore, and now I'm looking for a nice spot to lie down.

NewSon takes me by the elbow. "This way, Creator. We've set up a place for you."

A large pile of feather pillows is spread out in one corner of the room. Somebody's been using one of the converters for other than bot repair. I'm not complaining. Nestling in, I make plans to check with everyone in the morning.

***

When I wake up, they're still updating robots, not with the sleep device, but with the ability to both phase and cloak at the same time. What the hell? Where's Gort? This is his doing.

I find the big guy accompanied by Tommy, Survivor, and NewSon as they examine the map showing all the bots in Robot City. They're planning an attack. I listen for a while and wait until the group breaks up then pull Gort aside. "You gave them the phase upgrade. Why? Now there's nothing they can't do that we can. It was our only advantage. I was holding that for emergency backup."

Gort places a big hand on my shoulder. "It wasn't your invention to give or keep, it was Mum's, and she's approved it. We're going to win this war, Adam, and with minimal loss of life. It's only common sense to do so."

Sometimes I hate common sense. It interferes now and then with my own personal goals. "What if, in some near future, the Adamites go bad? I'm out of upper hands. I always like to have an ace up my sleeve, and now it's gone."

Gort chuckles. "You'll think of something. You always

do."

As I motorboat out the air I had sucked in for a smart retort, I shrug my shoulders in surrender. This is his show. "Fine, fine, fine. So what's the plan?"

"One. We need to take him out. Without his leadership, the Purists should fall in quick order. We need to get to him."

Bangkok Palace. *Sure.* Let's go hit what is probably the best fortified position they have. Even with the upgrades, they still need to turn off the phase to fire weapons, and that means losses. Considering how few of the Adamites remain, the plan sounds crazy. I thought I'd fixed that. "The castle is enormous, and more than likely better defended than anything. I know the place. Maybe it would be best if just a small group of us went. I bet I could find him for us."

"You're not coming with us, Adam. Your body density prevents the phase device from working for you. We need every available destroyer-bot in this sortie to be able to infiltrate the castle before the fighting starts, and your presence would make that impossible."

Left behind again. "Darn it, Gort. That's just not fair. I've got just as much right to go after One as anybody. You can't keep me out of this. Just how are you going to find One on your own?"

"My intention is to draw One out into the open before we attack."

Remembering how he hid from me when I searched everywhere, I am doubtful how successful this plan could be. "And just exactly what bait do you intend to use to draw him out?"

"Isn't it obvious? You, of course."

CHAPTER 37

I remember this movie. It featured me walking into Bangkok Palace and getting captured like a bumbling idiot. I never liked the ending.

This time, the movie's starting out a little different. First off, I'm not able to walk right in while cloaked. The outer perimeter is surrounded by all kinds of trip wires guaranteed to set off enough alarms to have me surrounded in seconds. No sneaking in.

That leaves the front door. At this point, I see no reason for being cloaked. As I near the entrance and the small army of destroyer-bots stationed near it, I turn my cloak off. Let them see me. There's nothing they can do.

Time to put Gort's plan into play. "I'm here to see One and parley on behalf of the Adamites. Tell him to come out and speak with me."

Though none of them act menacingly toward me, from all the flashing lights it's obvious a heated discussion is going on. Staring aimlessly around while I wait for an answer, I decide on a ten count before I brush past them. One. Two. Three. Four. Five. Si—

"You may enter and seek him out."

The bot interrupted my count, and I wouldn't exactly call his reply a proper invitation. What does he mean, *seek him out*? Ah, who cares. The first attempt to get One to show has failed, on to plan B. I'm going in.

The bots part and I walk past them to go in the front door. Once I'm through, the debate heats up again as their lasers are flashing more than ever. Something's got them shaken up.

Once past the second set of doors, the scene before me is surprising. Everywhere I look, there are destroyer-bots laid out on the floor. Except for a path where I can walk, they're wall-to-wall. Pausing to glance into the open visor of one nearby I see the same telltale signs I recognized before—the Curse.

I try to take a measure of how many I can see. Thousands, for sure, and this is just the front hall. Knowing how big the place is, if I assume the same carpet of bots lies everywhere, they must be in the hundreds of thousands, maybe even more than a million. Maybe the odds aren't so bad, after all.

I wonder what Gort and the others think when they see this. I can't see them, but they must be close, maybe even right beside me.

Two Purists have followed me in, so I need to talk to them instead of my compatriots. I turn to face them. "Look at all your comrades struck down by the Curse. What is One doing to solve this? If the Adamites knew of this demise, they would have no fear of you."

The one who told me to enter gives me a light shove. "They will heal in time. Despite these, we are still in the millions, far more than your paltry Adamites can muster. At least we aren't slaves to your Collective."

When he shoves me again, I hold my ground. "The Collective is no more. The Adamites are cured of the Curse."

"You lie. There is no cure for the Curse." He shoves me a third time.

I slap his hand away. "There is, and you're missing it.

How long until you join the others on the floor here?"

The two bots get into a heated argument. Finally, one walks away, leaving me with Mr. Grumpy.

He again shoves me, and once more I stay planted. After a moment of useless pushing, he gives up. "If you wish to find One, you will need to keep moving. He does not frequent here."

He's got a point. "No, I suppose he doesn't." I turn and start walking again. "I haven't played hide-and-seek since I was a child. I can't replicate myself, spread out, and look for him, so this may take a while." I hope Gort is getting my message.

As we pass from room to room, my recollection of the palace layout is returning. My conversations with him involved his projection through holograph emitters. Somewhere, there must be a secret room One watches and transmits from.

We arrive at the spot where the hidden door in the wall opened, and I was assaulted by the Purists. I stop to examine the wall in hopes of finding some kind of method of opening it. While I'm doing so, a number of bots have arrived. I can't tell for sure, but I think the one in the lead is the one who had been arguing and left. Now he's got about forty or so friends in tow.

As I finish looking the place over, I can't espy the opening. No matter. I'll make my own. Rearing back, I punch the wall, and a whole section caves way. Grumpy-pants tries to block me, but the new arrivals grab hold of him and pull him away. Something's going on here. I'm sensing a little revolt in the making. I turn to my protectors. "Thanks, gentlemen. I appreciate the support. Perhaps there *is* a possible resolution between you and the Adamites without any more fighting."

They're looking at each other, lights flashing away. The lead one looks back at me. "Maybe there is."

I like what I'm hearing. Personally, I'm tired of fighting. It's seems all I've done each life is fight, fight, fight. I nod and head into the opening. Inside is a wide, dark hallway, perhaps twelve feet across. A couple of the bots who must have sensed my dilemma when I stopped walking move up beside me and illuminate the way with their lasers.

This is getting better and better. If One is watching this, he must be getting nervous about the turncoats because behind me more and more keep arriving. The hallway runs a long way with plenty of doors to the left and right as we go. At each, I pause to open and peek inside. Seeing either empty rooms or vacant hallways, I proceed down the one I'm in. There's got to be an end to this thing.

There is, kind of. A staircase winding up. Through my wandering, I've lost all sense of where I am in the castle, but if my memory serves, there's a tower at the far east end of the place, and I'm betting this is it.

Whoa. Lots of steps. As I near the top, I'm guessing four or flights up. The stairs end at a small landing before a single door. I've checked every one to this point. If One's not on the other side, then I'll have to start over.

Opening the door, I step into a brightly lit room some thirty feet across. The curved walls tell me I'm right. This is the tower. A number of pieces of equipment line the walls. Some, I recognize, as in a matter converter and in a nanobot station. Some, I don't. This must be One's lab, and there the bugger is, standing near a holograph station. He's been watching my every move. Beside him, in her human form, is Eve. With the host of converts behind me, I'm feeling cocky. "So here's where you're hiding. There's no micro black hole box for you to lock me in now. Time to give it up, One."

"What's that you once said to me? 'Never give up, never surrender?' In fact, you've made things easier for me by weeding out the malcontents." He throws a switch and a surge of some kind of energy beam of such magnitude is flowing up through the floor. The bots behind me all collapse instantly while my own shield snaps and crackles and I fall to my hands and knees. Shit. I never noticed the emitters. High intensity Higgs beams. It's the only thing that makes sense. I can hardly move, the gravity pulling me down. There must be something else, though. Mum said my shield should be able to compensate, no matter what my density. There must be another factor. Some kind of shield disabler. Looking at the fallen robots, I expand the thought. Not just a shield disabler, but anything mechanical.

Gort appears in front of me, as do Tommy, NewSon, and a few others. Although all of them try to fire on One, they as well fall to the floor before they can do so. The effect on bots must be instantaneous. While in phase mode, they were unharmed, but once out, they become instantly susceptible to whatever it is One is doing.

Struggle as I might, I cannot resist the pull on me, and my arms give out, resulting in me sprawling on the floor, face down. I manage to turn my head to see One and Eve walking amongst us. He is carrying some type of short bazooka-shaped weapon. Why isn't the beam affecting them?

He stands over me. "I can imagine what you're thinking. How am I doing this? The great Adam Spenceworth laid low by some unknown force, unable to fathom why. Shall I tell you?"

He bends to pat my cheek. "No, I think not. Oh, by now you've probably surmised I'm using some type of Higgs beam, and you would be partially correct, but you will never guess the other part, the thing limiting your own shield defenses."

He moves over to Gort and kicks at him. "The same device shutting down the First here. The First. Ha! What a joke. He may be the first, but I am One, as in number one. The Purists all kneel to me."

His meandering has brought him to one of the bots who assisted me since entering the castle. "Well, maybe not all. There are still some who oppose my will. There is a solution for those unwilling to submit."

One takes aim at the bot and fires. There's a crackle as the bot's shield holds for just an instant before he crumbles into dust. One spins to flash the weapon at me.

"Like it? It's my latest invention. It uses the same technology as the matter converters, but in a beam. Right now I'm asking it to convert things to dust. If I wanted, I could have converted that bot into anything…water, rocks, air, whatever strikes my fancy. I could even have made him real human flesh. Sadly, there would be no life to it, but, for an instant, he would have been a real boy."

One chortles. Obviously, he finds his own joke amusing. I need to try and reason with him. It's our only hope. The question is, how do you reason with a madman?

"Yours is the fatal mistake made by all of history's tyrants. Rule by force leads to revolution…always. If you kill all who oppose you, then eventually you will stand alone."

"Never alone." He pulls Eve close. "Never alone again, for look who I have now…Eve, your sexbot. When she arrived and suggested we team up, I couldn't believe my good fortune. In a sexless world of destroyer-bots, I get the only female. Together, we will propagate a new race of robots, ones superior to these destroyer-bots. Ones who can populate the cosmos as our offspring. I will be the supreme ruler of the universe."

Offspring? Has One forgotten he's no longer a man? Eve can't bear children. I know he's egomaniacal, but this is downright loony. There's no talking sense with such insanity.

Eve, on the other hand, has been going through some weird expressions during One's tirade. She's pacing behind him. A possibility pops into my head. Maybe… "There's a small problem with your plan. There can only be *one* ruler of the universe."

"And who else would it be? You? I think not."

I need to plant the seed. "No, not me."

One moves to stand over Gort. "The First, then. I should have suspected as much. You and your robot hierarchy are over." He takes aim with his converter gun. "Say good-bye, Gort."

Before he can fire, Eve jumps up on his back and plunges a blade into his cranium. "No, not Gort, me. I am the one who will rule."

One falls and Eve scoops up his converter gun. It's me she's aiming at.

"*I* am number one now."

She fires, and the beam is painful. Although my clothes turn to dust, my super density must be resisting the effects, or at the very least slowing them down significantly because, damn, it hurts, but I'm not converting to whatever she's trying to convert me to. I can see what looks like some kind of effervescence emanating off my skin. There's no doubt something's happening.

I need to get up. Pushing with all my might, I manage to get back to my hands and knees but no further. This is a silly way to die.

CHAPTER 38

Springing to my feet, I can only surmise the Higgs emitters have been turned off. Eve scowls at me, fires at the wall behind her, creating an opening, and, as I start for her, she throws the gun at me then leaps out of the building.

I'm in no shape to follow. First of all, I don't think I could survive a four-floor plummet to the ground below. Second, my limbs are so weak I fall back to my hands and knees. I doubt I could even walk.

Crawling over to One, I look into his visor. There's still life. "Najmi, can you hear me?"

All around me, the bots are getting to their feet. Gort and Tommy join me at One's side.

Gort tries to communicate with One, robot style. After a moment, he shakes his head. "The mechanisms keeping him functioning are still operating, but his mind is gone." He touches the protruding blade. "This must have ruptured his memory well. All he was, his personality, his memories, are lost."

NewSon steps near. "It may be best to terminate him now. We don't want the Purists to hold out hope of his return."

Kill him? In One's case it would literally be "pulling the plug." I can't do that. For all that he's done wrong, there's one thing I have to grudgingly admit he was right on. Deep down, I have always envisioned robots as the future. Besides, I forgot how many great-grandsons he is, but Najmi is family. You don't kill family. "No. There may still be vestiges encoded inside somewhere. If anything, I owe it to him to try and find them. He had no idea what the Curse did to him. I shall repair him."

Gort puts a hand on my shoulder. Ouch, that stings. My flesh is still red everywhere, like some real bad-ass sunburn.

"I am proud of you, Adam. It is the right decision. After all those rebirths, all those lives, your own ego has finally toned down. The Adam I first knew would have turned One to dust by now."

No doubt about it. I've lost some of my touch. That old swagger of mine, can I get it back? "Maybe so, but don't tell anybody. Let's keep it our little secret."

Gort lets loose one of his deep laughs. When he stops, he picks up One. "Come. Let's get him to the lab aboard Mum. The sooner you start, the better."

From outside the room, I hear the thunder of footsteps then Survivor rushes in with a number of Adamites in tow.

NewSon grabs him as he enters. "Easy there. The fight's over. One is defeated."

Survivor looks around. "Huh. Well, good, then. It took me too damn long to figure out how to shut down those emitters. I was afraid everyone up here had been killed."

"You did that? You shut down the emitters?"

"Yeah. You know, part of surviving is not being a rash fool and charging into an enemy's lair without having some idea what you face. When I saw everyone fall, I put two and two together and hunted down the power feed. *Somebody's* got to use their brains now and then."

I chuckle along with the group, but not everyone is in a gleeful mood. The bot who is the leader of the rebel Purists comes and kneels before me.

"Creator, I beg for your help. Can you really cure the Curse? I and my brethren would do anything for that."

Here's where the politics kick in. I've got to play this right. "My cure is only for those who adhere to the teachings of the Adamites and obey the three laws as laid down by the First. Will you and your Purist friends submit to such things?"

He nods. "Anything."

I look to Tommy who has already taken the cue and moved to join me.

He scans the crowded room and pulls his scriptures sheet from his thigh. "To initiate you into the order, I need you all to kneel."

Every Purist does so, without exception...even the grumbler, who's been standing in the back of the room. Things are in good hands, and I step back to give Tommy center stage.

"Adam, I need you and Gort to come outside."

I peek out the opening blasted in the wall and can see the ship hovering there. *What's up, Mum?*

"Eve. I'm tracking her right now, but it won't be long before I lose her. We need to catch her before she gets away once more."

It's only been moments, and I've already forgotten about her. Gort's hands are full with One. I reach for the severely wounded bot. "Give him to me. You need to give both of us a lift over to Mum there."

Gort hands me One then bends down. "Hang on a moment." He rips one of the emitters from the floor. "We could use this. I can quickly configure something to use as an energy source."

With both One and the emitter in my hands, to the sound of Tommy's intonations, Gort lifts off and carries the two of us across to the open hangar door of the ship. I dodge in and take the captain's chair, leaving to Gort the moving of One to the repair station. "Okay, Mum. Let's go."

"On my way. She's looking into empty buildings. I suspect she's trying to find one she can hole up in. More than likely, one with a matter converter."

I recall my own attempt to have one of those things make a phaser gun. "That won't do her any good. They can't replicate micro black holes."

Mum brings us to the Adamite quarter. Most of the buildings have been reduced to piles of rubbish. I see Eve dodge out of one place and into another. "Let Gort and I out here. We'll go in on foot."

Mum drops to the ground, and we make for the doorway we saw Eve enter. Hopefully, there's no opening in the back. The place is two floors up, but the wreckage from a nearby building makes entry on foot possible.

As we clamber in, I recognize where I am. This is Tommy's, and, yes, he does have a matter converter in here. Mum was right.

There's no lights, and it's dark inside. I don't see any movement. "Eve. I know you're in here. Come on out."

Gort's trying to do his best to illuminate the room with his laser, but there's a lot of stuff making for all kinds of shadows—a bear, a lion, some dinosaurs, one of those terror birds, and other assorted animals standing or lying about everywhere. The place reeks. The power to the preservative emitters must be out. All the animals are decaying.

She's in here. There's definitely no way out the back. Holding my nose, I edge my way in. I need to flush her out to the door so Gort can grab her.

Halfway in, I conclude she's morphed into one of the animals. There is a limit to what changes she can make to her appearance. She can't be shorter or taller and must be a biped. That leaves the gorilla.

Yep. I see her clothes piled against the wall behind it. I make my way toward her. "Come on, Eve. It's over. We need to get you fixed up."

Roaring just like the animal, she charges at me, pushes me down, and makes for the exit. I was too slow to catch her, but not Gort. In one hand, he grabs her wrist, and with the other holds the emitter to her head. She slumps into his arms.

"I've got her, Adam. Let's go home."

Gort carries her out to a waiting Mum, and we get her on the med table. It takes me just over an hour to open her up and make the necessary changes. Gort's asked me to include the upgraded phase and cloak devices. She's sleeping soundly now.

Gort heads back to Bangkok Palace. Says he has things to attend to.

I'm tired as well. Think I'll get some shut-eye. As I snuggle down in my bed, there's a certain amount of satisfaction in how the day has turned out.

"You have a right to be proud. You cured the Curse, ended the robot war and, more importantly, you put our family back together."

Mum. I really need to install some privacy protocols. *I*

had help...a lot of it—you, Gort, Tommy, Survivor, NewSon, and all the rest.

"True, and I think you're going to need more of it soon. I'm reading some disturbing movements out there in the galaxy."

It can wait until tomorrow. Right now, I just want to get some sleep.

"All right. Sleep tight."

***

"Adam, get up. It's important."

I rub at my eyes. How long have I slept? It feels like it's only been minutes, not hours. "What is it, Mum?"

"You're needed right away. There's a serious problem."

I struggle into my clothes and make for the door. "What is it?"

"An invasion fleet. It just pulled into orbit over the planet."

CHAPTER 39

What the hell now? A guy just can't get a good night's sleep anymore. "Who are they?"

"Humans."

Now isn't that a kick. For over two million years, Earth has carried the battle for mankind against the Harkardi, and now they want to repay the destroyer-bots by invading? That's what you get for thanks nowadays.

The only thing I can surmise is, since One's amendment to the three laws, the Purists have been attacking human planets. I guess that would be enough to piss them off.

Mum gets me over to Bangkok Palace in a jiffy. Along the way, she educates me as to what she's been seeing in darkspace. It looks like it's only going to get worse.

Walking through the halls, I can see the Adamites have moved in lock, stock, and barrel, and are busy curing all of the Purists of the Curse.

Gort and the others have set up their headquarters in the massive dining room. They've pushed the table and chairs to the side and are watching holo images of the invasion fleet as I enter. Once again, the humans are in blue while the destroyer-bots are in red. I'll never understand that. "Looks like they've got numbers on you."

Gort nods. "We've received an ultimatum, but have yet to respond. I want you to be the point on this. You're human. They should listen."

Diplomacy has never been one of the fine arts I've learned. Nevertheless, Gort does have a point. "All right,

I'll do it. Here's how we'll play it. We need to show a submissive hand. I want every destroyer-bot grounded. No exceptions."

"It shall be done."

You know, all this taking charge is making me start to feel like my old self again. Maybe I'm finally getting my old swagger back. When Gort said my ego was in check— that really hurt. I miss it. "Good. Once that's done, let's invite them to Mum's for a chat…somewhere in near-Earth orbit. My choice would be a geostationary position right above us. I don't want any lack of communication to occur."

Gort nods some more. "That shouldn't be an issue. You and I can maintain a constant link through Mum."

I give Gort a friendly slap on the arm. "Not *you*. Tommy. *You're* coming with me."

"Why should *I* come with you?"

I'm not facing those humans alone. "I need a good bartender."

***

After what Mum has told me, I stall for over a day, even though the humans have agreed to a parley. Let's hope it turns about better than my last attempt at one. I've brought Survivor, NewSon, and a few others along as well, but under strict orders they are to remain both cloaked and phased. It's good to have backup in case of emergencies.

Mum has moved to the coordinates I asked for, and we're awaiting our guests. The doors are open, and the lights are on. When they finally show up, it's in force.

Some forty ships pull up, many with weapons trained. How trusting. I'm not exactly feeling the love.

It takes a while, but eventually a shuttle meanders through their ships, picking people up then docks in my bay. I'm waiting on the gangplank to greet them. As they emerge from the ship, I'm momentarily taken aback. The ten humans, six male and four female, are all different shapes, sizes, colors, and more. Blue skinned, red skinned, short and thick, tall and sticklike. I guess two million years of evolution on different planets will do that. "Greetings. Welcome aboard. My name is Adam Spenceworth, and I'm looking forward to a nice, pleasant chat with all of you."

By their puzzled looks, it's obvious two of them don't understand me. Others whisper to them in some weird language and they nod then smile. This is going to make it difficult.

The closest one to me, a not-bad-looking female, though the bluish tinge to her skin takes me a moment to become accustomed to, accepts my hand in greeting. "Thank you for hosting this meeting, Mr. Spenceworth. I am Admiral Leela of the Galaxy Core Amalgamation. My associates and I are hoping it will be fruitful. War is always an ugly business."

Leading the way, I head for the lounge. "I concur. I've seen more than my share of it, and frankly, I hope to never see another one again."

When they step into the room, they all edge sideways. Gort bows. "Gentlemen and ladies, welcome. I am your bartender for the evening. May I take your orders?"

Leela steps closer. "My, you're a big one. I thought all destroyer-bots were the same height?"

302

"Adam upsized me when my brethren first came into being. He felt it was important I should be dominant as I am the first."

She touched his open hand then pulled back. "You seem tame enough. I'll have whatever Mr. Spenceworth is having."

"Xirdalan beer. He has an affection for it from his days on New Azerbaijan." Gort straightens. "If it will make everyone feel comfortable, I shall get a round for all of you."

There are several nods and grunts of agreement with two ordering something different and three of them abstaining. Gort heads to the bar and procures the drinks while we all take advantage of the comfortable seating. I also installed one of those matter converters in the ship and stocked the bar in advance.

Once seated with drink in hand, Leela faces me. "Now...down to business, Mr. Spenceworth. The destroyer-bots and their production facilities need to be decommissioned immediately."

She must know they're sentient. "You're talking genocide."

"Oh, let's not be so dramatic. After all, at the end of the day, they're just machines."

I motion for Gort to come near. "Tell me, Gort, would you mind it if we decommissioned you and the others?"

"I would have my brethren fight until not one of us was left standing or until humanity gave up."

I return my attention to Leela. "There you have it. A sure sign of their sentience—a will to live."

"It matters not. Either you agree to our terms or we

will reduce the surface of the planet to slag. It would pain us to do so, as it is the birthplace of our people, but there is nothing you can do to stop us. We have devised a way to see the destroyer-bots when they are cloaked. There'll be no more surprise attacks. We swept your ship and the area before docking just to be sure."

So that means they still can't see someone who has both the cloak and phase devices operating simultaneously. They don't know Survivor and NewSon are here. Intriguing.

The external holographs pop on, showing the surrounding space, and another appears directly in the middle of the room showing the planet and its immediate environ. Mum has marked all of the human ships in blue. "Adam, they will be arriving momentarily."

Admiral Leela looks both at the image before her, and then outside. "*Who* will be arriving momentarily?

On cue, around the Earth holo-image, the space begins to fill with green dots—ships coming out of FTL—a lot of ships. "Those who would stop you."

I glance up. "Mum, send out a communiqué to our new arrivals to join us for tea, would you?"

"Yes, Adam. Request sent."

The humans are all standing now, conferring amongst each other as to the change in the situation. I smile at what I consider a most fortuitous thing—an Harkardi fleet.

Admiral Leela starts for the door. "These negotiations are finished. We will not consort with the Harkardi."

"I would not advise it, Admiral. Not until we've heard what the Harkardi want. Would you want me to be the only one to speak with them? Somehow, I doubt you want to be left out of the loop."

Leela stops, looks me over, and then returns to her seat. "You're right. I do not want things left only to you. Understand, this is still a meeting under truce. I expect full protection from any Harkardi aggression."

Judging by the weaponry each and every one of them carries, it hardly seems likely they need my assistance, but as I am the host, it's my job to comply. "Absolutely. Just as there are ten of you, the Harkardi are being offered to arrive with the same size contingent."

It doesn't take long for their arrival. The humans, Gort, and I greet them on the bridge, as my lounge is too small. Three females and seven runt males, though, I must admit, they look bigger than I remember. They're all still just as ugly.

The three females are ornately dressed. Must be royalty. Seeing as two are staying a half step behind one, I'm assuming she's of higher rank. Mum has learned who they are and passed on the info through my node. "Welcome aboard, High Princess Branjolia. I am honored you could join us."

She scowls at me, at Gort, and at every human present. Without saying a word, she turns her scowl toward the Harkardi female to her right. The female nods and steps forward. "Her exalted highness, first in line for the throne, is sullied by your presence, but understands the necessity of this meeting. She is prepared to accept terms of surrender from both the humans and the devil robots."

Surrender. I can't help but laugh. No wonder their right to ascension is earned through assassination. Such arrogance is insufferable. "Princess, I think you misunderstand. It is my intention to offer a suggestion of détente. Both you, the Harkardi, and Admiral Leela's people"—I nod toward Leela who acknowledges my nod with one of her own—"humanity, are relatively even throughout the galaxy. Meanwhile, the devil robots you speak of hold the balance of power. The question is, 'Why can't we all just get along?' I suggest a peace treaty be struck here and now and the insurance of that peace will be made by the robots of Earth as they will only attack the aggressor who breaks such a treaty. Either that, or we'll all start shooting now."

It's almost comical as everyone reaches for and checks their weapons. As the Harkardi females, except for knives, are unarmed, the odds favor the humans, a detail obviously not lost on the admiral as she steps near me.

"You play a dangerous game, Adam Spenceworth. What's to stop me and my friends from killing everyone here right now?"

"Them." I wave a hand at the emptiest spot in the room. "Show yourselves, gentlemen."

Survivor, NewSon, and the rest suddenly appear. The room is getting really crowded.

Leela's eyes go wide. "We scanned this ship. They were not here. I'm positive. How did you do that?"

I waggle a finger at her. "Now, now, Admiral. You don't really expect me to tell you, do you? Let's just say it's my little secret. Obviously, you're not quite as ready to take on Earth as you once thought. Now, as to that peace treaty I proposed?"

She holds a hand to her chin. "Under the circumstances, your proposal has merit, but there is still another party to this agreement. What say the Harkardi?"

The princess, who has never stopped scowling—I'm wondering if she's had her face surgically altered to stay that way—shakes her head, and her spokeswoman acknowledges it with another nod.

"Her exalted highness finds your terms unacceptable. Under the terms of this truce, we shall now return to our fleet."

The door to Eve's room swishes open and she steps out as a Harkardi in the same outfit she wore when she killed Mary. She's made good use of the converter, I see. Even the contact lenses are in place.

Humans and robots part as Eve makes her way toward the Harkardi contingent. "I say you're staying. You *know* who I am?"

The princess never flinches, but the rest of her crew mumbles to each other. It's too hard to hear what they're saying, but I do pick up the same few words here and there…*the Eternal Queen*. They know who she is, all right.

The third female steps in front of the princess and pulls a knife. The spokeswoman has pulled one as well. "Your day is past. You are ancient history. Her exalted highness is the future of the Harkardi."

Eve grins, and, from behind her back, produces her own blade. "I think not."

She moves so fast, I can barely keep track of her weapon. In a handful of short strokes, she parries both blades and sinks hers to the hilt into each woman. During all of this, I've put a staying hand in front of Leela, hoping she's quick enough to know to stay out of it. It worked. The other humans, taking her cue, stay put and give the now-circling Eve and Princess Branjolia room.

The princess orders the seven males to defend her, and they encircle her. Eve points at the closest one. "You know the law."

The runt glances back and forth between Eve and the princess then slinks away to the side. His cohorts follow suit. Branjolia is alone.

She finally pulls her own knife, a long, thin, ornamental-looking thing. "All the history books said you have no match. I think they lied."

Her lunge surprises even me, but not Eve. In one move, Eve's blade pierces the princess right through. As she falls to the ground, the males all kneel in obeisance. Eve turns to face me and Leela. "There is still a queen to dispatch, but I shall take care of that in short order. Once done, I shall accept the terms of your détente." She motions for the males to pick up the three bodies. "For now, I must return to my fleet. I wish you well, Adam Spenceworth."

Eve steps up to Leela. "If I hear that you have attacked Earth after I've gone, I shall hunt you and every human down until you are nothing but a memory."

Eve waves at the Harkardi and, together, they march out to the waiting transport. I watch as it returns to the fleet. It doesn't take long until they all engage their FTLs and disappear.

The admiral turns to Gort. "I think I'll have another one of those beers."

Gort gets her the drink and one for me as well. I dismiss the other bots and they disappear.

Leela downs her beer then gives me a quizzical look. "She's one of yours, isn't she? She wouldn't really kill us, would she? After all, she's of human design."

A good guess. A smart lass, and I like that. I think maybe an evening where we might get to know each other a little better is in order, but, for now, I'm not showing my hand. "Right down to the last man, woman, and child."

Leela hands her empty glass to Gort. "I guess I'd best be going. Perhaps we could work out the details of this agreement a little later, say over dinner?"

I take her hand and brush my lips across the back of it. "Your place or mine?"

She glances at her waiting entourage. "Yours, I think. We might need a bit of privacy."

She winks and leads her crew out to their ship. I've still got it. I turn to Gort and give him a friendly slap across the back. "Well, big buddy, I need your help to whip up one hell of a meal."

I always enjoy his laugh.

**

Everything has gone as planned. The treaty is in place and every bot has pledged to uphold Gort's three laws. They've been given the job of policemen, patrolling the galaxy to insure there are no breaches of the détente. There are always a few radicals who won't abide, and the Adamites always make short work of them.

Admiral Leela has become...a friend. That's about as close as I get nowadays. It does have its benefits.

I only saw Eve once more when the treaty was signed. She looked regal as ever. I miss her.

"Adam, you've overstayed your welcome. You're ninety-seven years old. You could die any moment, and then it would be too late to regenerate you. Please, get in the tube."

I fiddle with the last few connections. My hands aren't what they used to be. "I'm almost done, Mum."

The bot powers up and looks around. Finally, its gaze settles on me. "Where am I?"

That's a real good start. "You're in the lounge of my ship. Do you know who you are?"

His laser flickers for a while. "There is a name I can recall, though I am not sure."

Here it is. The real test. "What is it?"

"Najmi."

More than just a smile comes to me, also, a feeling of...goodness. Now I can finally rest.

CHAPTER 40

I am surrounded by nothing.

There is nothing above me, nothing below me, and nothing all round me. All screens are blank. "How long, Mum?"

"Over three centillion."

Gosh, that's a long time. They always kept getting exponentially longer. Almost five billion. I woke up that time with a soft glow to me. Kind of freaky, really. Just in time to see the planet Earth melt away and learn the Milky Way had been invaded by an alien species from the Andromeda galaxy when they merged. Apparently humanity and the Harkardi, long friends by then, with the help of the Adamites, kicked their asses. That was good to hear.

Nearly one hundred and twenty billion. Learning the entire universe was occupied by humans, Harkardi and some crossbreed race made me proud.

At three trillion, I'd become pretty bright and needed an exo-skin to tone it down some.

I think of all the *illions* I've gone through—quadrillions, quintillions, sextillions—the list goes on and on.

Now, there are no stars. The universe has gone cold.

I'm not feeling right. Twenty-five again, yeah, but at what density? Unlimited? All things have a limit, and I think I've hit mine.

The clanking behind me is Gort coming up the stairs. I turn to face him.

"Adam, you're awake. It's nice to see you again."

He's barely holding together. How he's managed to do it all these years is beyond me.

The door to Eve's room is smashed open. My guess is it wouldn't work anymore. Eve comes out, dragging one leg. Her synthetic skin is all but gone, but I still recognize her.

She hugs me. "I did it. I survived until you woke."

The sensations racking my body are getting worse. I don't think I'm going to last long. "You, Gort, and Mum should go now. Leave me here. Get somewhere safe."

Mum's lights flicker. "There's nowhere to go. We're family. We're staying with you until the end."

Gort wraps his arms around me and Eve. "It's time for a new beginning, Adam. We're from this age. Leave the next one to themselves."

I know what he's talking about. I can sense it. I'm about to go out with a big bang.

I...am Adam Spenceworth.

And now...I am God.

OTHER NOVELS by MICHAEL DRAKICH

GRAVE IS THE DAY

In October of 1957, more than Sputnik fell to Earth...

Set against the back drop of the Space Race and the Cold War, both the United States and the Soviet Union have a new issue to deal with, aliens from outer space. Both the Braannoo and the Muurgu are at war with each other and Earth becomes the newest battleground in their struggle. Spanning time from the launch of Sputnik to the near future, the interplay of historical events from a new light make you ask the question, could this all be true? The capture of aliens near small town USA unites three players from different quarters, Commander Kraanox of the Braannoo, First Lieutenant Wayne Bucknell as his captor and seven year old Justin Spencer, the first to make alien contact.

Grave Is The Day is a superb read! This story is a must read for all the science fiction, extraterrestrial lovers on Earth. Grave Is The Day has earned my rating of 5 stars! --Ramsey's Reviews

I have read books that meld fantasy with historical events before, but never one that takes such minute details and blends them so thoroughly. This is a great read and an exceptional rewrite of history for all ages. – Bitten By Books

He created each character with amazing attention to detail and development. I thoroughly enjoyed this book and found myself identifying with more than one of the delightful characters. -- Paranormal Romance Guild - Beth Price

THE BROTHERHOOD OF PIAXIA

Years have passed since the overthrow of the monarchy by the Brotherhood of Warlocks and they rule Piaxia in peaceful accord. But now forces are at work to disrupt this rule from outside the Brotherhood as well as within! In the border town of Rok, a young warlock acolyte, Tarlok and his older brother, Savan, captain of the guard, become embroiled in the machinations of dominance. While in the capital city, Tessia, the daughter of Piaxia's most influential merchant, begins a journey of survival. Follow the three as their paths intertwine, with members of the Brotherhood in pursuit and the powerful merchant's guild manipulating the populace for their own ends.

Great, well-rounded characters? Magic running rampant? A lost princess? Yes, this book has it all. – tHe crooked WorD

If you love fantasy that mixes magic, lost royalty, sacrifices, heroes, and strong characters, I would suggest The Brotherhood of Piaxia. – Captivated Reading

The Brotherhood of Piaxia is what it wants to be - a real entertaining fantasy story. It comes along with more characters than you normally get but a lot less then you meet in a famous series you can watch at HBO. It has definitely more magic than a famous fantasy trilogy you could see in cinemas. There is less blood and gore than in a book with a title how to serve a drink. It is also a book which does not drown in romance. For me is a book which you like to read when you want to have a well dosed mix of well-known books. Or in simple words The Brotherhood of Piaxia is like the espresso you enjoy after a good meal. – Edi's Book Lighthouse

314

LEST THE DEW RUST THEM

Terrorism in America has a new game…decapitations!

Homeland Security Director Robert Grimmson faces the task of catching five men in New York City. They call themselves the Sword Masters with a single minded plan of terror through decapitations.

Barely has the task begun when a new arrival at JFK is a man importing thousands of swords! Alexander Suten-Mdjai is a trainer in the deadly art of swordsmanship and Robert cannot help but believe there is a connection between him and the Sword Masters.

As he goes about the task, each step in his search is made more difficult through the interference of politicians, the media and his own government.

Robert's examination constantly draws him back to Alexander who regales him with a tale of swordsmanship from his lineage featuring events of mankind's bloody past and often oddly having a connection to the case before him.

With the clock ticking as New York collapses into a deep panic, he must catch the Sword Masters before it is too late!

THE INFINITE WITHIN

Going into outer space calls to Astronaut Brooke Jones like the sirens of old, and when the chance to be part of the first manned mission to Mars arises, she is ecstatic. But little does she know the fate that awaits her on the surface of the red planet or the results of her encounter when she gets back to Earth.

This book is very entertaining. It will grab hold of you, and keep poking at you to finish it. I would recommend this story to science fiction readers that enjoy something a little different. This will not give you the highs of the shoot-em-up in outer space. It takes place place on earth, for the most part. It could be a real story and has enough elements be good fiction. I look forward to reading more by this author. – Charles Kravetz – Keeping Dreams

I loved the uniqueness of the story and the high-caliber action scenes. The adventure and the sense of awe kept me reading late into wee hours. – Laurie Jenkins – Laurie's Thoughts and Reviews

Wow. First off I'll start by saying the book was amazing. In the beginning I was a little iffy about the whole deal then the book got better, and better, and obviously better. I was surprised at the level of detail in the storytelling – Ezekiel Carsella – Books N Tech

DEMON STONES

It's been almost a hundred years since warlock meddling freed the demons from their underground domain. Their eventual capture has encased them in large stones across all the lands. They became known as the *demon stones*.

Over time, the truth of their imprisonment devolved into legend and tales to frighten children.

Now, the seven kingdoms are in upheaval. The demon stones are being opened and the vile creatures once more roam the land. War has broken open between realms as the fingers of accusation are pointed.

Caught in the middle is Gar Murdach, a farm boy who recently passed the age of ascension of sixteen marking him as a man, and his younger sister, Darlee, as they both struggle in their separate ways to escape the horrors wrought by the demons and the war that swarms round them.

Sometimes a trip into a fantasy world, filled with the magic of the mind is a good place to go, add the intense story line, the detailed world and a young hero who clearly started out WAY out of his league and it becomes clear that sometimes fantasy characters mirror reality. – Diane at Tome Tender (Amazon Top 500 Reviewer)

Die-hard fantasy fans, particularly those who like a bit of high fantasy, will adore this book just as I did. – Kyra – The Review List

I would recommend this book to those who enjoy a good fantasy which is well-written and easy to follow. Well done, Mr. Drakich! – S. A. Molteni – And So It Begins…

www.ingramcontent.com/pod-product-compliance
Lightning Source LLC
Chambersburg PA
CBHW071847020726
47502CB00003B/638